The Collected Supernatural and Weird Fiction of W. W. Jacobs

The Collected Supernatural and Weird Fiction of W. W. Jacobs

Twenty-One Short Stories of the Strange and Unusual including 'The Monkey's Paw', 'The Brown Man's Servant', 'Sam's Ghost' and 'The Toll House'

W. W. Jacobs

LEONAUR

The Collected
Supernatural and Weird
Fiction of
W. W. Jacobs
Twenty-One Short Stories of the Strange and Unusual including 'The Monkey's Paw',
'The Brown Man's Servant', 'Sam's Ghost' and 'The Toll House'
by W. W. Jacobs

FIRST EDITION

Leonaur is an imprint of Oakpast Ltd

Copyright in this form © 2019 Oakpast Ltd

ISBN: 978-1-78282-814-3 (hardcover)
ISBN: 978-1-78282-815-0 (softcover)

http://www.leonaur.com

Contents

Captain Rogers

A man came slowly over the old stone bridge, and averting his gaze from the dark river with its silent craft, looked with some satisfaction toward the feeble lights of the small town on the other side. He walked with the painful, forced step of one who has already trudged far. His worsted hose, where they were not darned, were in holes, and his coat and knee-breeches were rusty with much wear, but he straightened himself as he reached the end of the bridge and stepped out bravely to the taverns which stood in a row facing the quay.

He passed the "Queen Anne"—a mere beershop—without pausing, and after a glance apiece at the "Royal George" and the "Trusty Anchor," kept on his way to where the "Golden Key" hung out a gilded emblem. It was the best house in Riverstone, and patronised by the gentry, but he adjusted his faded coat, and with a swaggering air entered and walked boldly into the coffee-room.

The room was empty, but a bright fire afforded a pleasant change to the chill October air outside. He drew up a chair, and placing his feet on the fender, exposed his tattered soles to the blaze, as a waiter who had just seen him enter the room came and stood aggressively inside the door.

"Brandy and water," said the stranger; "hot."

"The coffee-room is for gentlemen staying in the house," said the waiter.

The stranger took his feet from the fender, and rising slowly, walked toward him. He was a short man and thin, but there was something so menacing in his attitude, and something so fearsome in his stony brown eyes, that the other, despite his disgust for ill-dressed people, moved back uneasily.

"Brandy and water, hot," repeated the stranger; "and plenty of it. D'ye hear?"

The man turned slowly to depart.

"Stop!" said the other, imperiously. "What's the name of the landlord here?"

"Mullet," said the fellow, sulkily.

"Send him to me," said the other, resuming his seat; "and hark you, my friend, more civility, or 'twill be the worse for you."

He stirred the log on the fire with his foot until a shower of sparks whirled up the chimney. The door opened, and the landlord, with the waiter behind him, entered the room, but he still gazed placidly at the glowing embers.

"What do you want?" demanded the landlord, in a deep voice.

The stranger turned a little weazened yellow face and grinned at him familiarly.

"Send that fat rascal of yours away," he said, slowly.

The landlord started at his voice and eyed him closely; then he signed to the man to withdraw, and closing the door behind him, stood silently watching his visitor.

"You didn't expect to see me, Rogers," said the latter.

"My name's Mullet," said the other, sternly. "What do you want?"

"Oh, Mullet?" said the other, in surprise. "I'm afraid I've made a mistake, then. I thought you were my old shipmate, Captain Rogers. It's a foolish mistake of mine, as I've no doubt Rogers was hanged years ago. You never had a brother named Rogers, did you?"

"I say again, what do you want?" demanded the other, advancing upon him.

"Since you're so good," said the other. "I want new clothes, food, and lodging of the best, and my pockets filled with money."

"You had better go and look for all those things, then," said Mullet. "You won't find them here."

"Ay!" said the other, rising. "Well, well—There was a hundred guineas on the head of my old shipmate Rogers some fifteen years ago. I'll see whether it has been earned yet."

"If I gave you a hundred guineas," said the innkeeper, repressing his passion by a mighty effort, "you would not be satisfied."

"Reads like a book," said the stranger, in tones of pretended delight. "What a man it is!"

He fell back as he spoke, and thrusting his hand into his pocket, drew forth a long pistol as the innkeeper, a man of huge frame, edged toward him.

"Keep your distance," he said, in a sharp, quick voice.

The innkeeper, in no wise disturbed at the pistol, turned away calmly, and ringing the bell, ordered some spirits. Then taking a chair, he motioned to the other to do the same, and they sat in silence until the staring waiter had left the room again. The stranger raised his glass.

"My old friend Captain Rogers," he said, solemnly, "and may he never get his deserts!"

"From what jail have you come?" inquired Mullet, sternly.

"'Pon my soul," said the other, "I have been in so many—looking for Captain Rogers—that I almost forget the last, but I have just tramped from London, two hundred and eighty odd miles, for the pleasure of seeing your damned ugly figure-head again; and now I've found it, I'm going to stay. Give me some money."

The innkeeper, without a word, drew a little gold and silver from his pocket, and placing it on the table, pushed it toward him.

"Enough to go on with," said the other, pocketing it; "in future it is halves. D'ye hear me? *Halves!* And I'll stay here and see I get it."

He sat back in his chair, and meeting the other's hatred with a gaze as steady as his own, replaced his pistol.

"A nice snug harbour after our many voyages," he continued. "Shipmates we were, shipmates we'll be; while Nick Gunn is alive you shall never want for company. Lord! Do you remember the Dutch brig, and the fat frightened mate?"

"I have forgotten it," said the other, still eyeing him steadfastly. "I have forgotten many things. For fifteen years I have lived a decent, honest life. Pray God for your own sinful soul, that the devil in me does not wake again."

"Fifteen years is a long nap," said Gunn, carelessly; "what a godsend it 'll be for you to have me by you to remind you of old times! Why, you're looking smug, man; the honest innkeeper to the life! Gad! who's the girl?"

He rose and made a clumsy bow as a girl of eighteen, after a moment's hesitation at the door, crossed over to the innkeeper.

"I'm busy, my dear," said the latter, somewhat sternly.

"Our business," said Gunn, with another bow, "is finished. Is this your daughter, Rog— Mullet?"

"My stepdaughter," was the reply.

Gunn placed a hand, which lacked two fingers, on his breast, and bowed again.

"One of your father's oldest friends," he said smoothly; "and fallen on evil days; I'm sure your gentle heart will be pleased to hear that your good father has requested me—for a time—to make his house my home."

"Any friend of my father's is welcome to me, sir," said the girl, coldly. She looked from the innkeeper to his odd-looking guest, and conscious of something strained in the air, gave him a little bow and quitted the room.

"You insist upon staying, then?" said Mullet, after a pause.

"More than ever," replied Gunn, with a leer toward the door. "Why, you don't think I'm *afraid*, Captain? You should know me better than that."

"Life is sweet," said the other.

"Ay," assented Gunn, "so sweet that you will share things with me to keep it."

"No," said the other, with great calm. "I am man enough to have a better reason."

"No psalm singing," said Gunn, coarsely. "And look cheerful, you old buccaneer. Look as a man should look who has just met an old friend never to lose him again."

He eyed his man expectantly and put his hand to his pocket again, but the innkeeper's face was troubled, and he gazed stolidly at the fire.

"See what fifteen years' honest, decent life does for us," grinned the intruder.

The other made no reply, but rising slowly, walked to the door without a word.

"Landlord," cried Gunn, bringing his maimed hand sharply down on the table.

The innkeeper turned and regarded him.

"Send me in some supper," said Gunn; "the best you have, and plenty of it, and have a room prepared. The best."

The door closed silently, and was opened a little later by the dubious George coming in to set a bountiful repast. Gunn, after cursing him for his slowness and awkwardness, drew his chair to the table and made the meal of one seldom able to satisfy his hunger. He finished at last, and after sitting for some time smoking, with his legs sprawled on the fender, rang for a candle and demanded to be shown to his room.

His proceedings when he entered it were but a poor compliment to his host. Not until he had poked and pried into every corner did he close the door. Then, not content with locking it, he tilted a chair beneath the handle, and placing his pistol beneath his pillow, fell fast asleep.

Despite his fatigue he was early astir next morning. Breakfast was laid for him in the coffee-room, and his brow darkened. He walked into the hall, and after trying various doors entered a small sitting-room, where his host and daughter sat at breakfast, and with an easy assurance drew a chair to the table. The innkeeper helped him without a word, but the girl's hand shook under his gaze as she passed him some coffee.

"As soft a bed as ever I slept in," he remarked.

"I hope that you slept well," said the girl, civilly.

"Like a child," said Gunn, gravely; "an easy conscience. Eh, Mullet?"

The innkeeper nodded and went on eating. The other, after another remark or two, followed his example, glancing occasionally with warm approval at the beauty of the girl who sat at the head of the table.

"A sweet girl," he remarked, as she withdrew at the end of the meal; "and no mother, I presume?"

"No mother," repeated the other.

Gunn sighed and shook his head.

"A sad case, truly," he murmured. "No mother and such a guardian. Poor soul, if she but knew! Well, we must find her a husband."

He looked down as he spoke, and catching sight of his rusty clothes and broken shoes, clapped his hand to his pocket; and with a glance at his host, sallied out to renew his wardrobe. The innkeeper, with an inscrutable face, watched him down the quay, then with bent head he returned to the house and fell to work on his accounts.

In this work Gunn, returning an hour later, clad from head to foot in new apparel, offered to assist him. Mullet hesitated, but made no demur; neither did he join in the ecstasies which his new partner displayed at the sight of the profits. Gunn put some more gold into his new pockets, and throwing himself back in a chair, called loudly to George to bring him some drink.

In less than a month the intruder was the virtual master of the "Golden Key." Resistance on the part of the legitimate owner became more and more feeble, the slightest objection on his part drawing from the truculent Gunn dark allusions to his past and threats against his future, which for the sake of his daughter he could not ignore. His health began to fail, and Joan watched with perplexed terror the growth of a situation which was in a fair way of becoming unbearable.

The arrogance of Gunn knew no bounds. The maids learned to

11

tremble at his polite grin, or his worse freedom, and the men shrank appalled from his profane wrath. George, after ten years' service, was brutally dismissed, and refusing to accept dismissal from his hands, appealed to his master. The innkeeper confirmed it, and with lack-lustre eyes fenced feebly when his daughter, regardless of Gunn's presence, indignantly appealed to him.

"The man was rude to my friend, my dear," he said dispiritedly

"If he was rude, it was because Mr. Gunn deserved it," said Joan, hotly.

Gunn laughed uproariously.

"Gad, my dear, I like you!" he cried, slapping his leg. "You're a girl of spirit. Now I will make you a fair offer. If you ask for George to stay, stay he shall, as a favour to your sweet self."

The girl trembled.

"Who is master here?" she demanded, turning a full eye on her father.

Mullet laughed uneasily.

"This is business," he said, trying to speak lightly, "and women can't understand it. Gunn is—is valuable to me, and George must go."

"Unless you plead for him, sweet one?" said Gunn.

The girl looked at her father again, but he turned his head away and tapped on the floor with his foot. Then in perplexity, akin to tears, she walked from the room, carefully drawing her dress aside as Gunn held the door for her.

"A fine girl," said Gunn, his thin lips working; "a fine spirit. 'Twill be pleasant to break it; but she does not know who is master here."

"She is young yet," said the other, hurriedly.

"I will soon age her if she looks like that at me again," said Gunn. "By ——, I'll turn out the whole crew into the street, and her with them, an' I wish it. I'll lie in my bed warm o' nights and think of her huddled on a doorstep."

His voice rose and his fists clenched, but he kept his distance and watched the other warily. The innkeeper's face was contorted and his brow grew wet. For one moment something peeped out of his eyes; the next he sat down in his chair again and nervously fingered his chin.

"I have but to speak," said Gunn, regarding him with much satisfaction, "and you will hang, and your money go to the Crown. What will become of her then, think you?"

The other laughed nervously.

"'Twould be stopping the golden eggs," he ventured.

"Don't think too much of that," said Gunn, in a hard voice. "I was never one to be baulked, as you know."

"Come, come. Let us be friends," said Mullet; "the girl is young, and has had her way."

He looked almost pleadingly at the other, and his voice trembled. Gunn drew himself up, and regarding him with a satisfied sneer, quitted the room without a word.

Affairs at the "Golden Key" grew steadily worse and worse. Gunn dominated the place, and his vile personality hung over it like a shadow. Appeals to the innkeeper were in vain; his health was breaking fast, and he moodily declined to interfere. Gunn appointed servants of his own choosing-brazen maids and foul-mouthed men. The old patrons ceased to frequent the "Golden Key," and its bedrooms stood empty. The maids scarcely deigned to take an order from Joan, and the men spoke to her familiarly. In the midst of all this the innkeeper, who had complained once or twice of vertigo, was seized with a fit.

Joan, flying to him for protection against the brutal advances of Gunn, found him lying in a heap behind the door of his small office, and in her fear called loudly for assistance. A little knot of servants collected, and stood regarding him stupidly. One made a brutal jest. Gunn, pressing through the throng, turned the senseless body over with his foot, and cursing vilely, ordered them to carry it upstairs.

Until the surgeon came, Joan, kneeling by the bed, held on to the senseless hand as her only protection against the evil faces of Gunn and his proteges. Gunn himself was taken aback, the innkeeper's death at that time by no means suiting his aims.

The surgeon was a man of few words and fewer attainments, but under his ministrations the innkeeper, after a long interval, rallied. The half-closed eyes opened, and he looked in a dazed fashion at his surroundings. Gunn drove the servants away and questioned the man of medicine. The answers were vague and interspersed with Latin. Freedom from noise and troubles of all kinds was insisted upon and Joan was installed as nurse, with a promise of speedy assistance.

The assistance arrived late in the day in the shape of an elderly woman, whose Spartan treatment of her patients had helped many along the silent road. She commenced her reign by punching the sick man's pillows, and having shaken him into consciousness by this means, gave him a dose of physic, after first tasting it herself from the bottle.

After the first rally the innkeeper began to fail slowly. It was seldom that he understood what was said to him, and pitiful to the beholder to see in his intervals of consciousness his timid anxiety to earn the goodwill of the all-powerful Gunn. His strength declined until assistance was needed to turn him in the bed, and his great sinewy hands were forever trembling and fidgeting on the coverlet.

Joan, pale with grief and fear, tended him assiduously. Her stepfather's strength had been a proverb in the town, and many a hasty citizen had felt the strength of his arm. The increasing lawlessness of the house filled her with dismay, and the coarse attentions of Gunn became more persistent than ever. She took her meals in the sick-room, and divided her time between that and her own.

Gunn himself was in a dilemma. With Mullet dead, his power was at an end and his visions of wealth dissipated. He resolved to feather his nest immediately, and interviewed the surgeon. The surgeon was ominously reticent, the nurse cheerfully ghoulish.

"Four days I give him," she said, calmly; "four blessed days, not but what he might slip away at any moment."

Gunn let one day of the four pass, and then, choosing a time when Joan was from the room, entered it for a little quiet conversation. The innkeeper's eyes were open, and, what was more to the purpose, intelligent.

"You're cheating the hangman, after all," snarled Gunn. "I'm off to swear an information."

The other, by a great effort, turned his heavy head and fixed his wistful eyes on him.

"Mercy!" he whispered. "For her sake—give me—a little time!"

"To slip your cable, I suppose," quoth Gunn. "Where's your money? Where's your hoard, you miser?"

Mullet closed his eyes. He opened them again slowly and strove to think, while Gunn watched him narrowly. When he spoke, his utterance was thick and laboured.

"Come tonight," he muttered, slowly. "Give me—time—I will make your —your fortune. But the nurse-watches."

"I'll see to her," said Gunn, with a grin. "But tell me now, lest you die first."

"You will—let Joan—have a share?" panted the innkeeper.

"Yes, yes," said Gunn, hastily.

The innkeeper strove to raise himself in the bed, and then fell back again exhausted as Joan's step was heard on the stairs. Gunn gave a

14

savage glance of warning at him, and barring the progress of the girl at the door, attempted to salute her. Joan came in pale and trembling, and falling on her knees by the bedside, took her father's hand in hers and wept over it. The innkeeper gave a faint groan and a shiver ran through his body.

It was nearly an hour after midnight that Nick Gunn, kicking off his shoes, went stealthily out onto the landing. A little light came from the partly open door of the sick-room, but all else was in blackness. He moved along and peered in.

The nurse was sitting in a high-backed oak chair by the fire. She had slipped down in the seat, and her untidy head hung on her bosom. A glass stood on the small oak table by her side, and a solitary candle on the high mantelpiece diffused a sickly light. Gunn entered the room, and finding that the sick man was dozing, shook him roughly.

The innkeeper opened his eyes and gazed at him blankly.

"Wake, you fool," said Gunn, shaking him again.

The other roused and muttered something incoherently. Then he stirred slightly.

"The nurse," he whispered.

"She's safe enow," said Gunn. "I've seen to that."

He crossed the room lightly, and standing before the unconscious woman, inspected her closely and raised her in the chair. Her head fell limply over the arm.

"Dead?" inquired Mullet, in a fearful whisper.

"Drugged," said Gunn, shortly. "Now speak up, and be lively."

The innkeeper's eyes again travelled in the direction of the nurse.

"The men," he whispered; "the servants."

"Dead drunk and asleep," said Gunn, biting the words. "The last day would hardly rouse them. Now will you speak, damn you!"

"I must—take care—of Joan," said the father.

Gunn shook his clenched hand at him.

"My money—is—is—" said the other. "Promise me on—your oath—Joan."

"Ay, ay," growled Gunn; "how many more times? I'll marry her, and she shall have what I choose to give her. Speak up, you fool! It's not for you to make terms. Where is it?"

He bent over, but Mullet, exhausted with his efforts, had closed his eyes again, and half turned his head.

"Where is it, damn you?" said Gunn, from between his teeth.

Mullet opened his eyes again, glanced fearfully round the room, and whispered. Gunn, with a stifled oath, bent his ear almost to his mouth, and the next moment his neck was in the grip of the strongest man in Riverstone, and an arm like a bar of iron over his back pinned him down across the bed.

"You dog!" hissed a fierce voice in his ear. "I've got you—Captain Rogers at your service, and now you may tell his name to all you can. Shout it, you spawn of hell. Shout it!"

He rose in bed, and with a sudden movement flung the other over on his back. Gunn's eyes were starting from his head, and he writhed convulsively.

"I thought you were a sharper man, Gunn," said Rogers, still in the same hot whisper, as he relaxed his grip a little; "you are too simple, you hound! When you first threatened me, I resolved to kill you. Then you threatened my daughter. I wish that you had nine lives, that I might take them all. Keep still!"

He gave a half-glance over his shoulder at the silent figure of the nurse, and put his weight on the twisting figure on the bed.

"You drugged the hag, good Gunn," he continued. "Tomorrow morning, Gunn, they will find you in your room dead, and if one of the scum you brought into my house be charged with the murder, so much the better. When I am well, they will go. I am already feeling a little bit stronger, Gunn, as you see, and in a month, I hope to be about again."

He averted his face, and for a time gazed sternly and watchfully at the door. Then he rose slowly to his feet, and taking the dead man in his arms, bore him slowly and carefully to his room, and laid him a huddled heap on the floor. Swiftly and noiselessly he put the dead man's shoes on and turned his pockets inside out, kicked a rug out of place, and put a guinea on the floor. Then he stole cautiously down stairs and set a small door at the back open. A dog barked frantically, and he hurried back to his room. The nurse still slumbered by the fire.

She awoke in the morning shivering with the cold, and being jealous of her reputation, rekindled the fire, and measuring out the dose which the invalid should have taken, threw it away. On these unconscious preparations for an alibi Captain Rogers gazed through half-closed lids, and then turning his grim face to the wall, waited for the inevitable alarm.

In Mid-Atlantic

"No, sir," said the night-watchman, as he took a seat on a post at the end of the jetty, and stowed a huge piece of tobacco in his cheek. "No, man an' boy, I was at sea forty years afore I took on this job, but I can't say as ever I saw a real, downright ghost."

This was disappointing, and I said so. Previous experience of the power of Bill's vision had led me to expect something very different.

"Not but what I've known some queer things happen," said Bill, fixing his eyes on the Surrey side, and going off into a kind of trance. "Queer things."

I waited patiently; Bill's eyes, after resting for some time on Surrey, began to slowly cross the river, paused midway in reasonable hopes of a collision between a tug with its flotilla of barges and a penny steamer, and then came back to me.

"You heard that yarn old Cap'n Harris was telling the other day about the skipper he knew having a warning one night to alter his course, an' doing so, picked up five live men and three dead skeletons in a open boat?" he inquired.

I nodded.

"The yarn in various forms is an old one," said I.

"It's all founded on something I told him once," said Bill. "I don't wish to accuse Cap'n Harris of taking another man's true story an' spoiling it; he's got a bad memory, that's all. Fust of all, he forgets he ever heard the yarn; secondly, he goes and spoils it."

I gave a sympathetic murmur. Harris was as truthful an old man as ever breathed, but his tales were terribly restricted by this circumstance, whereas Bill's were limited by nothing but his own imagination.

"It was about fifteen years ago now," began Bill, getting the quid into a bye-way of his cheek, where it would not impede his utterance.

"I was A.B. on the *Swallow*, a barque, trading wherever we could pick up stuff. On this v'y'ge we was bound from London to Jamaica with a general cargo.

"The start of that v'y'ge was excellent. We was towed out of the St. Katherine's Docks here, to the Nore, an' the tug left us to a stiff breeze, which fairly raced us down Channel and out into the Atlantic. Everybody was saying what a fine v'y'ge we was having, an' what quick time we should make, an' the fust mate was in such a lovely temper that you might do anything with him a'most.

"We was about ten days out, an' still slipping along in this spanking way, when all of a sudden things changed. I was at the wheel with the second mate one night, when the skipper, whose name was Brown, came up from below in a uneasy sort o' fashion, and stood looking at us for some time without speaking. Then at last he sort o' makes up his mind, and ses he—

"'Mr. McMillan, I've just had a most remarkable experience, an' I don't know what to do about it.'

"'Yes, sir?' ses Mr. McMillan.

"'Three times I've been woke up this night by something shouting in my ear, "Steer nor'-nor'west!"' ses the cap'n very solemnly, '"Steer nor'nor'-west!" that's all it says. The first time I thought it was somebody got into my cabin skylarking, and I laid for 'em with a stick; but I've heard it three times, an' there's nothing there.'

"'It's a supernatural warning,' ses the second mate, who had a great uncle once who had the second sight, and was the most unpopular man of his family, because he always knew what to expect, and laid his plans according.

"'That's what I think,' ses the cap'n. 'There's some poor shipwrecked fellow creatures in distress.'

"'It's a verra grave responsebeelity.' ses Mr. McMillan. 'I should just ca' up the fairst mate.'

"'Bill,' ses the cap'n, 'just go down below, and tell Mr. Salmon I'd like a few words with him partikler.'

"Well, I went down below, and called up the first mate, and as soon as I'd explained to him what he was wanted for, he went right off into a fit of outrageous bad language, an' hit me. He came right up on deck in his pants an' socks. A most disrespekful way to come to the cap'n, but he was that hot and excited he didn't care what he did.

"'Mr. Salmon,' ses the cap'n gravely, 'I've just had a most solemn warning, and I want to'—

"'I know,' says the mate gruffly.

"'What! have you heard it too?' ses the cap'n, in surprise. 'Three times?'

"'I heard it from him.' ses the mate, pointing to me. 'Nightmare, sir, nightmare.'

"'It was not nightmare, sir,' ses the cap'n, very huffy, 'an' if I hear it again, I'm going to alter this ship's course.'

"Well, the fust mate was in a hole. He wanted to call the skipper something which he knew wasn't discipline. I knew what it was, an' I knew if the mate didn't do something, he'd be ill, he was that sort of man, everything flew to his head. He walked away, and put his head over the side for a bit, an' at last, when he came back, he was, comparatively speaking, calm.

"'You mustn't hear them words again, sir,' ses he; 'don't go to sleep again tonight. Stay up, an' we'll have a hand o' cards, and in the morning, you take a good stiff dose o' rhoobarb. Don't spoil one o' the best trips we've ever had for the sake of a pennyworth of rhoobarb,' ses he, pleading-like.

"'Mr. Salmon,' ses the cap'n, very angry, 'I shall not fly in the face o' Providence in any such way. I shall sleep as usual, an' as for your rhoobarb,' ses the cap'n, working hisself up into a passion—'damme, sir, I'll—I'll dose the whole crew with it, from first mate to cabin-boy, if I have any impertinence.'

"Well, Mr. Salmon, who was getting very mad, stalks down below, followed by the cap'n, an' Mr. McMillan was that excited that he even started talking to me about it. Half-an-hour arterwards the cap'n comes running up on deck again.

"'Mr. McMillan,' ses he excitedly, 'steer nor'nor'-west until further orders. I've heard it again, an' this time it nearly split the drum of my ear.'

"The ship's course was altered, an' after the old man was satisfied, he went back to bed again, an' almost directly arter eight bells went, an' I was relieved. I wasn't on deck when the fust mate come up, but those that were said he took it very calm. He didn't say a word. He just sat down on the poop, and blew his cheeks out.

"As soon as ever it was daylight the skipper was on deck with his glasses. He sent men up to the masthead to keep a good look-out, an' he was dancing about like a cat on hot bricks all the morning.

"'How long are we to go on this course, sir?' asks Mr. Salmon, about ten o'clock in the morning.

19

"'I've not made up my mind, sir,' ses the cap'n, very stately; but I could see he was looking a trifle foolish.

"At twelve o'clock in the day, the fust mate got a cough, and every time he coughed it seemed to act upon the skipper, and make him madder and madder. Now that it was broad daylight, Mr. McMillan didn't seem to be so creepy as the night before, an' I could see the cap'n was only waiting for the slightest excuse to get into our proper course again.

"'That's a nasty, bad cough o' yours, Mr. Salmon,' ses he, eyeing the mate very hard.

"'Yes, a nasty, irritating sort o' cough, sir,' ses the other; 'it worries me a great deal. It's this going up nor'ards what's sticking in my throat,' ses he.

"The cap'n give a gulp, and walked off, but he comes back in a minute, and ses he—

"'Mr. Salmon, I should think it a great pity to lose a valuable officer like yourself, even to do good to others. There's a hard ring about that cough I don't like, an' if you really think it's going up this bit north, why, I don't mind putting the ship in her course again.'

"Well, the mate thanked him kindly, and he was just about to give the orders when one o' the men who was at the masthead suddenly shouts out—

"'Ahoy! Small boat on the port bow!'

"The cap'n started as if he'd been shot, and ran up the rigging with his glasses. He came down again almost direckly, and his face was all in a glow with pleasure and excitement.

"'Mr. Salmon,' ses he, 'here's a small boat with a lug sail in the middle o' the Atlantic, with one pore man lying in the bottom of her. What do you think o' my warning now?'

"The mate didn't say anything at first, but he took the glasses and had a look, an' when he came back anyone could see his opinion of the skipper had gone up miles and miles.

"'It's a wonderful thing, sir,' ses he, 'and one I'll remember all my life. It's evident that you've been picked out as a instrument to do this good work.'

"I'd never heard the fust mate talk like that afore, 'cept once when he fell overboard, when he was full, and stuck in the Thames mud. He said it was Providence; though, as it was low water, according to the tide-table, I couldn't see what Providence had to do with it myself. He was as excited as anybody, and took the wheel himself, and put the

20

ship's head for the boat, and as she came closer, our boat was slung out, and me and the second mate and three other men dropped into her, an' pulled so as to meet the other.

"'Never mind the boat; we don't want to be bothered with her,' shouts out the cap'n as we pulled away—'Save the man!'

"I'll say this for Mr. McMillan, he steered that boat beautifully, and we ran alongside o' the other as clever as possible. Two of us shipped our oars, and gripped her tight, and then we saw that she was just an ordinary boat, partly decked in, with the head and shoulders of a man showing in the opening, fast asleep, and snoring like thunder.

"'Puir chap,' ses Mr. McMillan, standing up. 'Look how wasted he is.'

"He laid hold o' the man by the neck of his coat an' his belt, an', being a very powerful man, dragged him up and swung him into our boat, which was bobbing up and down, and grating against the side of the other. We let go then, an' the man we 'd rescued opened his eyes as Mr. McMillan tumbled over one of the thwarts with him, and, letting off a roar like a bull, tried to jump back into his boat.

"'Hold him!' shouted the second mate. 'Hold him tight! He's mad, puir feller.'

"By the way that man fought and yelled, we thought the mate was right, too. He was a short, stiff chap, hard as iron, and he bit and kicked and swore for all he was worth, until at last we tripped him up and tumbled him into the bottom of the boat, and held him there with his head hanging back over a thwart.

"'It's all right, my puir feller,' ses the second mate; 'ye're in good hands—ye're saved.'

"'Damme!' ses the man; 'what's your little game? Where's my boat—eh? Where's my boat?'

"He wriggled a bit, and got his head up, and, when he saw it bowling along two or three hundred yards away, his temper got the better of him, and he swore that if Mr. McMillan didn't row after it he'd knife him.

"'We can't bother about the boat,' ses the mate; 'we've had enough bother to rescue you.'

"'Who the devil wanted you to rescue me?' bellowed the man. 'I'll make you pay for this, you miserable swabs. If there's any law in Amurrica, you shall have it!'

"By this time, we had got to the ship, which had shortened sail, and the cap'n was standing by the side, looking down upon the stranger

21

with a big, kind smile which nearly sent him crazy.

"'Welcome aboard, my pore feller,' ses he, holding out his hand as the chap got up the side.

"'Are you the author of this outrage?' ses the man fiercely.

"'I don't understand you,' ses the cap'n, very dignified, and drawing himself up.

"'Did you send your chaps to sneak me out o' my boat while I was having forty winks?' roars the other. 'Damme! that's English, ain't it?'

"'Surely,' ses the cap'n, 'surely you didn't wish to be left to perish in that little craft. I had a supernatural warning to steer this course on purpose to pick you up, and this is your gratitude.'

"'Look here!' ses the other. 'My name's Cap'n Naskett, and I'm doing a record trip from New York to Liverpool in the smallest boat that has ever crossed the Atlantic, an' you go an' bust everything with your cussed officiousness. If you think I'm going to be kidnapped just to fulfil your beastly warnings, you've made a mistake. I'll have the law on you, that's what I'll do. Kidnapping's a punishable offence.'

"'What did you come here for, then?' ses the cap'n.

"'Come!' howls Cap'n Naskett. 'Come! A feller sneaks up alongside o' me with a boat-load of street-sweepings dressed as sailors, and snaps me up while I'm asleep, and you ask me what I come for. Look here. You clap on all sail and catch that boat o' mine, and put me back, and I'll call it quits. If you don't, I'll bring a law-suit agin you, and make you the laughing-stock of two continents into the bargain.'

"Well, to make the best of a bad bargain, the cap'n sailed after the cussed little boat, and Mr. Salmon, who thought more than enough time had been lost already, fell foul o' Cap'n Naskett. They was both pretty talkers, and the way they went on was a education for every sailorman afloat. Every man aboard got as near as they durst to listen to them; but I must say Cap'n Naskett had the best of it. He was a sarkastik man, and pretended to think the ship was fitted out just to pick up shipwrecked people, an' he also pretended to think we was castaways what had been saved by it. He said o' course anybody could see at a glance we wasn't sailormen, an' he supposed Mr. Salmon was a butcher what had been carried out to sea while paddling at Margate to strengthen his ankles. He said a lot more of this sort of thing, and all this time we was chasing his miserable little boat, an' he was admiring the way she sailed, while the fust mate was answering his reflexshuns, an' I'm sure that not even our skipper was more pleased than Mr. Salmon when we caught it at last, and shoved him back. He was ungrateful up to the last, an', just before leaving the ship, actually went up to Cap'n Brown, and advised him to shut his eyes an' turn round three times and catch what he could.

"I never saw the skipper so upset afore, but I heard him tell Mr. McMillan that night that if he ever went out of his way again after a craft, it would only be to run it down. Most people keep pretty quiet about supernatural things that happen to them, but he was about the quietest I ever heard of, an', what's more, he made everyone else keep quiet about it, too. Even when he had to steer nor'-nor'-west arter that in the way o' business he didn't like it, an' he was about the most cruelly disappointed man you ever saw when he heard afterwards that Cap'n Naskett got safe to Liverpool."

The Interruption

1

The last of the funeral guests had gone and Spencer Goddard, in decent black, sat alone in his small, well-furnished study. There was a queer sense of freedom in the house since the coffin had left it; the coffin which was now hidden in its solitary grave beneath the yellow earth. The air, which for the last three days had seemed stale and contaminated, now smelt fresh and clean. He went to the open window and, looking into the fading light of the autumn day, took a deep breath.

He closed the window and, stooping down, put a match to the fire, and, dropping into his easy chair, sat listening to the cheery crackle of the wood. At the age of thirty-eight he had turned over a fresh page. Life, free and unencumbered, was before him. His dead wife's money was at last his, to spend as he pleased, instead of being doled out in reluctant driblets.

He turned at a step at the door and his face assumed the appearance of gravity and sadness it had worn for the last four days. The cook, with the same air of decorous grief, entered the room quietly and, crossing to the mantelpiece, placed upon it a photograph.

"I thought you'd like to have it, sir," she said, in a low voice, "to remind you."

Goddard thanked her, and, rising, took it in his hand and stood regarding it. He noticed with satisfaction that his hand was absolutely steady.

"It is a very good likeness till she was taken ill," continued the woman. "I never saw anybody change so sudden."

"The nature of her disease, Hannah," said her master.

The woman nodded, and, dabbing at her eyes with her handkerchief, stood regarding him.

"Is there anything you want?" he inquired, after a time.

She shook her head. "I can't believe she's gone," she said, in a low voice. "Every now and then I have a queer feeling that she's still here—"

"It's your nerves," said her master sharply.

"—and wanting to tell me something."

By a great effort Goddard refrained from looking at her.

"Nerves," he said again. "Perhaps you ought to have a little holiday. It has been a great strain upon you."

"You, too, sir," said the woman respectfully. "Waiting on her hand and foot as you have done, I can't think how you stood it. If you'd only had a nurse—"

"I preferred to do it myself, Hannah," said her master.

"If I had had a nurse it would have alarmed her."

The woman assented. "And they are always peeking and prying into what doesn't concern them," she added. "Always think they know more than the doctors do."

Goddard turned a slow look upon her. The tall, angular figure was standing in an attitude of respectful attention; the cold slaty-brown eyes were cast down, the sullen face expressionless.

"She couldn't have had a better doctor," he said, looking at the fire again. "No man could have done more for her."

"And nobody could have done more for her than you did, sir," was the reply. "There's few husbands that would have done what you did."

Goddard stiffened in his chair. "That will do, Hannah," he said curtly.

"Or done it so well," said the woman, with measured slowness.

With a strange, sinking sensation, her master paused to regain his control. Then he turned and eyed her steadily. "Thank you," he said slowly; "you mean well, but at present I cannot discuss it."

For some time after the door had closed behind her, he sat in deep thought. The feeling of wellbeing of a few minutes before had vanished, leaving in its place an apprehension which he refused to consider, but which would not be allayed. He thought over his actions of the last few weeks, carefully, and could remember no flaw. His wife's illness, the doctor's diagnosis, his own solicitous care, were all in keeping with the ordinary. He tried to remember the woman's exact words—her manner. Something had shown him Fear. What?

He could have laughed at his fears next morning. The dining-room was full of sunshine and the fragrance of coffee and bacon was in the air. Better still, a worried and commonplace Hannah. Worried over two eggs with false birth certificates, over the vendor of which she became almost lyrical.

"The bacon is excellent," said her smiling master, "so is the coffee; but your coffee always is."

Hannah smiled in return, and, taking fresh eggs from a rosy-cheeked maid, put them before him.

A pipe, followed by a brisk walk, cheered him still further. He came home glowing with exercise and again possessed with that sense of freedom and freshness. He went into the garden—now his own—and planned alterations.

After lunch he went over the house. The windows of his wife's bedroom were open and the room neat and airy. His glance wandered from the made-up bed to the brightly polished furniture. Then he went to the dressing-table and opened the drawers, searching each in turn. With the exception of a few odds and ends they were empty. He went out on to the landing and called for Hannah.

"Do you know whether your mistress locked up any of her things?" he inquired.

"What things?" said the woman.

"Well, her jewellery mostly."

"Oh!" Hannah smiled. "She gave it all to me," she said quietly.

Goddard checked an exclamation. His heart was beating nervously, but he spoke sternly.

"When?"

"Just before she died—of gastroenteritis," said the woman.

There was a long silence. He turned and with great care mechanically closed the drawers of the dressing-table. The tilted glass showed him the pallor of his face, and he spoke without turning round.

"That is all right, then," he said huskily. "I only wanted to know what had become of it. I thought, perhaps, Milly—'

Hannah shook her head. "Milly's all right," she said, with a strange smile. "She's as honest as we are. Is there anything more you want, sir?"

She closed the door behind her with the quietness of the well-trained servant; Goddard, steadying himself with his hand on the rail of the bed, stood looking into the future.

2

The days passed monotonously, as they pass with a man in prison. Gone was the sense of freedom and the idea of a wider life. Instead

27

of a cell, a house with ten rooms—but Hannah, the jailer, guarding each one. Respectful and attentive, the model servant, he saw in every word a threat against his liberty his life. In the sullen face and cold eyes, he saw her knowledge of power; in her solicitude for his comfort and approval, a sardonic jest. It was the master playing at being the servant. The years of unwilling servitude were over, but she felt her way carefully with infinite zest in the game. Warped and bitter, with a cleverness which had never before had scope, she had entered into her kingdom. She took it little by little, savouring every morsel.

"I hope I've done right, sir," she said one morning. "I have given Milly notice."

Goddard looked up from his paper. "Isn't she satisfactory?" he inquired.

"Not to my thinking, sir," said the woman. "And she says she is coming to see you about it. I told her that would be no good."

"I had better see her and hear what she has to say," said her master.

"Of course, if you wish to," said Hannah; "only, after giving her notice, if she doesn't go I shall. I should be sorry to go I've been very comfortable here—but it's either her or me."

"I should be sorry to lose you," said Goddard in a hopeless voice.

"Thank you, sir," said Hannah. "I'm sure I've tried to do my best. I've been with you some time now—and I know all your little ways. I expect I understand you better than anybody else would. I do all I can to make you comfortable."

"Very well, I leave it to you," said Goddard in a voice which strove to be brisk and commanding. "You have my permission to dismiss her."

"There's another thing I wanted to see you about," said Hannah; "my wages. I was going to ask for a rise, seeing that I'm really housekeeper here now."

"Certainly," said her master, considering, "that only seems fair. Let me see what are you getting?"

"Thirty-six."

Goddard reflected for a moment and then turned with a benevolent smile. "Very well," he said cordially, "I'll make it forty-two. That's ten shillings a month more."

"I was thinking of a hundred," said Hannah dryly.

The significance of the demand appalled him. "Rather a big jump," he said at last. "I really don't know that I—"

"It doesn't matter," said Hannah. "I thought I was worth it—to you—that's all. You know best. Some people might think I was worth two hundred. That's a bigger jump, but after all a big jump is better than—"

She broke off and tittered. Goddard eyed her.

"—than a big drop," she concluded.

Her master's face set. The lips almost disappeared and something came into the pale eyes that was revolting. Still eyeing her, he rose and approached her. She stood her ground and met him eye to eye.

"You are jocular," he said at last.

"Short life and a merry one," said the woman.

"Mine or yours?"

"Both, perhaps," was the reply.

"If—if I give you a hundred," said Goddard, moistening his lips, "that ought to make your life merrier, at any rate."

Hannah nodded. "Merry and long, perhaps," she said slowly. "I'm careful, you know—very careful."

"I am sure you are," said Goddard, his face relaxing.

"Careful what I eat and drink, I mean," said the woman, eyeing him steadily.

"That is wise," he said slowly. "I am myself—that is why I am paying a good cook a large salary. But don't overdo things, Hannah; don't kill the goose that lays the golden eggs."

"I am not likely to do that," she said coldly. "Live and let live; that is my motto. Some people have different ones. But I'm careful; nobody won't catch me napping. I've left a letter with my sister, in case."

Goddard turned slowly and in a casual fashion put the flowers straight in a bowl on the table, and, wandering to the window, looked out. His face was white again and his hands trembled.

"To be opened after my death," continued Hannah. "I don't believe in doctors—not after what I've seen of them, I don't think they know enough; so, if I die, I shall be examined. I've given good reasons."

"And suppose," said Goddard, coming from the window, "suppose she is curious, and opens it before you die?"

"We must chance that," said Hannah, shrugging her shoulders; "but I don't think she will. I sealed it up with sealing-wax, with a mark on it."

"She might open it and say nothing about it," persisted her master.

An unwholesome grin spread slowly over Hannah's features. "I should know it soon enough," she declared boisterously, "and so would other people. Lord! there would be an upset! Chidham would have something to talk about for once. We should be in the paper—both of us."

Goddard forced a smile.

"Dear me!" he said gently. "Your pen seems to be a dangerous weapon, Hannah, but I hope that the need to open it will not happen for another fifty years. You look well and strong."

The woman nodded. "I don't take up my troubles before they come," she said, with a satisfied air; "but there's no harm in trying to prevent them coming. Prevention is better than cure."

"Exactly," said her master; "and, by the way, there's no need for this little financial arrangement to be known by anybody else. I might become unpopular with my neighbours for setting a bad example. Of course, I am giving you this sum because I really think you are worth it."

"I'm sure you do," said Hannah. "I'm not sure I ain't worth more, but this'll do to go on with. I shall get a girl for less than we are paying Milly, and that'll be another little bit extra for me."

"Certainly," said Goddard, and smiled again.

"Come to think of it," said Hannah, pausing at the door, "I ain't sure I shall get anybody else; then there'll be more than ever for me. If I do the work I might as well have the money."

Her master nodded, and, left to himself, sat down to think out a position which was as intolerable as it was dangerous. At a great risk he had escaped from the dominion of one woman only to fall, bound and helpless, into the hands of another. However vague and unconvincing the suspicions of Hannah might be, they would be sufficient. Evidence could be unearthed. Cold with fear one moment, and hot with fury the next, he sought in vain for some avenue of escape. It was his brain against that of a cunning, illiterate fool; a fool whose malicious stupidity only added to his danger. And she drank. With largely increased wages she would drink more and his very life might depend upon a hiccupped boast. It was clear that she was enjoying her supremacy; later on, her vanity would urge her to display it before others. He might have to obey the crack of her whip before witnesses, and that would cut off all possibility of escape.

He sat with his head in his hands. There must be a way out and he must find it. Soon. He must find it before gossip began; before the changed position of master and servant lent colour to her story when that story became known. Shaking with fury, he thought of her lean, ugly throat and the joy of choking her life out with his fingers. He started suddenly, and took a quick breath. No, no fingers—a rope.

Bright and cheerful outside and with his friends, in the house he was quiet and submissive. Milly had gone, and, if the service was poorer and the rooms neglected, he gave no sign. If a bell remained unanswered, he made no complaint, and to studied insolence turned the other cheek of politeness. When at this tribute to her power the woman smiled, he smiled in return. A smile which, for all its disarming softness, left her vaguely uneasy.

"I'm not afraid of you," she said once, with a menacing air.

"I hope not," said Goddard in a slightly surprised voice.

"Some people might be, but I'm not," she declared. "If anything happened to me—"Nothing could happen to such a careful woman as you are," he said, smiling again. "You ought to live to ninety—with luck."

It was clear to him that the situation was getting on his nerves. Unremembered but terrible dreams haunted his sleep. Dreams in which some great, inevitable disaster was always pressing upon him, although he could never discover what it was. Each morning he awoke unrefreshed to face another day of torment. He could not meet the woman's eyes for fear of revealing the threat that was in his own.

Delay was dangerous and foolish. He had thought out every move in that contest of wits which was to remove the shadow of the rope from his own neck and place it about that of the woman. There was a little risk, but the stake was a big one. He had but to set the ball rolling and others would keep it on its course. It was time to act.

He came in a little jaded from his afternoon walk, and left his tea untouched. He ate but little dinner, and, sitting hunched up over the fire, told the woman that he had taken a slight chill. Her concern, he felt grimly, might have been greater if she had known the cause.

He was no better next day, and after lunch called in to consult his doctor. He left with a clean bill of health except for a slight digestive derangement, the remedy for which he took away with him in a bottle. For two days he swallowed one tablespoonful three times a day in water, without result, then he took to his bed.

"A day or two in bed won't hurt you," said the doctor. "Show me that tongue of yours again.

"But what is the matter with me, Roberts?" inquired the patient.

The doctor pondered. "Nothing to trouble about nerves a bit

wrong—digestion a little bit impaired. You'll be all right in a day or two."

Goddard nodded. So far, so good; Roberts had not outlived his usefulness. He smiled grimly after the doctor had left, at the surprise he was preparing for him. A little rough on Roberts and his professional reputation, perhaps, but these things could not be avoided.

He lay back and visualised the programme. A day or two longer, getting gradually worse, then a little sickness. After that a nervous, somewhat shamefaced patient hinting at things. His food had a queer taste—he felt worse after taking it; he knew it was ridiculous, still—there was some of his beef-tea he had put aside, perhaps the doctor would like to examine it? and the medicine? Secretions, too; perhaps he would like to see those?

Propped on his elbow, he stared fixedly at the wall. There would be a trace—a faint trace—of arsenic in the secretions. There would be more than a trace in the other things. An attempt to poison him would be clearly indicated, and—his wife's symptoms had resembled his own—let Hannah get out of the web he was spinning if she could. As for the letter she had threatened him with, let her produce it; it could only recoil upon herself. Fifty letters could not save her from the doom he was preparing for her. It was her life or his, and he would show no mercy. For three days he doctored himself with sedulous care, watching himself anxiously the while. His nerve was going and he knew it. Before him was the strain of the discovery, the arrest, and the trial. The gruesome business of his wife's death. A long business. He would wait no longer, and he would open the proceedings with dramatic suddenness.

It was between nine and ten o'clock at night when he rang his bell, and it was not until he had rung four times that he heard the heavy steps of Hannah mounting the stairs.

"What d'you want?" she demanded, standing in the doorway.

"I'm very ill," he said, gasping. "Run for the doctor. Quick!"

The woman stared at him in genuine amazement. "What, at this time o' night?" she exclaimed. "Not likely."

"I'm dying!" said Goddard in a broken voice.

"Not you," she said roughly. "You'll be better in the morning."

"I'm dying," he repeated. "Go—for—the—doctor."

The woman hesitated. The rain beat in heavy squalls against the window, and the doctor's house was a mile distant on the lonely road. She glanced at the figure on the bed.

"I should catch my death o' cold," she grumbled.

She stood sullenly regarding him. He certainly looked very ill, and his death would by no means benefit her. She listened, scowling, to the wind and the rain.

"All right," she said at last, and went noisily from the room.

His face set in a mirthless smile, he heard her bustling about below. The front door slammed violently and he was alone.

He waited for a few minutes and then, getting out of bed, put on his dressing-gown and set about his preparations. With a steady hand he added a little white powder to the remains of his beef-tea and to the contents of his bottle of medicine. He stood listening a moment at some faint sound from below, and, having satisfied himself, lit a candle and made his way to Hannah's room. For a space he stood irresolute, looking about him. Then he opened one of the drawers and, placing the broken packet of powder under a pile of clothing at the back, made his way back to bed.

He was disturbed to find that he was trembling with excitement and nervousness. He longed for tobacco, but that was impossible. To reassure himself he began to rehearse his conversation with the doctor, and again he thought over every possible complication. The scene with the woman would be terrible; he would have to be too ill to take any part in it. The less he said the better. Others would do all that was necessary.

He lay for a long time listening to the sound of the wind and the rain. Inside, the house seemed unusually quiet, and with an odd sensation he suddenly realised that it was the first time he had been alone in it since his wife's death. He remembered that she would have to be disturbed. The thought was unwelcome. He did not want her to be disturbed. Let the dead sleep.

He sat up in bed and drew his watch from beneath the pillow. Hannah ought to have been back before; in any case she could not be long now. At any moment he might hear her key in the lock. He lay down again and reminded himself that things were shaping well. He had shaped them, and some of the satisfaction of the artist was his.

The silence was oppressive. The house seemed to be listening, waiting. He looked at his watch again and wondered, with a curse, what had happened to the woman. It was clear that the doctor must be out, but that was no reason for her delay. It was close on midnight, and the atmosphere of the house seemed in some strange fashion to be brooding and hostile.

In a lull in the wind he thought he heard footsteps outside, and his face cleared as he sat up listening for the sound of the key in the door below. In another moment the woman would be in the house and the fears engendered by a disordered fancy would have flown. The sound of the steps had ceased, but he could hear no sound of entrance. Until all hope had gone, he sat listening. He was certain he had heard footsteps. Whose?

Trembling and haggard he sat waiting, assailed by a crowd of murmuring fears. One whispered that he had failed and would have to pay the penalty of failing; that he had gambled with death and lost.

By a strong effort he fought down these fancies and, closing his eyes, tried to compose himself to rest. It was evident now that the doctor was out and that Hannah was waiting to return with him in his car. He was frightening himself for nothing. At any moment he might hear the sound of their arrival.

He heard something else, and, sitting up suddenly, tried to think what ii was and what had caused it. It was a very faint sound—stealthy. Holding his breath, he waited for it to be repeated. He heard it again, the mere ghost of a sound—the whisper of a sound, but significant as most whispers are.

He wiped his brow with his sleeve and told himself firmly that it was nerves, and nothing but nerves; but, against his will, he still listened. He fancied now that the sound came from his wife's room, the other side of the landing. It increased in loudness and became more insistent, but with his eyes fixed on the door of his room he still kept himself in hand, and tried to listen instead to the wind and the rain.

For a time, he heard nothing but that. Then there came a scraping, scurrying noise from his wife's room, and a sudden, terrific crash.

With a loud scream his nerve broke, and springing from the bed he sped downstairs and, flinging open the front-door, dashed into the night. The door, caught by the wind, slammed behind him.

With his hand holding the garden-gate open, ready for further flight, he stood sobbing for breath. His bare feet were bruised and the rain was very cold, but he took no heed. Then he ran a little way along the road and stood for some time, hoping and listening.

He came back slowly. The wind was bitter and he was soaked to the skin. The garden was black and forbidding, and unspeakable horror might be lurking in the bushes. He went up the road again, trembling with cold. Then, in desperation, he passed through the terrors of the garden to the house, only to find the door closed. The porch

34

gave a little protection from the icy rain, but none from the wind, and, shaking in every limb, he leaned in abject misery against the door. He pulled himself together after a time and stumbled round to the back-door. Locked! And all the lower windows were shuttered. He made his way back to the porch, and, crouching there in hopeless misery, waited for the woman to return.

4

He had a dim memory, when he awoke, of somebody questioning him, and then of being half pushed, half carried upstairs to bed. There was something wrong with his head and his chest and he was trembling violently, and very cold. Somebody was speaking.

"You must have taken leave of your senses," said the voice of Hannah. "I thought you were dead."

He forced his eyes to open. "Doctor," he muttered, "doctor."

"Out on a bad case," said Hannah. "I waited till I was tired of waiting, and then came along. Good thing for you I did. He'll be round first thing this morning. He ought to be here now."

She bustled about, tidying up the room, his leaden eyes following her as she collected the beef-tea and other things on a tray and carried them out.

"Nice thing I did yesterday," she remarked, as she came back. "Left the missus's bedroom window open. When I opened the door this morning, I found that beautiful Chippindale glass of hers had blown off the table and smashed to pieces. Did you hear it?"

Goddard made no reply. In a confused fashion he was trying to think. Accident or not, the fall of the glass had served its purpose. Were there such things as accidents? Or was life a puzzle—a puzzle into which every piece was made to fit? Fear and the wind. . . no: conscience and the wind. . . had saved the woman. He must get the powder back from her drawer. . . before she discovered it and denounced him. The medicine . . . he must remember not to take it. .

He was very ill, seriously ill. He must have taken a chill owing to that panic flight into the garden. Why didn't the doctor come? He had come . . . at last . . . he was doing something to his chest . . . it was cold.

Again . . . the doctor . . . there was something he wanted to tell him . . . Hannah and a powder . . . what was it?

Later on, he remembered, together with other things that he had hoped to forget. He lay watching an endless procession of memories, broken at times by a glance at the doctor, the nurse, and Hannah, who were all standing near the bed regarding him. They had been there a long time, and they were all very quiet. The last time he looked at Hannah was the first time for months that he had looked at her without loathing and hatred. Then he knew that he was dying.

The Castaway

Mrs. John Boxer stood at the door of the shop with her hands clasped on her apron. The short day had drawn to a close, and the lamps in the narrow little thoroughfares of Shinglesea were already lit. For a time, she stood listening to the regular beat of the sea on the beach some half-mile distant, and then with a slight shiver stepped back into the shop and closed the door.

The little shop with its wide-mouthed bottles of sweets was one of her earliest memories. Until her marriage she had known no other home, and when her husband was lost with the *North Star* some three years before, she gave up her home in Poplar and returned to assist her mother in the little shop.

In a restless mood she took up a piece of needlework, and a minute or two later put it down again. A glance through the glass of the door leading into the small parlour revealed Mrs. Gimpson, with a red shawl round her shoulders, asleep in her easy-chair.

Mrs. Boxer turned at the clang of the shop bell, and then, with a wild cry, stood gazing at the figure of a man standing in the doorway. He was short and bearded, with oddly shaped shoulders, and a left leg which was not a match; but the next moment Mrs. Boxer was in his arms sobbing and laughing together.

Mrs. Gimpson, whose nerves were still quivering owing to the suddenness with which she had been awakened, came into the shop; Mr. Boxer freed an arm, and placing it round her waist kissed her with some affection on the chin.

"He's come back!" cried Mrs. Boxer, hysterically.

"Thank goodness," said Mrs. Gimpson, after a moment's deliberation.

"He's alive!" cried Mrs. Boxer. "He's alive!"

She half-dragged and half-led him into the small parlour, and thrusting him into the easy-chair lately vacated by Mrs. Gimpson seated herself upon his knee, regardless in her excitement that the rightful owner was with elaborate care selecting the most uncomfortable chair in the room.

"Fancy his coming back!" said Mrs. Boxer, wiping her eyes. "How did you escape, John? Where have you been? Tell us all about it."

Mr. Boxer sighed. "It 'ud be a long story if I had the gift of telling of it," he said, slowly, "but I'll cut it short for the present. When the *North Star* went down in the South Pacific most o' the hands got away in the boats, but I was too late. I got this crack on the head with something falling on it from aloft. Look here."

He bent his head, and Mrs. Boxer, separating the stubble with her fingers, uttered an exclamation of pity and alarm at the extent of the scar; Mrs. Gimpson, craning forward, uttered a sound which might mean anything—even pity.

"When I come to my senses," continued Mr. Boxer, "the ship was sinking, and I just got to my feet when she went down and took me with her. How I escaped I don't know. I seemed to be choking and fighting for my breath for years, and then I found myself floating on the sea and clinging to a grating. I clung to it all night, and next day I was picked up by a native who was paddling about in a canoe, and taken ashore to an island, where I lived for over two years. It was right out o' the way o' craft, but at last I was picked up by a trading schooner named the *Pearl,* belonging to Sydney, and taken there. At Sydney I shipped aboard the *Marston Towers,* a steamer, and landed at the Albert Docks this morning."

"Poor John," said his wife, holding on to his arm. "How you must have suffered!"

"I did," said Mr. Boxer. "Mother got a cold?" he inquired, eying that lady.

"No, I ain't," said Mrs. Gimpson, answering for herself. "Why didn't you write when you got to Sydney?"

"Didn't know where to write to," replied Mr. Boxer, staring. "I didn't know where Mary had gone to."

"You might ha' wrote here," said Mrs. Gimpson.

"Didn't think of it at the time," said Mr. Boxer. "One thing is, I was very busy at Sydney, looking for a ship. However, I'm 'ere now."

"I always felt you'd turn up some day," said Mrs. Gimpson. "I felt certain of it in my own mind. Mary made sure you was dead, but I said 'no, I knew better.'"

There was something in Mrs. Gimpson's manner of saying this that impressed her listeners unfavourably. The impression was deepened when, after a short, dry laugh *à propos* of nothing, she sniffed again—three times.

"Well, you turned out to be right," said Mr. Boxer, shortly.

"I gin'rally am," was the reply; "there's very few people can take me in."

She sniffed again.

"Were the natives kind to you?" inquired Mrs. Boxer, hastily, as she turned to her husband.

"Very kind," said the latter. "Ah! you ought to have seen that island. Beautiful yellow sands and palm-trees; cocoa-nuts to be 'ad for the picking, and nothing to do all day but lay about in the sun and swim in the sea."

"Any public-'ouses there?" inquired Mrs. Gimpson.

"Cert'nly not," said her son-in-law. "This was an island—one o' the little islands in the South Pacific Ocean."

"What did you say the name o' the schooner was?" inquired Mrs. Gimpson.

"*Pearl*," replied Mr. Boxer, with the air of a resentful witness under cross-examination.

"And what was the name o' the captin?" said Mrs. Gimpson.

"Thomas—Henery—Walter—Smith," said Mr. Boxer, with somewhat unpleasant emphasis.

"An' the mate's name?"

"John Brown," was the reply.

"Common names," commented Mrs. Gimpson, "very common. But I knew you'd come back all right—I never 'ad no alarm. 'He's safe and happy, my dear,' I says. 'He'll come back all in his own good time.'"

"What d'you mean by that?" demanded the sensitive Mr. Boxer. "I come back as soon as I could."

"You know you were anxious, mother," interposed her daughter. "Why, you insisted upon our going to see old Mr. Silver about it."

"Ah! but I wasn't uneasy or anxious afterwards," said Mrs. Gimpson, compressing her lips.

"Who's old Mr. Silver, and what should he know about it?" inquired Mr. Boxer.

"He's a fortune-teller," replied his wife. "Reads the stars," said his mother-in-law.

Mr. Boxer laughed—a good ringing laugh. "What did he tell you?"

he inquired.

"Nothing," said his wife, hastily.

"Ah!" said Mr. Boxer, waggishly, "that was wise of 'im. Most of us could tell fortunes that way."

"That's wrong," said Mrs. Gimpson to her daughter, sharply. "Right's right any day, and truth's truth. He said that he knew all about John and what he'd been doing, but he wouldn't tell us for fear of 'urting our feelings and making mischief."

"Here, look 'ere," said Mr. Boxer, starting up; "I've 'ad about enough o' this. Why don't you speak out what you mean? I'll mischief 'im, the old humbug. Old rascal."

"Never mind, John," said his wife, laying her hand upon his arm. "Here you are safe and sound, and as for old Mr. Silver, there's a lot o' people don't believe in him."

"Ah! they don't want to," said Mrs. Gimpson, obstinately. "But don't forget that he foretold my cough last winter."

"Well, look 'ere," said Mr. Boxer, twisting his short, blunt nose into as near an imitation of a sneer as he could manage, "I've told you my story and I've got witnesses to prove it. You can write to the master of the *Marston Towers* if you like, and other people besides. Very well, then; let's go and see your precious old fortune-teller. You needn't say who I am; say I'm a friend, and tell 'im never to mind about making mischief, but to say right out where I am and what I've been doing all this time. I have my 'opes it'll cure you of your superstitiousness."

"We'll go round after we've shut up, mother," said Mrs. Boxer. "We'll have a bit o' supper first and then start early."

Mrs. Gimpson hesitated. It is never pleasant to submit one's superstitions to the tests of the unbelieving, but after the attitude she had taken up she was extremely loath to allow her son-in-law a triumph.

"Never mind, we'll say no more about it," she said, primly, "but I 'ave my own ideas."

"I dessay," said Mr. Boxer; "but you're afraid for us to go to your old fortune-teller. It would be too much of a show-up for 'im."

"It's no good your trying to aggravate me, John Boxer, because you can't do it," said Mrs. Gimpson, in a voice trembling with passion.

"O' course, if people like being deceived they must be," said Mr. Boxer; "we've all got to live, and if we'd all got our common-sense fortune-tellers couldn't. Does he tell fortunes by tea-leaves or by the colour of your eyes?"

"Laugh away, John Boxer," said Mrs. Gimpson, icily; "but I shouldn't have been alive now if it hadn't ha' been for Mr. Silver's warnings."

"Mother stayed in bed for the first ten days in July," explained Mrs. Boxer, "to avoid being bit by a mad dog."

"*Tchee—tchee—tchee*," said the hapless Mr. Boxer, putting his hand over his mouth and making noble efforts to restrain himself; "*tchee—tch—*

"I s'pose you'd ha' laughed more if I 'ad been bit?" said the glaring Mrs. Gimpson.

"Well, who did the dog bite after all?" inquired Mr. Boxer, recovering.

"You don't understand," replied Mrs. Gimpson, pityingly; "me being safe up in bed and the door locked, there was no mad dog. There was no use for it."

"Well," said Mr. Boxer, "me and Mary's going round to see that old deceiver after supper, whether you come or not. Mary shall tell 'im I'm a friend, and ask him to tell her everything about 'er husband. Nobody knows me here, and Mary and me'll be affectionate like, and give 'im to understand we want to marry. Then he won't mind making mischief."

"You'd better leave well alone," said Mrs. Gimpson.

Mr. Boxer shook his head. "I was always one for a bit o' fun," he said, slowly. "I want to see his face when he finds out who I am."

Mrs. Gimpson made no reply; she was looking round for the market-basket, and having found it she left the reunited couple to keep house while she went out to obtain a supper which should, in her daughter's eyes, be worthy of the occasion.

She went to the High Street first and made her purchases, and was on the way back again when, in response to a sudden impulse, as she passed the end of Crowner's Alley, she turned into that small by-way and knocked at the astrologer's door.

A slow, dragging footstep was heard approaching in reply to the summons, and the astrologer, recognising his visitor as one of his most faithful and credulous clients, invited her to step inside. Mrs. Gimpson complied, and, taking a chair, gazed at the venerable white beard and small, red-rimmed eyes of her host in some perplexity as to how to begin.

"My daughter's coming round to see you presently," she said, at last. The astrologer nodded.

"She—she wants to ask you about 'er husband," faltered' Mrs. Gimpson; "she's going to bring a friend with her—a man who doesn't believe in your knowledge. He—he knows all about my daughter's husband, and he wants to see what you say you know about him."

The old man put on a pair of huge horn spectacles and eyed her carefully.

"You've got something on your mind," he said, at last; "you'd better tell me everything."

Mrs. Gimpson shook her head.

"There's some danger hanging over you," continued Mr. Silver, in a low, thrilling voice; "some danger in connection with your son-in-law. There" he waved a lean, shrivelled hand backward and forward as though dispelling a fog, and peered into distance—"there is something forming over you. You—or somebody—are hiding something from me."

Mrs. Gimpson, aghast at such omniscience, sank backward in her chair.

"Speak," said the old man, gently; "there is no reason why you should be sacrificed for others."

Mrs. Gimpson was of the same opinion, and in some haste, she reeled off the events of the evening. She had a good memory, and no detail was lost.

"Strange, strange," said the venerable Mr. Silver, when he had finished. "He is an ingenious man."

"Isn't it true?" inquired his listener. "He says he can prove it. And he is going to find out what you meant by saying you were afraid of making mischief."

"He can prove some of it," said the old man, his eyes snapping spitefully. "I can guarantee that."

"But it wouldn't have made mischief if you had told us that," ventured Mrs. Gimpson. "A man can't help being cast away."

"True," said the astrologer, slowly; "true. But let them come and question me; and whatever you do, for your own sake don't let a soul know that you have been here. If you do, the danger to yourself will be so terrible that even I may be unable to help you."

Mrs. Gimpson shivered, and more than ever impressed by his marvellous powers made her way slowly home, where she found the unconscious Mr. Boxer relating his adventures again with much gusto to a married couple from next door.

"It's a wonder he's alive," said Mr. Jem Thompson, looking up as the old woman entered the room; "it sounds like a storybook. Show us that cut on your head again, mate."

The obliging Mr. Boxer complied.

"We're going on with 'em after they've 'ad supper," continued Mr. Thompson, as he and his wife rose to depart. "It'll be a fair treat to me to see old Silver bowled out."

Mrs. Gimpson sniffed and eyed his retreating figure disparagingly; Mrs. Boxer, prompted by her husband, began to set the table for supper.

It was a lengthy meal, owing principally to Mr. Boxer, but it was over at last, and after that gentleman had assisted in shutting up the shop, they joined the Thompsons, who were waiting outside, and set off for Crowner's Alley. The way was enlivened by Mr. Boxer, who had thrills of horror every ten yards at the idea of the supernatural things he was about to witness, and by Mr. Thompson, who, not to be outdone, persisted in standing stock still at frequent intervals until he had received the assurances of his giggling better-half that he would not be made to vanish in a cloud of smoke.

By the time they reached Mr. Silver's abode the party had regained its decorum, and, except for a tremendous shudder on the part of Mr. Boxer as his gaze fell on a couple of skulls which decorated the magician's table, their behaviour left nothing to be desired. Mrs. Gimpson, in a few awkward words, announced the occasion of their visit. Mr. Boxer she introduced as a friend of the family from London.

"I will do what I can," said the old man, slowly, as his visitors seated themselves, "but I can only tell you what I see. If I do not see all, or see clearly, it cannot be helped."

Mr. Boxer winked at Mr. Thompson, and received an understanding pinch in return; Mrs. Thompson in a hot whisper told them to behave themselves.

The mystic preparations were soon complete. A little cloud of smoke, through which the fierce red eyes of the astrologer peered keenly at Mr. Boxer, rose from the table. Then he poured various liquids into a small china bowl and, holding up his hand to command silence, gazed steadfastly into it. "I see pictures," he announced, in a deep voice. "The docks of a great city; London. I see an ill-shaped man with a bent left leg standing on the deck of a ship."

Mr. Thompson, his eyes wide open with surprise, jerked Mr. Boxer in the ribs, but Mr. Boxer, whose figure was a sore point with him, made no response.

"The ship leaves the docks," continued Mr. Silver, still peering into the bowl. "As she passes through the entrance her stern comes into view with the name painted on it. The—the—the——"

"Look agin, old chap," growled Mr. Boxer, in an undertone.

"The *North Star*," said the astrologer. "The ill-shaped man is still standing on the fore-part of the ship; I do not know his name or who he is. He takes the portrait of a beautiful young woman from his pocket and gazes at it earnestly."

Mrs. Boxer, who had no illusions on the subject of her personal appearance, sat up as though she had been stung; Mr. Thompson, who was about to nudge Mr. Boxer in the ribs again, thought better of it and assumed an air of uncompromising virtue.

"The picture disappears," said Mr. Silver. "Ah! I see; I see. A ship in a gale at sea. It is the *North Star*; it is sinking. The ill-shaped man sheds tears and loses his head. I cannot discover the name of this man."

Mr. Boxer, who had been several times on the point of interrupting, cleared his throat and endeavoured to look unconcerned.

"The ship sinks," continued the astrologer, in thrilling tones. "Ah! what is this? a piece of wreckage with a monkey clinging to it? No, no-o. The ill-shaped man again. Dear me!"

His listeners sat spellbound. Only the laboured and intense breathing of Mr. Boxer broke the silence.

"He is alone on the boundless sea," pursued the seer; "night falls. Day breaks, and a canoe propelled by a slender and pretty but dusky maiden approaches the castaway. She assists him into the canoe and his head sinks on her lap, as with vigorous strokes of her paddle she propels the canoe toward a small island fringed with palm trees."

"Here, look 'ere—" began the overwrought Mr. Boxer.

"*H'sh, h'sh!*" ejaculated the keenly interested Mr. Thompson. "W'y don't you keep quiet?"

"The picture fades," continued the old man. "I see another: a native wedding. It is the dusky maiden and the man she rescued. Ah! the wedding is interrupted; a young man, a native, breaks into the group. He has a long knife in his hand. He springs upon the ill-shaped man and wounds him in the head."

Involuntarily Mr. Boxer's hand went up to his honourable scar, and the heads of the others swung round to gaze at it. Mrs. Boxer's face was terrible in its expression, but Mrs. Gimpson's bore the look of sad and patient triumph of one who knew men and could not be surprised at anything they do.

"The scene vanishes," resumed the monotonous voice, "and another one forms. The same man stands on the deck of a small ship.

The name on the stern is the *Peer*—no, *Paris*—no, no, no, *Pearl*. It fades from the shore where the dusky maiden stands with hands stretched out imploringly. The ill-shaped man smiles and takes the portrait of the young and beautiful girl from his pocket."

"Look 'ere," said the infuriated Mr. Boxer, "I think we've 'ad about enough of this rubbish. I have—more than enough."

"I don't wonder at it," said his wife, trembling furiously. "You can go if you like. I'm going to stay and hear all that there is to hear."

"You sit quiet," urged the intensely interested Mr. Thompson. "He ain't said it's you. There's more than one misshaped man in the world, I s'pose?"

"I see an ocean liner," said the seer, who had appeared to be in a trance state during this colloquy. "She is sailing for England from Australia. I see the name distinctly: the *Marston Towers*. The same man is on board of her. The ship arrives at London. The scene closes; another one forms. The ill-shaped man is sitting with a woman with a beautiful face—not the same as the photograph."

"What they can see in him I can't think," muttered Mr. Thompson, in an envious whisper. "He's a perfick terror, and to look at him——"

"They sit hand in hand," continued the astrologer, raising his voice. "She smiles up at him and gently strokes his head; he——"

A loud smack rang through the room and startled the entire company; Mrs. Boxer, unable to contain herself any longer, had, so far from profiting by the example, gone to the other extreme and slapped her husband's head with hearty good-will. Mr. Boxer sprang raging to his feet, and in the confusion, which ensued the fortune-teller, to the great regret of Mr. Thompson, upset the contents of the magic bowl.

"I can see no more," he said, sinking hastily into his chair behind the table as Mr. Boxer advanced upon him.

Mrs. Gimpson pushed her son-in-law aside, and laying a modest fee upon the table took her daughter's arm and led her out. The Thompsons followed, and Mr. Boxer, after an irresolute glance in the direction of the ingenuous Mr. Silver, made his way after them and fell into the rear. The people in front walked on for some time in silence, and then the voice of the greatly impressed Mrs. Thompson was heard, to the effect that if there were only more fortune-tellers in the world there would be a lot more better men.

Mr. Boxer trotted up to his wife's side. "Look here, Mary," he began.

"Don't you speak to me," said his wife, drawing closer to her mother, "because I won't answer you."

Mr. Boxer laughed, bitterly. "This is a nice home-coming," he remarked.

He fell to the rear again and walked along raging, his temper by no means being improved by observing that Mrs. Thompson, doubtless with a firm belief in the saying that "Evil communications corrupt good manners," kept a tight hold of her husband's arm. His position as an outcast was clearly defined, and he ground his teeth with rage as he observed the virtuous uprightness of Mrs. Gimpson's back. By the time they reached home he was in a spirit of mad recklessness far in advance of the character given him by the astrologer.

His wife gazed at him with a look of such strong interrogation as he was about to follow her into the house that he paused with his foot on the step and eyed her dumbly.

"Have you left anything inside that you want?" she inquired.

Mr. Boxer shook his head. "I only wanted to come in and make a clean breast of it," he said, in a curious voice; "then I'll go."

Mrs. Gimpson stood aside to let him pass, and Mr. Thompson, not to be denied, followed close behind with his faintly protesting wife. They sat down in a row against the wall, and Mr. Boxer, sitting opposite in a hang-dog fashion, eyed them with scornful wrath.

"Well?" said Mrs. Boxer, at last.

"All that he said was quite true," said her husband, defiantly. "The only thing is, he didn't tell the arf of it. Altogether, I married three dusky maidens."

Everybody but Mr. Thompson shuddered with horror.

"Then I married a white girl in Australia," pursued Mr. Boxer, musingly. "I wonder old Silver didn't see that in the bowl; not 'arf a fortune-teller, I call 'im."

"What they *see* in 'im!" whispered the astounded Mr. Thompson to his wife.

"And did you marry the beautiful girl in the photograph?" demanded Mrs. Boxer, in trembling accents.

"I did," said her husband.

"Hussy," cried Mrs. Boxer.

"I married her," said Mr. Boxer, considering—"I married her at Camberwell, in eighteen ninety-three."

"Eighteen *ninety-three!*" said his wife, in a startled voice. "But you couldn't. Why, you didn't marry me till eighteen ninety-*four.*"

"What's that got to do with it?" inquired the monster, calmly.

Mrs. Boxer, pale as ashes, rose from her seat and stood gazing at him with horror-struck eyes, trying in vain to speak.

"You villain!" cried Mrs. Gimpson, violently. "I always distrusted you."

"I know you did," said Mr. Boxer, calmly.

"You've been committing bigamy," cried Mrs. Gimpson.

"Over and over agin," assented Mr. Boxer, cheerfully. "It's got to be a 'obby with me."

"Was the first wife alive when you married my daughter?" demanded Mrs. Gimpson.

"Alive?" said Mr. Boxer. "O' course she was. She's alive now—bless her."

He leaned back in his chair and regarded with intense satisfaction the horrified faces of the group in front.

"You—you'll go to jail for this," cried Mrs. Gimpson, breathlessly. "What is your first wife's address?"

"I decline to answer that question," said her son-in-law.

"What is your first wife's address?" repeated Mrs. Gimpson.

"Ask the fortune-teller," said Mr. Boxer, with an aggravating smile. "And then get 'im up in the box as a witness, little bowl and all. He can tell you more than I can."

"I demand to know her name and address," cried Mrs. Gimpson, putting a bony arm around the waist of the trembling Mrs. Boxer.

"I decline to give it," said Mr. Boxer, with great relish. "It ain't likely I'm going to give myself away like that; besides, it's agin the law for a man to criminate himself. You go on and start your bigamy case, and call old red-eyes as a witness."

Mrs. Gimpson gazed at him in speechless wrath and then stooping down conversed in excited whispers with Mrs. Thompson. Mrs. Boxer crossed over to her husband.

"Oh, John," she wailed, "say it isn't true, say it isn't true."

Mr. Boxer hesitated. "What's the good o' me saying anything?" he said, doggedly.

"It isn't true," persisted his wife. "Say it isn't true."

"What I told you when I first came in this evening was quite true," said her husband, slowly. "And what I've just told you is as true as what that lying old fortune-teller told you. You can please yourself what you believe."

"I believe you, John," said his wife, humbly.

Mr. Boxer's countenance cleared and he drew her on to his knee.

"That's right," he said, cheerfully. "So long as you believe in me, I don't care what other people think. And before I'm much older I'll find out how that old rascal got to know the names of the ships I was aboard. Seems to me somebody's been talking."

The Monkey's Paw

Without, the night was cold and wet, but in the small parlour of Laburnam Villa the blinds were drawn and the fire burned brightly. Father and son were at chess, the former, who possessed ideas about the game involving radical changes, putting his king into such sharp and unnecessary perils that it even provoked comment from the white-haired old lady knitting placidly by the fire.

"Hark at the wind," said Mr. White, who, having seen a fatal mistake after it was too late, was amiably desirous of preventing his son from seeing it.

"I'm listening," said the latter, grimly surveying the board as he stretched out his hand. "Check."

"I should hardly think that he'd come tonight," said his father, with his hand poised over the board.

"Mate," replied the son.

"That's the worst of living so far out," bawled Mr. White, with sudden and unlooked-for violence; "of all the beastly, slushy, out-of-the-way places to live in, this is the worst. Pathway's a bog, and the road's a torrent. I don't know what people are thinking about. I suppose because only two houses in the road are let, they think it doesn't matter."

"Never mind, dear," said his wife, soothingly; "perhaps you'll win the next one."

Mr. White looked up sharply, just in time to intercept a knowing glance between mother and son. The words died away on his lips, and he hid a guilty grin in his thin grey beard.

"There he is," said Herbert White, as the gate banged to loudly and heavy footsteps came toward the door.

The old man rose with hospitable haste, and opening the door, was heard condoling with the new arrival. The new arrival also condoled with himself, so that Mrs. White said, "Tut, tut!" and coughed gently as her husband entered the room, followed by a tall, burly man, beady of eye and rubicund of visage.

"Sergeant-Major Morris," he said, introducing him.

The sergeant-major shook hands, and taking the proffered seat by the fire, watched contentedly while his host got out whiskey and tumblers and stood a small copper kettle on the fire.

At the third glass his eyes got brighter, and he began to talk, the little family circle regarding with eager interest this visitor from distant parts, as he squared his broad shoulders in the chair and spoke of wild scenes and doughty deeds; of wars and plagues and strange peoples.

"Twenty-one years of it," said Mr. White, nodding at his wife and son. "When he went away, he was a slip of a youth in the warehouse. Now look at him."

"He don't look to have taken much harm," said Mrs. White, politely.

"I'd like to go to India myself," said the old man, "just to look round a bit, you know."

"Better where you are," said the sergeant-major, shaking his head. He put down the empty glass, and sighing softly, shook it again.

"I should like to see those old temples and *fakirs* and jugglers," said the old man. "What was that you started telling me the other day about a monkey's paw or something, Morris?"

"Nothing," said the soldier, hastily. "Leastways nothing worth hearing."

"Monkey's paw?" said Mrs. White, curiously.

"Well, it's just a bit of what you might call magic, perhaps," said the sergeant-major, offhandedly.

His three listeners leaned forward eagerly. The visitor absent-mindedly put his empty glass to his lips and then set it down again. His host filled it for him.

"To look at," said the sergeant-major, fumbling in his pocket, "it's just an ordinary little paw, dried to a mummy."

He took something out of his pocket and proffered it. Mrs. White drew back with a grimace, but her son, taking it, examined it curiously.

"And what is there special about it?" inquired Mr. White as he took it from his son, and having examined it, placed it upon the table.

"It had a spell put on it by an old *fakir*," said the sergeant-major, "a very holy man. He wanted to show that fate ruled people's lives, and that those who interfered with it did so to their sorrow. He put a spell on it so that three separate men could each have three wishes from it."

His manner was so impressive that his hearers were conscious that their light laughter jarred somewhat.

"Well, why don't you have three, sir?" said Herbert White, cleverly.

The soldier regarded him in the way that middle age is wont to regard presumptuous youth. "I have," he said, quietly, and his blotchy face whitened.

"And did you really have the three wishes granted?" asked Mrs. White.

"I did," said the sergeant-major, and his glass tapped against his strong teeth.

"And has anybody else wished?" persisted the old lady.

"The first man had his three wishes. Yes," was the reply; "I don't know what the first two were, but the third was for death. That's how I got the paw."

His tones were so grave that a hush fell upon the group.

"If you've had your three wishes, it's no good to you now, then, Morris," said the old man at last. "What do you keep it for?"

The soldier shook his head. "Fancy, I suppose," he said, slowly. "I did have some idea of selling it, but I don't think I will. It has caused enough mischief already. Besides, people won't buy. They think it's a fairy tale; some of them, and those who do think anything of it want to try it first and pay me afterward."

"If you could have another three wishes," said the old man, eyeing him keenly, "would you have them?"

"I don't know," said the other. "I don't know."

He took the paw, and dangling it between his forefinger and thumb, suddenly threw it upon the fire. White, with a slight cry, stooped down and snatched it off.

"Better let it burn," said the soldier, solemnly.

"If you don't want it, Morris," said the other, "give it to me."

"I won't," said his friend, doggedly. "I threw it on the fire. If you keep it, don't blame me for what happens. Pitch it on the fire again like a sensible man."

The other shook his head and examined his new possession closely. "How do you do it?" he inquired.

"Hold it up in your right hand and wish aloud," said the sergeant-major, "but I warn you of the consequences."

"Sounds like the *Arabian Nights*," said Mrs. White, as she rose and began to set the supper. "Don't you think you might wish for four pairs of hands for me?"

Her husband drew the talisman from pocket, and then all three burst into laughter as the sergeant-major, with a look of alarm on his face, caught him by the arm.

"If you must wish," he said, gruffly, "wish for something sensible."

Mr. White dropped it back in his pocket, and placing chairs, motioned his friend to the table. In the business of supper, the talisman was partly forgotten, and afterward the three sat listening in an enthralled fashion to a second instalment of the soldier's adventures in India.

"If the tale about the monkey's paw is not more truthful than those he has been telling us," said Herbert, as the door closed behind their guest, just in time for him to catch the last train, "we sha'nt make much out of it."

"Did you give him anything for it, father?" inquired Mrs. White, regarding her husband closely.

"A trifle," said he, colouring slightly. "He didn't want it, but I made him take it. And he pressed me again to throw it away."

"Likely," said Herbert, with pretended horror. "Why, we're going to be rich, and famous and happy. Wish to be an emperor, father, to begin with; then you can't be henpecked."

He darted round the table, pursued by the maligned Mrs. White armed with an antimacassar.

Mr. White took the paw from his pocket and eyed it dubiously. "I don't know what to wish for, and that's a fact," he said, slowly. "It seems to me I've got all I want."

"If you only cleared the house, you'd be quite happy, wouldn't you?" said Herbert, with his hand on his shoulder. "Well, wish for two hundred pounds, then; that 'll just do it."

His father, smiling shamefacedly at his own credulity, held up the talisman, as his son, with a solemn face, somewhat marred by a wink at his mother, sat down at the piano and struck a few impressive chords.

"I wish for two hundred pounds," said the old man distinctly.

A fine crash from the piano greeted the words, interrupted by a shuddering cry from the old man. His wife and son ran toward him.

"It moved," he cried, with a glance of disgust at the object as it lay on the floor.

"As I wished, it twisted in my hand like a snake."

"Well, I don't see the money," said his son as he picked it up and placed it on the table, "and I bet I never shall."

"It must have been your fancy, father," said his wife, regarding him anxiously.

He shook his head. "Never mind, though; there's no harm done, but it gave me a shock all the same."

They sat down by the fire again while the two men finished their pipes. Outside, the wind was higher than ever, and the old man started nervously at the sound of a door banging upstairs. A silence unusual and depressing settled upon all three, which lasted until the old couple rose to retire for the night.

"I expect you'll find the cash tied up in a big bag in the middle of your bed," said Herbert, as he bade them goodnight, "and something horrible squatting up on top of the wardrobe watching you as you pocket your ill-gotten gains."

He sat alone in the darkness, gazing at the dying fire, and seeing faces in it. The last face was so horrible and so simian that he gazed at it in amazement. It got so vivid that, with a little uneasy laugh, he felt on the table for a glass containing a little water to throw over it. His hand grasped the monkey's paw, and with a little shiver he wiped his hand on his coat and went up to bed.

2

In the brightness of the wintry sun next morning as it streamed over the breakfast table he laughed at his fears. There was an air of prosaic wholesomeness about the room which it had lacked on the previous night, and the dirty, shrivelled little paw was pitched on the sideboard with a carelessness which betokened no great belief in its virtues.

"I suppose all old soldiers are the same," said Mrs. White. "The idea of our listening to such nonsense! How could wishes be granted in these days? And if they could, how could two hundred pounds hurt you, father?"

"Might drop on his head from the sky," said the frivolous Herbert.

"Morris said the things happened so naturally," said his father, "that you might if you so wished attribute it to coincidence."

"Well, don't break into the money before I come back," said Herbert as he rose from the table. "I'm afraid it'll turn you into a mean, avaricious man, and we shall have to disown you."

His mother laughed, and following him to the door, watched him down the road; and returning to the breakfast table, was very happy at the expense of her husband's credulity. All of which did not prevent her from scurrying to the door at the postman's knock, nor prevent her from referring somewhat shortly to retired sergeant-majors of bibulous habits when she found that the post brought a tailor's bill.

"Herbert will have some more of his funny remarks, I expect, when he comes home," she said, as they sat at dinner.

"I dare say," said Mr. White, pouring himself out some beer; "but for all that, the thing moved in my hand; that I'll swear to."

"You thought it did," said the old lady soothingly.

"I say it did," replied the other. "There was no thought about it; I had just—What's the matter?"

His wife made no reply. She was watching the mysterious movements of a man outside, who, peering in an undecided fashion at the house, appeared to be trying to make up his mind to enter. In mental connection with the two hundred pounds, she noticed that the stranger was well dressed, and wore a silk hat of glossy newness. Three times he paused at the gate, and then walked on again. The fourth time he stood with his hand upon it, and then with sudden resolution flung it open and walked up the path. Mrs. White at the same moment placed her hands behind her, and hurriedly unfastening the strings of her apron, put that useful article of apparel beneath the cushion of her chair.

She brought the stranger, who seemed ill at ease, into the room. He gazed at her furtively, and listened in a preoccupied fashion as the old lady apologized for the appearance of the room, and her husband's coat, a garment which he usually reserved for the garden. She then waited as patiently as her sex would permit, for him to broach his business, but he was at first strangely silent.

"I—was asked to call," he said at last, and stooped and picked a piece of cotton from his trousers. "I come from 'Maw and Meggins.'"

The old lady started. "Is anything the matter?" she asked, breathlessly. "Has anything happened to Herbert? What is it? What is it?"

Her husband interposed. "There, there, mother," he said, hastily. "Sit down, and don't jump to conclusions. You've not brought bad news, I'm sure, sir;" and he eyed the other wistfully.

"I'm sorry—" began the visitor.

"Is he hurt?" demanded the mother, wildly.

The visitor bowed in assent. "Badly hurt," he said, quietly, "but he is not in any pain."

"Oh, thank God!" said the old woman, clasping her hands. "Thank

God for that! Thank—"

She broke off suddenly as the sinister meaning of the assurance dawned upon her and she saw the awful confirmation of her fears in the other's averted face. She caught her breath, and turning to her slower-witted husband, laid her trembling old hand upon his. There was a long silence.

"He was caught in the machinery," said the visitor at length in a low voice.

"Caught in the machinery," repeated Mr. White, in a dazed fashion, "yes."

He sat staring blankly out at the window, and taking his wife's hand between his own, pressed it as he had been wont to do in their old courting-days nearly forty years before.

"He was the only one left to us," he said, turning gently to the visitor. "It is hard."

The other coughed, and rising, walked slowly to the window. "The firm wished me to convey their sincere sympathy with you in your great loss," he said, without looking round. "I beg that you will understand I am only their servant and merely obeying orders."

There was no reply; the old woman's face was white, her eyes staring, and her breath inaudible; on the husband's face was a look such as his friend the sergeant might have carried into his first action.

"I was to say that 'Maw and Meggins' disclaim all responsibility," continued the other. "They admit no liability at all, but in consideration of your son's services, they wish to present you with a certain sum as compensation."

Mr. White dropped his wife's hand, and rising to his feet, gazed with a look of horror at his visitor. His dry lips shaped the words, "How much?"

"Two hundred pounds," was the answer.

Unconscious of his wife's shriek, the old man smiled faintly, put out his hands like a sightless man, and dropped, a senseless heap, to the floor.

3

In the huge new cemetery, some two miles distant, the old people buried their dead, and came back to a house steeped in shadow and silence. It was all over so quickly that at first, they could hardly realise it, and remained in a state of expectation as though of something else to happen—something else which was to lighten this load, too heavy for old hearts to bear.

But the days passed, and expectation gave place to resignation—the hopeless resignation of the old, sometimes miscalled, apathy. Sometimes they hardly exchanged a word, for now they had nothing to talk about, and their days were long to weariness.

It was about a week after that the old man, waking suddenly in the night, stretched out his hand and found himself alone. The room was in darkness, and the sound of subdued weeping came from the window. He raised himself in bed and listened.

"Come back," he said, tenderly. "You will be cold."

"It is colder for my son," said the old woman, and wept afresh.

The sound of her sobs died away on his ears. The bed was warm, and his eyes heavy with sleep. He dozed fitfully, and then slept until a sudden wild cry from his wife awoke him with a start.

"*The paw!*" she cried wildly. "The monkey's paw!"

He started up in alarm. "Where? Where is it? What's the matter?"

She came stumbling across the room toward him. "I want it," she said, quietly. "You've not destroyed it?"

"It's in the parlour, on the bracket," he replied, marvelling. "Why?"

She cried and laughed together, and bending over, kissed his cheek.

"I only just thought of it," she said, hysterically. "Why didn't I think of it before? Why didn't *you* think of it?"

"Think of what?" he questioned.

"The other two wishes," she replied, rapidly. "We've only had one."

"Was not that enough?" he demanded, fiercely.

"No," she cried, triumphantly; "we'll have one more. Go down and get it quickly, and wish our boy alive again."

The man sat up in bed and flung the bedclothes from his quaking limbs. "Good God, you are mad!" he cried, aghast.

"Get it," she panted; "get it quickly, and wish—Oh, my boy, my boy!"

Her husband struck a match and lit the candle. "Get back to bed," he said, unsteadily. "You don't know what you are saying."

"We had the first wish granted," said the old woman, feverishly; "why not the second?"

"A coincidence," stammered the old man.

"Go and get it and wish," cried his wife, quivering with excitement.

The old man turned and regarded her, and his voice shook. "He has been dead ten days, and besides he—I would not tell you else, but—I could only recognise him by his clothing. If he was too terrible for you to see then, how now?"

"Bring him back," cried the old woman, and dragged him toward the door. "Do you think I fear the child I have nursed?"

He went down in the darkness, and felt his way to the parlour, and then to the mantelpiece. The talisman was in its place, and a horrible fear that the unspoken wish might bring his mutilated son before him ere he could escape from the room seized upon him, and he caught his breath as he found that he had lost the direction of the door. His brow cold with sweat, he felt his way round the table, and groped along the wall until he found himself in the small passage with the unwholesome thing in his hand.

Even his wife's face seemed changed as he entered the room. It was white and expectant, and to his fears seemed to have an unnatural look upon it. He was afraid of her.

"*Wish!*" she cried, in a strong voice.

"It is foolish and wicked," he faltered.

"*Wish!*" repeated his wife.

He raised his hand. "I wish my son alive again."

The talisman fell to the floor, and he regarded it fearfully. Then he sank trembling into a chair as the old woman, with burning eyes, walked to the window and raised the blind.

He sat until he was chilled with the cold, glancing occasionally at the figure of the old woman peering through the window. The candle-end, which had burned below the rim of the china candlestick, was throwing pulsating shadows on the ceiling and walls, until, with a flicker larger than the rest, it expired. The old man, with an unspeakable sense of relief at the failure of the talisman, crept back to his bed, and a minute or two afterward the old woman came silently and apathetically beside him.

Neither spoke, but lay silently listening to the ticking of the clock. A stair creaked, and a squeaky mouse scurried noisily through the wall. The darkness was oppressive, and after lying for some time screwing up his courage, he took the box of matches, and striking one, went downstairs for a candle.

At the foot of the stairs the match went out, and he paused to strike another; and at the same moment a knock, so quiet and stealthy as to be scarcely audible, sounded on the front door.

The matches fell from his hand and spilled in the passage. He stood motionless, his breath suspended until the knock was repeated. Then he turned and fled swiftly back to his room, and closed the door behind him. A third knock sounded through the house.

"*What's that?*" cried the old woman, starting up.

"A rat," said the old man in shaking tones—"a rat. It passed me on the stairs."

His wife sat up in bed listening. A loud knock resounded through the house.

"It's Herbert!" she screamed. "It's Herbert!"

She ran to the door, but her husband was before her, and catching her by the arm, held her tightly.

"What are you going to do?" he whispered hoarsely.

"It's my boy; it's Herbert!" she cried, struggling mechanically. "I forgot it was two miles away. What are you holding me for? Let go. I must open the door."

"For God's sake don't let it in," cried the old man, trembling.

"You're afraid of your own son," she cried, struggling. "Let me go. I'm coming, Herbert; I'm coming."

There was another knock, and another. The old woman with a sudden wrench broke free and ran from the room. Her husband followed to the landing, and called after her appealingly as she hurried downstairs. He heard the chain rattle back and the bottom bolt drawn slowly and stiffly from the socket. Then the old woman's voice, strained and panting.

"The bolt," she cried, loudly. "Come down. I can't reach it."

But her husband was on his hands and knees groping wildly on the floor in search of the paw. If he could only find it before the thing outside got in. A perfect fusillade of knocks reverberated through the house, and he heard the scraping of a chair as his wife put it down in the passage against the door. He heard the creaking of the bolt as it came slowly back, and at the same moment he found the monkey's paw, and frantically breathed his third and last wish.

The knocking ceased suddenly, although the echoes of it were still in the house. He heard the chair drawn back, and the door opened. A cold wind rushed up the staircase, and a long loud wail of disappointment and misery from his wife gave him courage to run down to her side, and then to the gate beyond. The street lamp flickering opposite shone on a quiet and deserted road.

Sam's Ghost

"Yes, I know", said the night-watchman, thoughtfully, as he sat with a cold pipe in his mouth gazing across the river. "I've 'eard it afore. People tell me they don't believe in ghosts and make a laugh of 'em, and all I say is: let them take on a night-watchman's job. Let 'em sit 'ere all alone of a night with the water lapping against the posts and the wind moaning in the corners; especially if a pal of theirs has slipped overboard, and there is little nasty bills stuck up just outside in the High Street offering a reward for the body. Twice men 'ave fallen overboard from this jetty, and I've 'ad to stand my watch here the same night, and not a farthing more for it.

"One of the worst and artfullest ghosts I ever 'ad anything to do with was Sam Bullet. He was a waterman at the stairs nearby 'ere; the sort o' man that 'ud get you to pay for drinkst and drink yours up by mistake arter he 'ad finished his own. The sort of man that 'ad always left his baccy-box at 'ome, but always 'ad a big pipe in 'is pocket. He fell overboard off of a lighter one evening, and all that his mates could save was 'is cap. It was on'y two nights afore that he 'ad knocked down an old man and bit a policeman's little finger to the bone, so that, as they pointed out to the widder, p'r'aps he was taken for a wise purpose. P'r'aps he was 'appier where he was than doing six months."

"He was the sort o' chap that'll make himself 'appy anywhere," ses one of 'em, comfortinglike.

"Not without me," ses Mrs. Bullet, sobbing, and wiping her eyes on something she used for a pocket-hankercher. "He never could bear to be away from me. Was there no last words?"

"On'y one," ses one o' the chaps, Joe Peel by name.

"As 'e fell overboard," ses the other.

Mrs. Bullet began to cry agin, and say wot a good 'usband he 'ad been. "Seventeen years come Michaelmas," she ses, "and never a cross

59

word. Nothing was too good for me. Nothing. I 'ad only to ask to 'ave."

"Well, he's gorn now," ses Joe, "and we thought we ought to come round and tell you."

"So, as you can tell the police," ses the other chap.

That was 'ow I came to hear of it fust; a policeman told me that night as I stood outside the gate 'aving a quiet pipe. He wasn't shedding tears; his only idea was that Sam 'ad got off too easy.

"Well, well," I ses, trying to pacify 'im, "he won't bite no more fingers; there's no policemen where he's gorn to."

He went off grumbling and telling me to be careful, and I put my pipe out and walked up and down the wharf thinking. On'y a month afore I 'ad lent Sam fifteen shillings on a gold watch and chain wot he said an uncle 'ad left 'im. I wasn't wearing it because 'e said 'is uncle wouldn't like it, but I 'ad it in my pocket, and I took it out under one of the lamps and wondered wot I ought to do.

My fust idea was to take it to Mrs. Bullet, and then, all of a sudden, the thought struck me: "Suppose he 'and't come by it honest?"

I walked up and down agin, thinking. If he 'adn't, and it was found out, it would blacken his good name and break 'is pore wife's 'art. That's the way I looked at it, and for his sake and 'er sake I determined to stick to it.

I felt 'appier in my mind when I 'ad decided on that, and I went round to the Bear's Head and 'ad a pint. Arter that I 'ad another, and then I come back to the wharf and put the watch and chain on and went on with my work.

Every time I looked down at the chain on my waistcoat it reminded me of Sam. I looked on to the river and thought of 'im going down on the ebb. Then I got a sort o' lonesome feeling standing on the end of the jetty all alone, and I went back to the Bear's Head and 'ad another pint.

They didn't find the body, and I was a'most forgetting about Sam when one evening, as I was sitting on a box waiting to get my breath back to 'ave another go at sweeping, Joe Peel, Sam's mate, came on to the wharf to see me.

He came in a mysterious sort o' way that I didn't like: looking be'ind 'im as though he was afraid of being follered, and speaking in a whisper as If 'e was afraid of being heard. He wasn't a man I liked, and I was glad that the watch and chain was stowed safe away in my trowsis-pocket.

"I've 'ad a shock, watchman," he ses.

"Oh!" I ses.

"A shock wot's shook me all up," he ses, working up a shiver. "I've seen something wot I thought people never could see, and wot I never want to see agin. *I've seen Sam!*"

I thought a bit afore I spoke. "Why, I thought he was drownded," I ses.

"So 'e is," ses Joe. "When I say I've seen 'im I mean that I 'ave seen his *ghost!*"

He began to shiver agin, all over.

"Wot was it like?" I ses, very calm.

"Like Sam," he ses, rather short.

"When was it?" I ses.

"Last night at a quarter to twelve," he ses. "It was standing at my front door waiting for me.

"And 'ave you been shivering like that ever since?" I ses.

"Worse than that," ses Joe, looking at me very 'ard. "It's wearing off now. The ghost gave me a message for you."

I put my 'and in my trowsis-pocket and looked at 'im. Then I walked very slow, towards the gate.

"It gave me a message for you," ses Joe, walking beside me. "'We was always pals, Joe,' it ses, 'you and me, and I want you to pay up fifteen bob for me wot I borrowed off of Bill the watchman. I can't rest until it's paid', it ses. 'So, here's the fifteen bob, watchman.'"

He put his 'and in 'is pocket and takes out fifteen bob and 'olds it out to me.

"No, no," I ses. "I can't take your money, Joe Peel. It wouldn't be right. Pore Sam is welcome to the fifteen bob—I don't want it."

"You must take it," ses Joe. "The ghost said if you didn't it would come to me agin and agin till you did, and I can't stand any more of it."

"I can't 'elp your troubles," I ses.

"You must," ses Joe. "'Give Bill the fifteen bob,' it ses, 'and he'll give you a gold watch and chain wot I gave 'im to mind till it was paid.'"

I see his little game then. "Gold watch and chain," I ses, laughing. "You must ha' nusunderstood it, Joe."

"I understood It right enough," ses Joe, getting a bit closer to me as I stepped outside the gate. "Here's your fifteen bob; are you going to give me that watch and chain?"

"Sartainly not," I ses. "I don't know wot you mean by a watch and chain. *If* I 'ad it and I gave it to anybody, I should give It to Sam's widder, not to you."

"It's nothing to do with 'er," ses Joe, very quick. "Sam was most pertikler about that."

"I expect you dreamt it all," I ses. "Where would pore Sam get a gold watch and chain from? And why should 'e go to you about it? Why didn't 'e come to me? If 'e thinks I 'ave got it let 'im come to me."

"All right, I'll go to the police-station," ses Joe.

"I'll come with you," I ses. "But 'ere's a policeman coming along. Let's go to 'im."

I moved towards 'im, but Joe hung back, and, arter using one or two words that would ha' made any ghost ashamed to know 'im, he sheered off. I 'ad a word or two with the policeman about the weather, and then I went inside and locked the gate.

My idea was that Sam 'ad told Joe about the watch and chain afore he fell overboard. Joe was a nasty customer, and I could see that I should 'ave to be a bit careful. Some men might ha' told the police about it—but I never cared much for them. They're like kids in a way, always asking questions—most of which you can't answer.

It was a little bit creepy all alone on the wharf that night. I don't deny it. Twice I thought I 'eard something coming up on tiptoe behind me. The second time I was so nervous that I began to sing to keep my spirits up, and I went on singing till three of the hands of the Susan Emily, wot was lying alongside, came up from the fo'c'sle and offered to fight me. I was thankful when daylight came.

Five nights arterwards I 'ad the shock of my life. It was the fust night for some time that there was no craft up. A dark night, and a nasty moaning sort of a wind. I 'ad just lighted the lamp at the corner of the warehouse, wot 'ad blown out, and was sitting down to rest afore putting the ladder away, when I 'appened to look along the jetty and saw a head coming up over the edge of it. In the light of the lamp I saw the dead white face of Sam Bullet's ghost making faces at me.

I just caught my breath, sharp like, and then turned and ran for the gate like a racehorse. I 'ad left the key in the padlock, in case of anything happening, and I just gave it one turn, flung the wicket open and slammed it in the ghost's face, and tumbled out into the road.

I ran slap into the arms of a young policeman wot was passing. Nasty, short-tempered chap he was, but I don't think I was more glad to see anybody in my life. I hugged 'im till 'e nearly lost 'is breath, and then he sat me down on the kerb-stone and asked me wot I meant by it.

Wot with the excitement and the running I couldn't speak at fust, and when I did he said I was trying to deceive 'im.

"There ain't no such thing as ghosts," he ses; "you've been drinking."

"It came up out o' the river and run arter me like the wind," I ses.

"Why didn't it catch you, then?" he ses, looking me up and down and all round about. "Talk sense."

He went up to the gate and peeped in, and, arter watching a moment, stepped inside and walked down the wharf, with me follering. It was my dooty; besides, I didn't like being left all alone by myself.

Twice we walked up and down and all over the wharf. He flashed his lantern into all the dark corners, into empty barrels and boxes, and then he turned and flashed It right into my face and shook his 'ead at me.

"You've been having a bit of a lark with me," he ses, "and for two pins I'd take you. Mind, if you say a word about this to anybody, I will."

He stalked off with his 'ead in the air, and left me all alone in charge of a wharf with a ghost on it. I stayed outside in the street, of course, but every now and then I fancied I heard something moving about the other side of the gate, and once it was so distinct that I run along to the Bear's Head and knocked 'em up and asked them for a little brandy, for illness.

I didn't get it, of course; I didn't expect to; but I 'ad a little conversation with the landlord from 'is bedroom winder that did me more good than the brandy would ha' done. Once or twice I thought he would 'ave fallen out, and many a man has 'ad his licence taken away for less than a quarter of wot 'e said to me that night. Arter he thought he 'ad finished and was going back to bed agin, I pointed out to 'im that he 'adn't kissed me "goodnight," and if it 'adn't ha' been for 'is missis and two grown-up daughters and the potman I believe he'd ha' talked to me till daylight.

'Ow I got through the rest of the night I don't know. It seemed to be twenty nights instead of one, but the day came at last, and when the hands came on at six o'clock, they found the gate open and me on dooty same as usual.

I slept like a tired child when I got 'ome, and arter a steak and onions for dinner I sat down and lit my pipe and tried to think wot was to be done. One thing I was quite certain about: I wasn't going to spend another night on that wharf alone.

I went out arter a bit, as far as the Clarendon Arms, for a breath of fresh air, and I 'ad just finished a pint and was wondering whether I ought to 'ave another, when Ted Dennis came in, and my mind was made up. He 'ad been in the army all 'is life, and, so far, he 'ad never seen anything that 'ad frightened 'im. I've seen him myself take on men twice 'is size just for the love of the thing, and, arter knocking them silly, stand 'em a pint out of 'is own pocket. When I asked 'im whether he was afraid of ghosts he laughed so 'ard that the landlord came from the other end of the bar to see wot was the matter.

I stood Ted a pint, and arter he 'ad finished it I told 'im just how things was. I didn't say anything about the watch and chain, because there was no need to, and when we came outside agin I 'ad engaged an assistant-watchman for ninepence a night.

"All you've got to do," I ses, "is to keep me company. You needn't turn up till eight o'clock of a night, and you can leave 'arf an hour afore me in the morning."

"Right-o!" ses Ted. "And if I see the ghost, I'll make It wish it 'ad never been born."

It was a load off my mind, and I went 'ome and ate a tea that made my missis talk about the work'ouse, and orstritches in 'uman shape wot would eat a woman out of 'ouse and 'ome if she would let 'em.

I got to the wharf just as it was striking six, and at a quarter to seven the wicket was pushed open gentle and the ugly 'ead of Mr. Joe Peel was shoved inside.

Hullo!" I ses. "Wot do you want?'

"I want to save your life," he ses, in a solemn voice. "You was within a inch of death last night, watchman."

"Oh!" I ses, careless-like. "'Ow do you know!"

"The ghost o' Sam Bullet told me," ses Joe. "Arter it 'ad chased you up the wharf screaming for 'elp, it came round and told me all about it."

"It seems fond of you," I ses. "I wonder why?"

"It was in a terrible temper," ses Joe, "and its face was awful to look at. 'Tell the watchman,' it ses, 'that if he don't give you the watch and chain I shall appear to 'im agin and kill 'im.'"

"All right," I ses, looking behind me to where three of the 'ands of the *Daisy* was sitting on the fo'c'sle smoking. "I've got plenty of company tonight."

"Company won't save you," ses Joe. "For the last time, are you going to give me that watch and chain, or not? Here's your fifteen bob."

"No," I ses; "even if I 'ad got it I shouldn't give it to you; and it's no use giving it to the ghost, because, being made of air, he 'asn't got anywhere to put it."

"Very good," ses Joe, giving me a black look. "I've done all I can to save you, but if you won't listen to sense, you won't. You'll see Sam Bullet agin, and you'll not on'y lose the watch and chain but your life as well."

"All right," I ses, "and thank you kindly, but I've got an assistant, as it 'appens—a man wot wants to see a ghost."

"An assistant?" ses Joe, staring.

"An old soldier," I ses. "A man wot likes trouble and danger. His idea is to shoot the ghost and see wot 'appens."

"Shoot," ses Joe. "Shoot a pore 'armless ghost. Does he want to be 'ung? Ain't it enough for a pore man to be drownded, but wot you must try and shoot 'im arterwards? Why, you ought to be ashamed o' yourself. Where's your 'art?"

"It won't be shot if it don't come on my wharf," I ses. "Though I don't mind if it does when I've got somebody with me. I ain't afraid of anything living, and I don't mind ghosts when there's two of us. Besides which, the noise of the pistol'll wake up 'arf the river."

"You take care you don't get woke up," ses Joe, 'ardly able to speak for temper.

He went off stamping, and grinding 'is teeth, and at eight o'clock to the minute, Ted Dennis turned up with 'is pistol and helped me take care of the wharf. Happy as a skylark 'e was, and to see him 'iding behind a barrel with his pistol ready, waiting for the ghost, a'most made me forget the expense of it all.

It never came near us that night, and Ted was a bit disappointed next morning as he took 'is ninepence and went off. Next night was the same, and the next, and then Ted gave up hiding on the wharf for it, and sat and snoozed in the office instead.

A week went by, and then another, and still there was no sign of Sam Bullet's ghost, or Joe Peel, and every morning I 'ad to try and work up a smile as I shelled out ninepence for Ted. It nearly ruined me, and, worse than that, I couldn't explain why I was short to the missis. Fust of all she asked me *wot* I was spending it on, then she asked me *who* I was spending it on. It nearly broke up my 'ome—she did smash one kitchen-chair and a vase off the parlour mantelpiece—but I wouldn't tell 'er, and then, led away by some men on strike at Smith's wharf, Ted went on strike for a bob a night.

That was arter he 'ad been with me for three weeks, and when Saturday came, of course I was more short than ever, and people came and stood at their doors all the way down our street to listen to the missis taking my character away.

I stood it as long as I could, and then, when 'er back was turned for 'arf a moment, I slipped out. While she'd been talking I'd been thinking, and it came to me dear as daylight that there was no need for me to sacrifice myself any longer looking arter a dead man's watch and chain.

I didn't know exactly where Joe Peel lived, but I knew the part, and arter peeping into seven public-'ouses I see the man I wanted sitting by 'imself in a little bar. I walked in quiet-like, and sat down opposite 'im.

"Morning," I ses.

Joe Peel grunted.

"'Ave one with me?" I ses.

He grunted agin, but not quite so fierce, and I fetched the two pints from the counter and took a seat alongside of 'im.

"I've been looking for you," I ses.

"Oh!" he ses, looking me up and down and all over. "Well, you've found me now."

"I want to talk to you about the ghost of pore Sam Bullet," I ses.

Joe Peel put 'is mug down sudden and looked at me fierce. "Look 'ere! Don't you come and try to be funny with me," he ses. "'Cos I won't 'ave it,"

"I don't want to be funny," I ses. "Wot I want to know is, are you in the same mind about that watch and chain as you was the other day?"

He didn't seem to be able to speak at fust, but arter a time 'e gives a gasp. "Wot's the game?" he ses.

"Wot I want to know is, if I give you that watch and chain for fifteen bob, will that keep the ghost from 'anging round my wharf agin?" I ses.

"Why, o' course," he ses, staring; "but you ain't been seeing it agin, 'ave you?"

"I've not, and I don't want to," I ses. "If it wants you to 'ave the watch and chain, give me the fifteen bob, and it's yours."

He looked at me for a moment as if he couldn't believe 'is eyesight, and then 'e puts his 'and into 'is trowsis-pocket and pulls out one shilling and fourpence, 'arf a day-pipe, and a bit o' lead-pencil.

"That's all I've got with me," he ses. "I'll owe you the rest. You ought to ha' took the fifteen bob when I 'ad it."

There was no 'elp for it, and arter making 'im swear to give me the rest o' the money when 'e got it, and that I shouldn't see the ghost agin, I 'anded the things over to 'im and came away. He came to the door to see me off, and if ever a man looked puzzled, 'e did. Pleased at the same time.

It was a load off of my mind. My conscience told me I'd done right, and arter sending a little boy with a note to Ted Dennis to tell 'im not to come any more, I felt 'appier than I 'ad done for a long time. When I got to the wharf that evening it seemed like a different place, and I was whistling and smiling over my work quite in my old way, when the young policeman passed.

"Hullo!" he ses. "'Ave you seen the ghost agin?"

"I 'ave not," I ses, drawing myself up. "'Ave you?"

"No," he ses. "We missed it."

"Missed it?" I ses, staring at 'im.

"Yes," he ses, nodding. "The day arter you came out screaming, and cuddling me like a frightened baby, it shipped as A.B. on the barque *Ocean King*, for Valparaiso. We missed it by a few hours. Next time you see a ghost, knock it down fust and go and cuddle the police arterwards."

Three at Table

The talk in the coffee-room had been of ghosts and apparitions, and nearly everybody present had contributed his mite to the stock of information upon a hazy and somewhat thread-bare subject. Opinions ranged from rank incredulity to childlike faith, one believer going so far as to denounce unbelief as impious, with a reference to the Witch of Endor, which was somewhat marred by being complicated in an inexplicable fashion with the story of Jonah.

"Talking of Jonah," he said solemnly, with a happy disregard of the fact that he had declined to answer several eager questions put to him on the subject, "look at the strange tales sailors tell us."

"I wouldn't advise you to believe all those," said a bluff, clean-shaven man, who had been listening without speaking much. "You see when a sailor gets ashore, he's expected to have something to tell, and his friends would be rather disappointed if he had not."

"It's a well-known fact," interrupted the first speaker firmly, "that sailors are very prone to see visions."

"They are," said the other dryly, "they generally see them in pairs, and the shock to the nervous system frequently causes headache next morning."

"You never saw anything yourself?" suggested an unbeliever.

"Man, and boy," said the other, "I've been at sea thirty years, and the only unpleasant incident of that kind occurred in a quiet English countryside."

"And that?" said another man.

"I was a young man at the time," said the narrator, drawing at his pipe and glancing good-humouredly at the company. "I, had just come back from China, and my own people being away I went down into the country to invite myself to stay with an uncle. When I got down to the place, I found it closed and the family in the South of

France; but as they were due back in a couple of days I decided to put up at the Royal George, a very decent inn, and await their return.

"The first day I passed well enough; but in the evening the dullness of the rambling old place, in which I was the only visitor, began to weigh upon my spirits, and the next morning after a late breakfast I set out with the intention of having a brisk day's walk.

"I started off in excellent spirits, for the day was bright and frosty, with a powdering of snow on the iron-bound roads and nipped hedges, and the country had to me all the charm of novelty. It was certainly flat, but there was plenty of timber, and the villages through which I passed were old and picturesque.

"I lunched luxuriously on bread and cheese and beer in the bar of a small inn, and resolved to go a little further before turning back. When at length I found I had gone far enough, I turned up a lane at right angles to the road I was passing, and resolved to find my way back by another route. It is a long lane that has no turning, but this had several, each of which had turnings of its own, which generally led, as I found by trying two or three of them, into the open marshes. Then, tired of lanes, I resolved to rely upon the small compass which hung from my watch chain and go across country home.

"I had got well into the marshes when a white fog, which had been for some time hovering round the edge of the ditches, began gradually to spread. There was no escaping it, but by aid of my compass I was saved from making a circular tour and fell instead into frozen ditches or stumbled over roots in the grass. I kept my course, however, until at four o'clock, when night was coming rapidly up to lend a hand to the fog, I was fain to confess myself lost.

"The compass was now no good to me, and I wandered about miserably, occasionally giving a shout on the chance of being heard by some passing shepherd or farmhand. At length by great good luck I found my feet on a rough road driven through the marshes, and by walking slowly and tapping with my stick managed to keep to it. I had followed it for some distance when I heard footsteps approaching me.

"We stopped as we met, and the new arrival, a sturdy-looking countryman, hearing of my plight, walked back with me for nearly a mile, and putting me on to a road gave me minute instructions how to reach a village some three miles distant.

"I was so tired that three miles sounded like ten, and besides that, a little way off from the road I saw dimly a lighted window. I pointed it out, but my companion shuddered and looked round him uneasily.

"'You won't get no good there,' he said, hastily.

"'Why not?' I asked.

"'There's a something there, sir,' he replied, 'what 'tis I dunno, but the little 'un belonging to a gamekeeper as used to live in these parts see it, and it was never much good afterward. Some say as it's a poor mad thing, others says as it's a kind of animal; but whatever it is, it ain't good to see.'

"'Well, I'll keep on, then,' I said. 'Goodnight.'

"He went back whistling cheerily until his footsteps died away in the distance, and I followed the road he had indicated until it divided into three, any one of which to a stranger might be said to lead straight on. I was now cold and tired, and having half made up my mind walked slowly back toward the house.

"At first all I could see of it was the little patch of light at the window. I made for that until it disappeared suddenly, and I found myself walking into a tall hedge. I felt my way round this until I came to a small gate, and opening it cautiously, walked, not without some little nervousness, up a long path which led to the door. There was no light and no sound from within. Half repenting of my temerity I shortened my stick and knocked lightly upon the door.

"I waited a couple of minutes and then knocked again, and my stick was still beating the door when it opened suddenly and a tall bony old woman, holding a candle, confronted me.

"'What do you want?' she demanded gruffly.

"'I've lost my way,' I said, civilly; 'I want to get to Ashville.'

"'Don't know it,' said the old woman.

"She was about to close the door when a man emerged from a room at the side of the hall and came toward us. An old man of great height and breadth of shoulder.

"'Ashville is fifteen miles distant,' he said slowly.

"'If you will direct me to the nearest village, I shall be grateful,' I remarked.

"He made no reply, but exchanged a quick, furtive glance with the woman. She made a gesture of dissent.

"'The nearest place is three miles off,' he said, turning to me and apparently trying to soften a naturally harsh voice; 'if you will give me the pleasure of your company, I will make you as comfortable as I can.'

"I hesitated. They were certainly a queer-looking couple, and the gloomy hall with the shadows thrown by the candle looked hardly more inviting than the darkness outside.

"'You are very kind,' I murmured, irresolutely, 'but—'

"'Come in,' he said quickly; 'shut the door, Anne.'

"Almost before I knew it, I was standing inside and the old woman, muttering to herself, had closed the door behind me. With a queer sensation of being trapped I followed my host into the room, and taking the proffered chair warmed my frozen fingers at the fire.

"'Dinner will soon be ready,' said the old man, regarding me closely. 'If you will excuse me.'

"I bowed and he left the room. A minute afterward I heard voices; his and the old woman's, and, I fancied, a third. Before I had finished my inspection of the room he returned, and regarded me with the same strange look I had noticed before.

"'There will be three of us at dinner,' he said, at length. 'We two and my son.'

"I bowed again, and secretly hoped that that look didn't run in the family.

"'I suppose you don't mind dining in the dark,' he said, abruptly.

"'Not at all,' I replied, hiding my surprise as well as I could, 'but really, I'm afraid I'm intruding. If you'll allow me—'

"He waved his huge gaunt hands. 'We're not going to lose you now we've got you,' he said, with a dry laugh. 'It's seldom we have company, and now we've got you we'll keep you. My son's eyes are bad, and he can't stand the light. Ah, here is Anne.'

"As he spoke the old woman entered, and, eyeing me stealthily, began to lay the cloth, while my host, taking a chair the other side of the hearth, sat looking silently into the fire. The table set, the old woman brought in a pair of fowls ready carved in a dish, and placing three chairs, left the room. The old man hesitated a moment, and then, rising from his chair, placed a large screen in front of the fire and slowly extinguished the candles.

"'Blind man's holiday,' he said, with clumsy jocosity, and groping his way to the door opened it. Somebody came back into the room with him, and in a slow, uncertain fashion took a seat at the table, and the strangest voice I have ever heard broke a silence which was fast becoming oppressive.

"'A cold night,' it said slowly.

"I replied in the affirmative, and light or no light, fell to with an appetite which had only been sharpened by the snack in the middle of the day. It was somewhat difficult eating in the dark, and it was evident from the behaviour of my invisible companions that they were as unused to dining under such circumstances as I was. We ate in silence until the old woman blundered into the room with some sweets and put them with a crash upon the table.

"'Are you a stranger about here?' inquired the curious voice again.

"I replied in the affirmative, and murmured something about my luck in stumbling upon such a good dinner.

"'Stumbling is a very good word for it,' said the voice grimly. 'You have forgotten the port, father.'

"'So, I have,' said the old man, rising. 'It's a bottle of the "Celebrated" today; I will get it myself.'

"He felt his way to the door, and closing it behind him, left me alone with my unseen neighbour. There was something so strange about the whole business that I must confess to more than a slight feeling of uneasiness.

"My host seemed to be absent a long time. I heard the man opposite lay down his fork and spoon, and half fancied I could see a pair of wild eyes shining through the gloom like a cat's.

"With a growing sense of uneasiness, I pushed my chair back. It caught the hearthrug, and in my efforts to disentangle it the screen fell over with a crash and in the flickering light of the fire I saw the face of the creature opposite. With a sharp catch of my breath I left my chair and stood with clenched fists beside it. Man, or beast, which was it? The flame leaped up and then went out, and in the mere red glow of the fire it looked more devilish than before.

"For a few moments we regarded each other in silence; then the door opened and the old man returned. He stood aghast as he saw the warm firelight, and then approaching the table mechanically put down a couple of bottles.

"'I beg your pardon,' said I, reassured by his presence, 'but I have accidentally overturned the screen. Allow me to replace it.'

"'No,' said the old man, gently, 'let it be.

"'We have had enough of the dark. I'll give you a light.'

"He struck a match and slowly lit the candles. Then—I saw that the man opposite had but the remnant of a face, a gaunt wolfish face in which one unquenched eye, the sole remaining feature, still glittered. I was greatly moved, some suspicion of the truth occurring to me.

"'My son was injured some years ago in a burning house,' said the old man. 'Since then we have lived a very retired life. When you came to the door, we—' his voice trembled, 'that is—my son—'

"'I thought," said the son simply, 'that it would be better for me not to come to the dinner-table. But it happens to be my birthday, and my father would not hear of my dining alone, so we hit upon this foolish plan of dining in the dark. I'm sorry I startled you.'

"'I am sorry,' said I, as I reached across the table and gripped his hand, 'that I am such a fool; but it was only in the dark that you startled me.'

"From a faint tinge in the old man's cheek and a certain pleasant softening of the poor solitary eye in front of me I secretly congratulated myself upon this last remark.

"'We never see a friend,' said the old man, apologetically, 'and the temptation to have company was too much for us. Besides, I don't know what else you could have done.'

"'Nothing else half so good, I'm sure,' said I.

"'Come,' said my host, with almost a sprightly air. 'Now we know each other, draw our chairs to the fire and let's keep this birthday in a proper fashion.'

"He drew a small table to the fire for the glasses and produced a box of cigars, and placing a chair for the old servant, sternly bade her to sit down and drink. If the talk was not sparkling, it did not lack for vivacity, and we were soon as merry a party as I have ever seen. The night wore on so rapidly that we could hardly believe our ears when in a lull in the conversation a clock in the hall struck twelve.

"'A last toast before we retire,' said my host, pitching the end of his cigar into the fire and turning to the small table.

"We had drunk several before this, but there was something impressive in the old man's manner as he rose and took up his glass. His tall figure seemed to get taller, and his voice rang as he gazed proudly at his disfigured son.

"'The health of the children my boy saved!' he said, and drained his glass at a draught."

Brevet Rank

The crew of the *Elisabeth Hopkins* sat on deck in the gloaming, gazing idly at the dusky shapes of the barges as they dropped silently down on the tide, or violently discussing the identity of various steamers as they came swiftly past Even with these amusements the time hung heavily, and they thought longingly of certain cosy bars by the riverside to which they were wont to betake themselves in their spare time.

Tonight, in deference to the wishes of the skipper, wishes which approximated closely to those of Royalty in their effects, they remained on board. A new acquaintance of his, a brother captain, who dabbled in mesmerism, was coming to give them a taste of his quality, and the skipper, sitting on the side of the schooner in the faint light which streamed from the galley, was condescendingly explaining to them the marvels of hypnotism.

"I never 'eard the likes of it," said one, with a deep breath, as the skipper concluded a marvellous example.

"There's a lot you ain't 'eard of, Bill," said another, whose temper was suffering from lack of beer. "But 'ave you seen all this, sir?"

"Everything," said the skipper, impressively. "He wanted to mesmerise me, an' I said, 'All right,' I ses, 'do it an' welcome—if you can, but I expect my head's a bit too strong for you.'"

"And it was, sir, I'll bet," said the man who had been so candid with Bill.

"He tried everything," said the skipper, "then he give it up; but he's coming aboard tonight, so any of you that likes can come down the cabin and be mesmerised free."

"Why can't he do it on deck?" said the mate, rising from the hatches and stretching his gigantic form.

"'Cos he must have artificial light, George," said the skipper. "He lets me a little bit into the secret, you know, an' he told me he likes to have the men a bit dazed-like first."

Voices sounded from the wharf, and the night-watchman appeared piloting Captain Zingall to the schooner. The crew noticed that he came aboard quite like any other man, descending the ladder with even more care than usual. He was a small man, of much dignity, with light grey eyes which had been so strained by the exercise of his favourite hobby that they appeared to be starting from his head. He chatted agreeably about freights for some time, and then, at his brother skipper's urgent entreaty, consented to go below and give them a taste of his awful powers.

At first, he was not very successful. The men stared at the discs he put into their hands until their eyes ached, but for some time without effect. Bill was the first to yield, and to the astonishment of his friends passed into a soft magnetic slumber, from which he emerged to perform the usual idiotic tricks peculiar to mesmerised subjects.

"It's wonderful what power you 'ave over 'em," said Captain Bradd, respectfully.

Captain Zingall smiled affably. "At the present moment," he said, "that man is my unthinkin' slave, an' whatever I wish him to do he does. Would any of you like him to do anything?"

"Well, sir," said one of the men, "'e owes me 'arf a crown, an' I think it would be a 'ighly interestin' experiment if you could get 'im to pay me. If anything 'ud make me believe in mesmerism, that would."

"An' he owes me eighteenpence, sir," said another seaman, eagerly.

"One at a time," said the first speaker, sharply.

"An' 'e's owed me five shillin's since I don't know when," said the cook, with dishonest truthfulness.

Captain Zingall turned to his subject. "You owe that man half a crown," he said, pointing, "that one eighteenpence, and that one five shillings. Pay them."

In the most matter-of-fact way in the world Bill groped in his pockets, and, producing some greasy coins, payed the sums mentioned, to the intense delight of everybody.

"Well, I'm blest," said the mate, staring. "I thought mesmerism was all rubbish. Now bring him to again."

"But don't tell 'im wot 'e's been doin'," said the cook.

Zingall with a few passes brought his subject round, and with a subdued air he took his place with the others.

"What'd it feel like, Bill?" asked Joe. "Can you remember what you did?"

Bill shook his head.

"Don't try to," said the cook, feelingly.

"I should like to put you under the influence," said Zingall, eyeing the mate.

"You couldn't," said that gentleman, promptly.

"Let me try," said Zingall, persuasively.

"Do," said the skipper, "to oblige me, George."

"Well, I don't mind much," said the mate, hesitating; "but no making *me* give those chaps money, you know."

"No, no," said Zingall.

"Wot does 'e mean? Give the chaps money?" said Bill, turning with a startled air to the cook.

"I dunno," said the cook airily. "Just watch 'im, Bill," he added, anxiously.

But Bill had something better to do, and feeling in his pockets hurriedly strove to balance his cash account. It was impossible to do anything else while he was doing it, and the situation became so strained and his language so weird that the skipper was compelled in the interest of law and morality to order him from the cabin.

"Look at me," said Zingall to the mate after quiet had been restored.

The mate complied, and everybody gazed spellbound at the tussle for supremacy between brute force and occult science. Slowly, very slowly, science triumphed, being interrupted several times by the bloodcurdling threats of Bill, as they floated down the companion-way. Then the mate suddenly lurched forward, and would have fallen but that strong hands caught him and restored him to his seat.

"I'm going to show you something now, if I can," said Zingall, wiping his brow; "but I don't know how it'll come off, because I'm only a beginner at this sort of thing, and I've never tried this before. If you don't mind, cap'n, I'm going to tell him he is Cap'n Bradd, and that you are the mate."

"Go ahead," said the delighted Bradd.

Captain Zingall went ahead full speed. With a few rapid passes he roused the mate from his torpor and fixed him with his glittering eye.

"You are Cap'n Bradd, master o' this ship," he said slowly.

"Ay, ay," said the mate, earnestly.

"And that's your mate, George, said Zingall, pointing to the deeply interested Bradd.

"Ay, ay," said the mate again, with a sigh.

"Take command, then," said Zingall, leaving him with a satisfied air and seating himself on the locker.

The mate sat up and looked about him with an air of quiet authority.

"George," he said, turning suddenly to the skipper with a very passable imitation of his voice.

"Sir," said the skipper, with a playful glance at Zingall.

"A friend o' mine named Cap'n Zingall is coming aboard tonight," said the mate, slowly. "Get a little whisky for him out o' my state-room."

"Ay, ay, sir," said the amused Bradd.

"Just a little in the bottom of the bottle'll do," continued the mate; "don't put more in, for he drinks like a fish."

"I never said such a thing, cap'n," said Bradd, in an agitated whisper. "I never thought o' such a thing."

"No, I know you wouldn't," said Zingall, who was staring hard at a nearly empty whisky bottle on the table.

"And don't leave your baccy pouch lying about, George," continued the mate, in a thrilling whisper.

The skipper gave a faint, mirthless little laugh, and looked at him uneasily.

"If ever there was a sponger for baccy, George, it's him," said the mate, in a confidential whisper.

Captain Zingall, who was at that very moment filling his pipe from the pouch which the skipper had himself pushed towards him, laid it carefully on the table again, and gazing steadily at his friend, took out the tobacco already in his pipe and replaced it. In the silence which ensued the mate took up the whisky bottle, and pouring the contents into a tumbler, added a little water, and drank it with relish.

He leaned back on the locker and smacked his lips. There was a faint laugh from one of the crew, and looking up smartly he seemed to be aware for the first time of their presence. "What are you doin' down here?" he roared. "What do you want?"

"Nothin', sir," said the cook. "Only we thought—"

"Get out at once," vociferated the mate, rising.

"Stay where you are," said the skipper, sharply.

"George!" said the mate, in the squeaky voice in which he chose to personate the skipper.

78

"Bring him round, Zingall," said the skipper, irritably. "I've had enough o' this. I'll let 'im know who's who."

With a confident smile Zingall got up quietly from the locker, and fixed his terrible gaze on the mate. The mate fell back and gazed at him open-mouthed.

"Who the devil are you staring at?" he demanded, rudely.

Still holding him with his gaze, Zingall clapped his hands together, and stepping up to him blew strongly in his face. The mate, with a perfect scream of rage, picked him up by the middle, and dumping him heavily on the floor, held him there and worried him.

"Help!" cried Zingall, in a smothered voice; "take him off!"

"Why don't you bring him round?" yelled the skipper, excitably. "What's the good of playing with him?"

Zingall's reply, which was quite irrelevant, consisted almost entirely of adjectives and improper nouns.

"Blow in 'is face agin, sir," said the cook, bending down kindly.

"Take him off!" yelled Zingall; "he's killing me!"

The skipper flew to the assistance of his friend, but the mate, who was of gigantic strength and stature, simply backed, and crushed him against a bulkhead. Then, as if satisfied, he released the crestfallen Zingall, and stood looking at him.

"Why—don't—you—bring—him—round?" panted the skipper.

"He's out of my control," said Zingall, rising nimbly to his feet. "I've heard of such cases before. I'm only new at the work, you know, but I dare say, in a couple of years' time—"

The skipper howled at him, and the mate, suddenly alive again to the obnoxious presence of the crew, drove them up the companion ladder, and pursued them to the forecastle.

"This is a pretty kettle o' fish," said Bradd, indignantly. "Why don't you bring him round?"

"Because I can't," said Zingall, shortly. "It'll have to wear off."

"Wear off!" repeated the skipper.

"He's under a delusion now," said Zingall, "an' o' course I can't say how long it'll last, but whatever you do don't cross him in any way."

"Oh, don't cross him," repeated Bradd, with sarcastic inflection, "and you call yourself a mesmerist."

Zingall drew himself up with a little pride. "Well, see what I've done," he said. "The fact is, I was charged full with electricity when I came aboard, and he's got it all now. It's left me weak, and until my will wears off him, he's captain o' this ship."

"And what about me?" said Bradd.

"You're the mate," said Zingall, "and mind, for your own sake, you act up to it. If you don't cross him I haven't any doubt it'll be all right, but if you do, he'll very likely murder you in a fit of frenzy, and—he wouldn't be responsible. Goodnight."

"You're not going?" said Bradd, clutching him by the sleeve.

"I am," said the other. "He seems to have took a violent dislike to me, and if I stay here it'll only make him worse."

He ran lightly up on deck, and avoiding an ugly rush on the part of the mate, who had been listening, sprang on to the ladder and hastily clambered ashore.

The skipper, worn and scared, looked up as the bogus skipper came below.

"I'm going to bed, George," said the mate, staring at him. "I feel a bit heavy. Give me a call just afore high water."

"Where are you goin' to sleep?" demanded the skipper.

"Goin' to sleep?" said the mate, "why, in my state-room, to be sure."

He took the empty bottle from the table, and opening the door of the state-room, closed it in the face of its frenzied owner, and turned the key in the lock. Then he leaned over the berth, and, cramming the pillow against his mouth, gave way to his feelings until he was nearly suffocated.

Any idea that the skipper might have had of the healing effects of sleep were rudely dispelled when the mate came on deck next morning, and found that they had taken the schooner out without arousing him. His delusion seemed to be stronger than ever, and pushing the skipper from the wheel he took it himself, and read him a short and sharp lecture on the virtues of obedience.

"I know you're a good sort, George Smith," he said, leniently, "nobody could wish for a better, but while I'm master of this here ship it don't become you to take things upon yourself in the way you do."

"But you don't understand," said the skipper, trying to conquer his temper. "Now look me in the eye, George."

"Who are you calling George?" said the mate sharply.

"Well, look me in the eye, then," said the skipper, waiving the point.

"I'll look at you in a way you won't like in a minute," said the mate, ferociously.

"I want to explain the position of affairs to you," said the skipper. "Do you remember Cap'n Zingall what was aboard last night?"

"Little dirty-looking man what kept staring at me?" demanded the mate.

"Well, I don't know about 'is being dirty," said the skipper, "but that's the man. Do you know what he did to you, Geo—"

"Eh!" said the mate, sharply.

"He mesmerised you," said the skipper, hastily. "Now keep quite calm. You say you're Benjamin Bradd, master o' this vessel, don't you?"

"I do," said the mate. "Let me hear anybody say as I ain't."

"Yesterday," said the skipper, plucking up courage and speaking very slowly and impressively, "you were George Smith, the mate, but my friend, Captain Zingall, mesmerised you and made you think you were me."

"I see what it is," said the mate severely. "You've been drinking; you've been up to my whisky."

"Call the crew up and ask 'em then," said Bradd, desperately.

"Call 'em up yourself, you lunatic," said the mate, loudly enough for the men to hear. "If anybody dares to play the fool with me, I won't leave a whole bone in his body, that's all."

In obedience to the summons of Captain Bradd the crew came up, and being requested by him to tell the mate that he was the mate, and that he was at present labouring under a delusion, stood silently nudging each other and eyeing him uneasily.

"Well," said the latter at length, "why don't you speak and tell George he's gone off his 'ead a bit?"

"It ain't nothing to do with us, sir," said Bill, very respectfully.

"But, damn it all, man," said the mate, taking a mighty grip of his collar, "you know I'm the cap'n, don't you?"

"O' course I do, sir," said Bill.

"There you are, George," said the mate, releasing him, and turning to the frantic Bradd; "you hear that? Now, look here, you listen to me. Either you've been drinking, or else your 'ead's gone a little bit off. You go down and turn in, and if you don't give me any more of your nonsense, I'll overlook it for this once."

He ordered the crew forward again, and being desirous of leaving some permanent mark of his command on the ship, had the galley fresh painted in red and blue, and a lot of old stores, which he had vainly condemned when mate, thrown overboard. The skipper stood by helplessly while it was done, and then went below of his own accord and turned in, as being the only way to retain his sanity, or, at any rate, the clearness of head which he felt to be indispensable at this juncture.

Time, instead of restoring the mate to his senses, only appeared to confirm him in his folly, and the skipper, after another attempt to convince him, let things drift, resolving to have him put under restraint as soon as they got to port.

They reached Tidescroft in the early afternoon, but before they entered the harbour the mate, as though he had had some subtle intuition that this would be his last command, called the crew to him and read them a touching little homily upon their behaviour when they should land. He warned them of public-houses and other dangers, and reminded them affectingly of their duties as husbands and fathers. "Always go home to your wife and children, my lads," he continued with some emotion, "as I go home to mine."

"Why, he ain't got none," whispered Bill, staring.

"Don't be a fool, Bill," said the cook, "he means the cap'n's. Don't you see he's the cap'n now?"

It was as clear as noonday, and the agitation of the skipper—a perfect Othello in his way—was awful. He paced the deck incessantly, casting fretful glances ashore, and, as the schooner touched the side of the quay, sprang on to the bulwarks and jumped ashore. The mate watched him with an ill-concealed grin, and then, having made the vessel snug, went below to strengthen himself with a drop of the skipper's whisky for the crowning scene of his play. He came on deck again, and, taking no heed of the whispers of the crew, went ashore.

Meantime, Captain Bradd had reached his house, and was discussing the situation with his astonished spouse. She pooh-poohed the idea of the police and the medical faculty as being likely to cause complications with the owners, and, despite the remonstrances of her husband, insisted upon facing the mate alone.

"Now you go in the kitchen," she said, looking from the window. "Here he comes. You see how I'll settle him."

The skipper looked out of the window and saw the unhappy victim of Captain Zingall slowly approaching. His wife drew him away, and, despite his remonstrances, pushed him into the next room and closed the door.

She sat on the sofa calmly sewing, as the mate, whose hardihood was rapidly failing him, entered Her manner gave him no assistance whatever, and coming sheepishly in he took a chair.

"I've come home," he said at last

"So, I see, Ben," said Mrs. Bradd, calmly.

"He's told her," said the mate to himself.

"Children all right?" he inquired, after another pause.

"Yes," said Mrs. Bradd, simply. "Little Joe's boots are almost off his feet, though."

"Ah," said the mate, blankly.

"I've been waiting for you to come, Ben," said Mrs. Bradd after a pause. "I want you to change a five-pound note Uncle Dick gave me."

"Can't do it," said the mate, briefly. The absence of Captain Bradd was disquieting to a bashful man in such a position, and he had looked forward to a stormy scene which was to bring him to his senses again.

"Show me what you've got," said Mrs. Bradd, leaning forward.

The mate pulled out an old leather purse and counted the contents, two pounds and a little silver.

"There isn't five pounds there," said Mrs. Bradd, "but I may as well take last week's housekeeping while you've got it out."

Before the mate could prevent her, she had taken the two pounds and put it in her pocket. He looked at her placid face in amazement, but she met his gaze calmly and drummed on the table with her thimble.

"No, no, I want the money myself," said the mate at last. He put his hands to his head and began to prepare for the grand transformation scene. "My head's gone," he said, in a gurgling voice. "What am I doing here? Where am I?"

"Good gracious, what's the matter with the man?" said Mrs. Bradd, with a scream. She snatched up a bowl of flowers and flung the contents in his face as her husband burst into the room. The mate sprang to his feet, spluttering.

"What am I doing here, Cap'n Bradd?" he said in his usual voice.

"He's come round!" said Bradd, ecstatically. "He's come round. Oh, George, you have been playing the fool. Don't you know what you've been doing?"

The mate shook his head, and stared round the room. "I thought we were in London," he said, putting his hand to his head. "You said Cap'n Zingall was coming aboard. How did we get here? Where am I?"

In a hurried, breathless fashion the skipper told him, the mate regarding him the while with a stare of fixed incredulity.

"I can't understand it," he said at length. "My mind's a perfect blank."

"A perfect blank," said Mrs. Bradd, cheerfully. It might have been accident, but she tapped her pocket as she spoke, and the outwitted mate bit his lip as he realised his blunder, and turned to the door. The couple watched him as he slowly passed up the street.

"It's most extraordinary," said the skipper; "the most extraordinary case I ever heard of."

"So, it is," said his wife, "and what's more extraordinary still for you, Ben, you're going to church on Sunday, and what's more extraordinary even than that, you are going to put two golden sovereigns in the plate."

The Vigil

"I'm the happiest man in the world," said Mr. Farrer, in accents of dreamy tenderness.

Miss Ward sighed. "Wait till father comes in," she said.

Mr. Farrer peered through the plants which formed a welcome screen to the window and listened with some uneasiness. He was waiting for the firm, springy step that should herald the approach of ex-Sergeant-Major Ward. A squeeze of Miss Ward's hand renewed his courage.

"Perhaps I had better light the lamp," said the girl, after a long pause. "I wonder where mother's got to?"

"She's on my side, at any rate," said Mr. Farrer.

"Poor mother!" said the girl. "She daren't call her soul her own. I expect she's sitting in her bedroom with the door shut. She hates unpleasantness. And there's sure to be some."

"So do I," said the young man, with a slight shiver. "But why should there be any? He doesn't want you to keep single all your life, does he?"

"He'd like me to marry a soldier," said Miss Ward. "He says that the young men of the present day are too soft. The only thing he thinks about is courage and strength."

She rose and, placing the lamp on the table, removed the chimney, and then sought round the room for the matches. Mr. Farrer, who had two boxes in his pocket, helped her.

They found a box at last on the mantelpiece, and Mr. Farrer steadied her by placing one arm round her waist while she lit the lamp. A sudden exclamation from outside reminded them that the blind was not yet drawn, and they sprang apart in dismay as a grizzled and upright old warrior burst into the room and confronted them.

"Pull that blind down!" he roared. "Not you," he continued, as Mr.

85

Farrer hastened to help. "What do you mean by touching my blind? What do you mean by embracing my daughter? Eh? Why don't you answer?"

"We—we are going to be married," said Mr. Farrer, trying to speak boldly.

The sergeant-major drew himself up, and the young man gazed in dismay at a chest which seemed as though it would never cease expanding.

"Married!" exclaimed the sergeant-major, with a grim laugh. "Married to a little tame bunny-rabbit! Not if I know it. Where's your mother?" he demanded, turning to the girl.

"Upstairs," was the reply.

Her father raised his voice, and a nervous reply came from above. A minute later Mrs. Ward, pale of cheek, entered the room.

"Here's fine goings-on!" said the sergeant major, sharply. "I go for a little walk, and when I come back this—this infernal cockroach has got its arm round my daughter's waist. Why don't you look after her? Do you know anything about it?"

His wife shook her head.

"Five feet four and about thirty round the chest, and wants to marry my daughter!" said the sergeant-major, with a sneer. "Eh? What's that? What did you say? What?"

"I said that's a pretty good size for a cockroach," murmured Mr. Farrer, defiantly. "Besides, size isn't everything. If it was, you'd be a general instead of only a sergeant-major."

"You get out of my house," said the other, as soon as he could get his breath. "Go on. Sharp with it."

"I'm going," said the mortified Mr. Farrer. "I'm sorry if I was rude. I came on purpose to see you tonight. Bertha—Miss Ward, I mean—told me your ideas, but I couldn't believe her. I said you'd got more common sense than to object to a man just because he wasn't a soldier."

"I want a man for a son-in-law," said the other. "I don't say he's got to be a soldier."

"Just so," said Mr. Farrer. "You're a man, ain't you? Well, I'll do anything that you'll do."

"Pph!" said the sergeant-major. "I've done my little lot. I've been in action four times, and wounded in three places. That's my tally."

"The colonel said once that my husband doesn't know what fear is," said Mrs. Ward, timidly. "He's afraid of nothing."

"Except ghosts," remarked her daughter, softly.

"Hold your tongue, miss," said her father, twisting his moustache. "No sensible man is afraid of what doesn't exist."

"A lot of people believe they do, though," said Mr. Farrer, breaking in. "I heard the other night that old Smith's ghost has been seen again swinging from the apple tree. Three people have seen it."

"Rubbish!" said the sergeant-major.

"Maybe," said the young man; "but I'll bet you, Mr. Ward, for all your courage, that you won't go up there alone at twelve o'clock one night to see."

"I thought I ordered you out of my house just now," said the sergeant-major, glaring at him.

"Going into action," said Mr. Farrer, pausing at the door, "is one thing —you have to obey orders and you can't help yourself; but going to a lonely cottage two miles off to see the ghost of a man that hanged himself is another."

"Do you mean to say I'm afraid?" blustered the other.

Mr. Farrer shook his head. "I don't say anything," he remarked; "but even a cockroach does a bit of thinking sometimes."

"Perhaps *you'd* like to go," said the sergeant-major.

"I don't mind," said the young man; "and perhaps you'll think a little better of me, Mr. Ward. If I do what you're afraid to do—"

Mrs. Ward and her daughter flung themselves hastily between the sergeant-major and his intended sacrifice. Mr. Farrer, pale but determined, stood his ground.

"I'll dare you to go up and spend a night there alone," he said.

"I'll dare you," said the incensed warrior, weakly.

"All right; I'll spend Wednesday night there," said Mr. Farrer, "and I'll come round on Thursday and let you know how I got on."

"I dare say," said the other; "but I don't want you here, and, what's more, I won't have you. You can go to Smith's cottage on Wednesday at twelve o'clock if you like, and I'll go up any time between twelve and three and make sure you're there. D'ye understand? I'll show you whether I'm afraid or not."

"There's no reason for you to be afraid," said Mr. Farrer. "I shall be there to protect you. That's very different to being there alone, as I shall be. But, of course, you can go up the next night by yourself, and wait for me, if you like. If you like to prove your courage, I mean."

"When I want to be ordered about," said the sergeant-major, in a magnificent voice, "I'll let you know. Now go, before I do anything I might be sorry for afterwards."

He stood at the door, erect as a ramrod, and watched the young man up the road. His conversation at the supper-table that night related almost entirely to puppy-dogs and the best way of training them.

He kept a close eye upon his daughter for the next day or two, but human nature has its limits. He tried to sleep one afternoon in his easy-chair with one eye open, but the exquisite silence maintained by Miss Ward was too much for it. A hum of perfect content arose from the feature below, and five minutes later Miss Ward was speeding in search of Mr. Farrer.

"I had to come, Ted," she said, breathlessly, "because tomorrow's Wednesday. I've got something to tell you, but I don't know whether I ought to."

"Tell me and let me decide," said Mr. Farrer, tenderly.

"I—I'm so afraid you might be frightened," said the girl. "I won't tell you, but I'll give you a hint. If you see anything awful, don't be frightened."

Mr. Farrer stroked her hand. "The only thing I'm afraid of is your father," he said, softly.

"Oh!" said the girl, clasping her hands together. "You have guessed it."

"Guessed it?" said Mr. Farrer.

Miss Ward nodded. "I happened to pass his door this morning," she said, in a low voice. "It was open a little way, and he was standing up and measuring one of mother's nightgowns against his chest. I couldn't think what he was doing it for at first."

Mr. Farrer whistled and his face hardened.

"That's not fair play," he said at last. "All right; I'll be ready for him."

"He doesn't like to be put in the wrong," said Miss Ward. "He wants to prove that you haven't got any courage. He'd be disappointed if he found you had."

"All right," said Mr. Farrer again. "You're an angel for coming to tell me."

"Father would call me something else, I expect," said Miss Ward, with a smile. "Goodbye. I want to get back before he wakes up."

She was back in her chair, listening to her father's slumbers, half an hour before he awoke.

"I'm making up for tomorrow night," he said, opening his eyes suddenly.

His daughter nodded.

"Shows strength of will," continued the sergeant-major, amiably. "Wellington could go to sleep at any time by just willing it. I'm the same way; I can go to sleep at five minutes' notice."

"It's a very useful gift," said Miss Ward, piously, "very."

Mr. Ward had two naps the next day. He awoke from the second at twelve-thirty a.m., and in a somewhat disagreeable frame of mind rose and stretched himself. The house was very still. He took a small brown-paper parcel from behind the sofa and, extinguishing the lamp, put on his cap and opened the front door.

If the house was quiet, the little street seemed dead. He closed the door softly and stepped into the darkness. In terms which would have been understood by "our army in Flanders" he execrated the forefathers, the name, and the upbringing of Mr. Edward Farrer.

Not a soul in the streets; not a light in a window. He left the little town behind, passed the last isolated house on the road, and walked into the greater blackness of a road between tall hedges. He had put on canvas shoes with rubber soles, for the better surprise of Mr. Farrer, and his own progress seemed to partake of a ghostly nature. Every ghost story he had ever heard or read crowded into his memory. For the first time in his experience even the idea of the company of Mr. Farrer seemed better than no company at all.

The night was so dark that he nearly missed the turning that led to the cottage. For the first few yards he had almost to feel his way; then, with a greater yearning than ever for the society of Mr. Farrer, he straightened his back and marched swiftly and noiselessly towards the cottage.

It was a small, tumble-down place, set well back in an overgrown garden. The sergeant-major came to a halt just before reaching the gate, and, hidden by the hedge, unfastened his parcel and shook out his wife's best nightgown.

He got it over his head with some difficulty, and, with his arms in the sleeves, tried in vain to get his big hands through the small, lace-trimmed wristbands. Despite his utmost efforts he could only get two or three fingers through, and after a vain search for his cap, which had fallen off in the struggle, he made his way to the gate and stood there waiting. It was at this moment that the thought occurred to him that Mr. Farrer might have failed to keep the appointment.

His knees trembled slightly and he listened anxiously for any sound from the house. He rattled the gate and, standing with white arms outstretched, waited. Nothing happened. He shook it again, and then, pulling himself together, opened it and slipped into the garden. As he did so a large bough which lay in the centre of the footpath thoughtfully drew on one side to let him pass.

Mr. Ward stopped suddenly and, with his gaze fixed on the bough, watched it glide over the grass until it was swallowed up in the darkness. His own ideas of frightening Mr. Farrer were forgotten, and in a dry, choking voice he called loudly upon the name of that gentleman.

He called two or three times, with no response, and then, in a state of panic, backed slowly towards the gate with his eyes fixed on the house. A loud crash sounded from somewhere inside, the door was flung violently open, and a gruesome figure in white hopped out and squatted on the step.

It was evident to Sergeant-Major Ward that Mr. Farrer was not there, and that no useful purpose could be served by remaining. It was clear that the young man's courage had failed him, and, with grey head erect, elbows working like the sails of a windmill, and the ends of the nightgown streaming behind him, the sergeant-major bent his steps towards home.

He dropped into a walk after a time and looked carefully over his shoulder. So far as he could see he was alone, but the silence and loneliness were oppressive. He looked again, and, without stopping to inquire whether his eyes had deceived him, broke into a run again. Alternately walking and running, he got back to the town, and walked swiftly along the streets to his house. Police-Constable Burgess, who was approaching from the other direction, reached it at almost the same moment, and, turning on his lantern, stood gaping with astonishment. "Anything wrong?" he demanded.

"Wrong?" panted the sergeant-major, trying to put a little surprise and dignity into his voice. "No."

"I thought it was a lady walking in her sleep at first," said the constable. "A tall lady."

The sergeant-major suddenly became conscious of the nightgown. "I've been—for a little walk," he said, still breathing hard. "I felt a bit chilly—so I—put this on."

"Suits you, too," said the constable, stiffly. "But you Army men always was a bit dressy. Now if I put that on, I should look ridikerlous."

The door opened before Mr. Ward could reply, and revealed, in the light of a bedroom candle, the astonished countenances of his wife and daughter.

"*George!*" exclaimed Mrs. Ward.

"*Father!*" said Miss Ward.

The sergeant-major tottered in and, gaining the front room, flung himself into his armchair. A stiff glass of whisky and water, handed him by his daughter, was swallowed at a gulp.

"Did you go?" inquired Mrs. Ward, clasping her hands.

The sergeant-major, fully conscious of the suspicions aroused by his disordered appearance, rallied his faculties. "Not likely," he said, with a short laugh. "After I got outside, I knew it was no good going there to look for that young snippet. He'd no more think of going there than he would of flying. I walked a little way down the road—for exercise—and then strolled back."

"But—my nightgown?" said the wondering Mrs. Ward.

"Put it on to frighten the constable," said her husband.

He stood up and allowed her to help him pull it off. His face was flushed and his hair tousled, but the bright fierceness of his eye was unquenched. In submissive silence she followed him to bed.

He was up late next morning, and made but a poor breakfast. His after-dinner nap was disturbed, and tea was over before he had regained his wonted calm. An hour later the arrival of a dignified and reproachful Mr. Farrer set him blazing again.

"I have come to see you about last night," said Mr. Farrer, before the other could speak. "A joke's a joke, but when you said you would come, I naturally expected you would keep your word."

"Keep my word?" repeated the sergeant-major, almost choking with wrath.

"I stayed there in that lonely cottage from twelve to three, as per agreement, waiting for you," said Mr. Farrer.

"You were not there," shouted the sergeant-major.

"How do you know?" inquired the other.

The sergeant-major looked round helplessly at his wife and daughter.

"Prove it," said Mr. Farrer, pushing his advantage. "You questioned my courage, and I stayed there three hours. Where were you?"

"You were not there," said the sergeant-major. "I *know*. You can't bluff me. You were afraid."

"I was there, and I'll swear it," said Mr. Farrer. "Still, there's no harm done. I'll go there again tonight, and I'll dare you to come for me?"

"Dare?" said the sergeant-major, choking. "Dare?"

"Dare," repeated the other; "and if you don't come this time, I'll spread it all over Marcham. Tomorrow night you can go there and wait for me. If you see what I saw—"

"Oh, Ted!" said Miss Ward, with a shiver.

"Saw?" said the sergeant-major, starting.

"Nothing harmful," said Mr. Farrer, calmly. "As a matter of fact, it was very interesting."

"What was?" demanded the sergeant-major.

"It sounds rather silly, as a matter of fact," said Mr. Farrer, slowly. "Still, I did see a broken bough moving about the garden."

Mr. Ward regarded him open-mouthed.

"Anything else?" he inquired, in a husky voice.

"A figure in white," said Mr. Farrer, "with long waving arms, hopping about like a frog. I don't suppose you believe me, but if you come tonight, perhaps you'll see it yourself. It's very interesting.

"Wer—weren't you frightened?" inquired the staring Mrs. Ward.

Mr. Farrer shook his head. "It would take more than that to frighten me," he said, simply. "I should be ashamed of myself to be afraid of a poor thing like that. It couldn't do me any harm."

"Did you see its face?" inquired Mrs. Ward, nervously.

Mr. Farrer shook his head.

"What sort of a body had it got?" said her daughter.

"So far as I could see, very good," said Mr. Farrer. "Very good figure—not tall, but well made."

An incredible suspicion that had been forming in the sergeant-major's mind began to take shape. "Did you see anything else?" he asked, sharply.

"One more," said Mr. Farrer, regarding him pleasantly. "One I call the Running Ghost."

"Run—" began the sergeant-major, and stopped suddenly.

"It came in at the front gate," pursued Mr. Farrer. "A tall, well-knit figure of martial bearing—much about your height, Mr. Ward—with a beautiful filmy white robe down to its knees—"

He broke off in mild surprise, and stood gazing at Miss Ward, who, with her handkerchief to her mouth, was rocking helplessly in her chair.

"Knees," he repeated, quietly. "It came slowly down the path, and halfway to the house it stopped, and in a frightened sort of voice called out my name. I was surprised, naturally, but before I could get to it—to reassure it—"

"That'll do," said the sergeant-major, rising hastily and drawing himself up to his full height.

"You asked me," said Mr. Farrer, in an aggrieved voice.

"I know I did," said the sergeant-major, breathing heavily. "I know I did; but if I sit here listening to any more of your lies, I shall be ill. The best thing you can do is to take that giggling girl out and give her a breath of fresh air. I have done with her."

Twin Spirits

The "Terrace," consisting of eight gaunt houses, faced the sea, while the back rooms commanded a view of the ancient little town some half mile distant. The beach, a waste of shingle, was desolate and bare except for a ruined bathing machine and a few pieces of linen drying in the winter sunshine. In the offing tiny steamers left a trail of smoke, while sailing-craft, their canvas glistening in the sun, slowly melted from the sight. On all these things the "Terrace" turned a stolid eye, and, counting up its gains of the previous season, wondered whether it could hold on to the next. It was a discontented "Terrace," and had become prematurely soured by a Board which refused them a pier, a bandstand, and illuminated gardens.

From the front windows of the third storey of No. 1 Mrs. Cox, gazing out to sea, sighed softly.

The season had been a bad one, and Mr. Cox had been even more troublesome than usual owing to tightness in the money market and the avowed preference of local publicans for cash transactions to assets in chalk and slate. In Mr. Cox's memory there never had been such a drought, and his crop of patience was nearly exhausted.

He had in his earlier days attempted to do a little work, but his health had suffered so much that his wife had become alarmed for his safety. Work invariably brought on a cough, and as he came from a family whose lungs had formed the staple conversation of their lives, he had been compelled to abandon it, and at last it came to be understood that if he would only consent to amuse himself, and not get into trouble, nothing more would be expected of him. It was not much of a life for a man of spirit, and at times it became so unbearable that Mr. Cox would disappear for days together in search of work, returning unsuccessful after many days with nerves shattered in the pursuit.

Mrs. Cox's meditations were disturbed by a knock at the front door, and, the servants having been discharged for the season, she hurried downstairs to open it, not without a hope of belated lodgers—invalids in search of an east wind. A stout, middle-aged woman in widow's weeds stood on the doorstep.

"Glad to see you, my dear," said the visitor, kissing her loudly.

Mrs. Cox gave her a subdued caress in return, not from any lack of feeling, but because she did everything in a quiet and spiritless fashion.

"I've got my Uncle Joseph from London staying with us," continued the visitor, following her into the hall, "so I just got into the train and brought him down for a blow at the sea."

A question on Mrs. Cox's lips died away as a very small man who had been hidden by his niece came into sight.

"My Uncle Joseph," said Mrs. Berry; "Mr. Joseph Piper," she added.

Mr. Piper shook hands, and after a performance on the doormat, protracted by reason of a festoon of hemp, followed his hostess into the faded drawing-room.

"And Mr. Cox?" inquired Mrs. Berry, in a cold voice.

Mrs. Cox shook her head. "He's been away this last three days," she said, flushing slightly.

"Looking for work?" suggested the visitor.

Mrs. Cox nodded, and, placing the tips of her fingers together, fidgeted gently.

"Well, I hope he finds it," said Mrs. Berry, with more venom than the remark seemed to require. "Why, where's your marble clock?"

Mrs. Cox coughed. "It's being mended," she said, confusedly.

Mrs. Berry eyed her anxiously. "Don't mind him, my dear," she said, with a jerk of her head in the direction of Mr. Piper, "he's nobody. Wouldn't you like to go out on the beach a little while, uncle?"

"No," said Mr. Piper.

"I suppose Mr. Cox took the clock for company," remarked Mrs. Berry, after a hostile stare at her relative.

Mrs. Cox sighed and shook her head. It was no use pretending with Mrs. Berry.

"He'll pawn the clock and anything else he can lay his hands on, and when he's drunk it up come home to be made a fuss of," continued Mrs. Berry, heatedly; "that's you men."

Her glance was so fiery that Mr. Joseph Piper was unable to allow the remark to pass unchallenged.

"*I* never pawned a clock," he said, stroking his little grey head.

"That's a lot to boast of, isn't it?" demanded his niece; "if I hadn't got anything better than that to boast of, I wouldn't boast at all."

Mr. Piper said that he was not boasting.

"It'll go on like this, my dear, till you're ruined," said the sympathetic Mrs. Berry, turning to her friend again; "what'll you do then?"

"Yes, I know," said Mrs. Cox. "I've had a bad season, too, and I'm so anxious about him in spite of it all. I can't sleep at nights for fearing that he's in some trouble. I'm sure I laid awake half last night crying."

Mrs. Berry sniffed loudly, and Mr. Piper making a remark in a low voice, turned on him with ferocity.

"What did you say?" she demanded.

"I said it does her credit," said Mr. Piper, firmly.

"I might have known it was nonsense," retorted his niece, hotly. "Can't you get him to take the pledge, Mary?"

"I couldn't insult him like that," said Mrs. Cox, with a shiver; "you don't know his pride. He never admits that he drinks; he says that he only takes a little for his indigestion. He'd never forgive me. When he pawns the things, he pretends that somebody has stolen them, and the way he goes on at me for my carelessness is alarming. He gets worked up to such a pitch that sometimes I almost think he believes it himself."

"Rubbish," said Mrs. Berry, tartly, "you're too easy with him."

Mrs. Cox sighed, and, leaving the room, returned with a bottle of wine which was port to the look and red-currant to the taste, and a seedcake of formidable appearance. The visitors attacked these refreshments mildly, Mr. Piper sipping his wine with an obtrusive carefulness which his niece rightly regarded as a reflection upon her friend's hospitality.

"What Cox wants is a shock," she said; "you've dropped some crumbs on the carpet, uncle."

Mr. Piper apologised and said he had got his eye on them, and would pick them up when he had finished and pick up his niece's at the same time to prevent her stooping. Mrs. Berry, in an aside to Mrs. Cox, said that her Uncle Joseph's tongue had got itself disliked on both sides of the family.

"And I'd give him one," said Mrs. Berry, returning again to the subject of Mr. Cox and shocks. "He has a gentleman's life of it here, and he would look rather silly if you were sold up and he had to do something for his living."

"It's putting away the things that is so bad," said Mrs. Cox, shaking her head; "that clock won't last him out, I know; he'll come back and take some of the other things. Every spring I have to go through his pockets for the tickets and get the things out again, and I mustn't say a word for fear of hurting his feelings. If I do, he goes off again."

"If I were you," said Mrs. Berry, emphatically, "I'd get behind with the rent or something and have the brokers in. He'd look rather astonished if he came home and saw a broker's man sitting in a chair—"

"He'd look more astonished if he saw him sitting in a flower-pot," suggested the caustic Mr. Piper.

"I couldn't do that," said Mrs. Cox. "I couldn't stand the disgrace, even though I knew I could pay him out. As it is, Cox is always setting his family above mine."

Mrs. Berry, without ceasing to stare Mr. Piper out of countenance, shook her head, and, folding her arms, again stated her opinion that Mr. Cox wanted a shock, and expressed a great yearning to be the humble means of giving him one.

"If you can't have the brokers in, get somebody to pretend to be one," she said, sharply; "that would prevent him pawning any more things, at any rate. Why wouldn't he do?" she added, nodding at her uncle.

Anxiety on Mrs. Cox's face was exaggerated on that of Mr. Piper.

"Let uncle pretend to be a broker's man in for the rent," continued the excitable lady, rapidly. "When Mr. Cox turns up after his spree, tell him what his doings have brought you to, and say you'll have to go to the workhouse."

"I look like a broker's man, don't I?" said Mr. Piper, in a voice more than tinged with sarcasm.

"Yes," said his niece, "that's what put it into my head."

"It's very kind of you, dear, and very kind of Mr. Piper," said Mrs. Cox, "but I couldn't think of it, I really couldn't."

"Uncle would be delighted," said Mrs. Berry, with a wilful blinking of plain facts. "He's got nothing better to do; it's a nice house and good food, and he could sit at the open window and sniff at the sea all day long."

Mr. Piper sniffed even as she spoke, but not at the sea.

"And I'll come for him the day after tomorrow," said Mrs. Berry.

It was the old story of the stronger will: Mrs. Cox after a feeble stand gave way altogether, and Mr. Piper's objections were demolished before he had given them full utterance. Mrs. Berry went off alone after dinner, secretly glad to have got rid of Mr. Piper, who was making a self-invited stay at her house of indefinite duration; and Mr. Piper, in his new role of broker's man, essayed the part with as much help as a clay pipe and a pint of beer could afford him.

That day and the following he spent amid the faded grandeurs of the drawing-room, gazing longingly at the wide expanse of beach and the tumbling sea beyond. The house was almost uncannily quiet, an occasional tinkle of metal or crash of china from the basement giving the only indication of the industrious Mrs. Cox; but on the day after the quiet of the house was broken by the return of its master, whose annoyance, when he found the drawing-room clock stolen and a man in possession, was alarming in its vehemence. He lectured his wife severely on her mismanagement, and after some hesitation announced his intention of going through her books. Mrs. Cox gave them to him, and, armed with pen and ink and four square inches of pink blotting-paper, he performed feats of balancing which made him a very Blondin of finance.

"I shall have to get something to do," he said, gloomily, laying down his pen.

"Yes, dear," said his wife.

Mr. Cox leaned back in his chair and, wiping his pen on the blotting-paper, gazed in a speculative fashion round the room. "Have you any money?" he inquired.

For reply his wife rummaged in her pocket and after a lengthy search produced a bunch of keys, a thimble, a needle-case, two pocket-handkerchiefs, and a halfpenny. She put this last on the table, and Mr. Cox, whose temper had been mounting steadily, threw it to the other end of the room.

"I can't help it," said Mrs. Cox, wiping her eyes. "I'm sure I've done all I could to keep a home together. I can't even raise money on anything."

Mr. Cox, who had been glancing round the room again, looked up sharply.

"Why not?" he inquired.

"The broker's man," said Mrs. Cox, nervously; "he's made an inventory of everything, and he holds us responsible."

Mr. Cox leaned back in his chair. "This is a pretty state of things," he blurted, wildly. "Here have I been walking my legs off looking for work, any work so long as it's honest labour, and I come back to find a broker's man sitting in my own house and drinking up my beer."

He rose and walked up and down the room, and Mrs. Cox, whose nerves were hardly equal to the occasion, slipped on her bonnet and announced her intention of trying to obtain a few necessaries on credit. Her husband waited in indignant silence until he heard the front door close behind her, and then stole softly upstairs to have a look at the fell destroyer of his domestic happiness.

Mr. Piper, who was already very tired of his imprisonment, looked up curiously as he heard the door pushed open, and discovered an elderly gentleman with an appearance of great stateliness staring at him. In the ordinary way he was one of the meekest of men, but the insolence of this stare was outrageous. Mr. Piper, opening his mild blue eyes wide, stared back. Whereupon Mr. Cox, fumbling in his vest pocket, found a pair of folders, and putting them astride his nose, gazed at the pseudo-broker's man with crushing effect.

"What do you want here?" he asked, at length. "Are you the father of one of the servants?"

"I'm the father of all the servants in the house," said Mr. Piper, sweetly.

"Don't answer me, sir," said Mr. Cox, with much pomposity; "you're an eyesore to an honest man, a vulture, a harpy."

Mr. Piper pondered.

"How do you know what's an eyesore to an honest man?" he asked, at length.

Mr. Cox smiled scornfully.

"Where is your warrant or order, or whatever you call it?" he demanded.

"I've shown it to Mrs. Cox," said Mr. Piper.

"Show it to me," said the other.

"I've complied with the law by showing it once," said Mr. Piper, bluffing, "and I'm not going to show it again."

Mr. Cox stared at him disdainfully, beginning at his little sleek grey head and travelling slowly downwards to his untidy boots and then back again. He repeated this several times, until Mr. Piper, unable to bear it patiently, began to eye him in the same fashion.

"What are you looking at, vulture?" demanded the incensed Mr. Cox.

"Three spots o' grease on a dirty weskit," replied Mr. Piper, readily, "a pair o' bow legs in a pair o' somebody else's trousers, and a shabby coat wore under the right arm, with carrying off"—he paused a moment as though to make sure—"with carrying off of a drawing-room clock."

He regretted this retort almost before he had finished it, and rose to his feet with a faint cry of alarm as the heated Mr. Cox first locked the door and put the key in his pocket and then threw up the window.

"Vulture!" he cried, in a terrible voice.

"Yes, sir," said the trembling Mr. Piper.

Mr. Cox waved his hand towards the window.

"Fly," he said, briefly.

Mr. Piper tried to form his white lips into a smile, and his knees trembled beneath him.

"Did you hear what I said?" demanded Mr. Cox. "What are you waiting for? If you don't fly out of the window, I'll throw you out."

"Don't touch me," screamed Mr. Piper, retreating behind a table, "it's all a mistake. All a joke. I'm not a broker's man. Ha! ha!"

"Eh?" said the other; "not a broker's man? What are you, then?"

In eager, trembling tones Mr. Piper told him, and, gathering confidence as he proceeded, related the conversation which had led up to his imposture. Mr. Cox listened in a dazed fashion, and as he concluded threw himself into a chair, and gave way to a terrible outburst of grief.

"The way I've worked for that woman," he said, brokenly, "to think it should come to this! The deceit of the thing; the wickedness of it My heart is broken; I shall never be the same man again—never!"

Mr. Piper made a sympathetic noise.

"It's been very unpleasant for me," he said, "but my niece is so masterful."

"I don't blame you," said Mr. Cox, kindly; "shake hands."

They shook hands solemnly, and Mr. Piper, muttering something about a draught, closed the window.

"You might have been killed in trying to jump out of that window," said Mr. Cox; "fancy the feelings of those two deceitful women then."

"Fancy my feelings!" said Mr. Piper, with a shudder. "Playing with fire, that's what I call it. My niece is coming this afternoon; it would serve her right if you gave her a fright by telling her you had killed me. Perhaps it would be a lesson to her not to be so officious."

"It would serve 'em both right," agreed Mr. Cox; "only Mrs. Berry might send for the police."

"I never thought of that," said Mr. Piper, fondling his chin.

"I might frighten my wife," mused the amiable Mr. Cox; "it would be a lesson to her not to be deceitful again. And, by Jove, I'll get some money from her to escape with; I know she's got some, and if she hasn't, she will have in a day or two. There's a little pub at Newstead, eight miles from here, where we could be as happy as fighting cocks with a fiver or two. And while we're there enjoying ourselves my wife'll be half out of her mind trying to account for your disappearance to Mrs. Berry."

"It sounds all right," said Mr. Piper, cautiously, "but she won't believe you. You don't look wild enough to have killed anybody."

"I'll look wild enough when the time comes," said the other, nodding. "You get on to the White Horse at Newstead and wait for me. I'll let you out at the back way. Come along."

"But you said it was eight miles," said Mr. Piper.

"Eight miles easy walking," rejoined Mr. Cox. "Or there's a train at three o'clock. There's a signpost at the corner there, and if you don't hurry, I shall be able to catch you up. Goodbye."

He patted the hesitating Mr. Piper on the back, and letting him out through the garden, indicated the road. Then he returned to the drawing-room, and carefully rumpling his hair, tore his collar from the stud, overturned a couple of chairs and a small table, and sat down to wait as patiently as he could for the return of his wife.

He waited about twenty minutes, and then he heard a key turn in the door below and his wife's footsteps slowly mounting the stairs. By the time she reached the drawing-room his tableau was complete, and she fell back with a faint shriek at the frenzied figure which met her eyes.

"Hush," said the tragedian, putting his finger to his lips.

"Henry, what is it?" cried Mrs. Cox. "What is the matter?"

"The broker's man," said her husband, in a thrilling whisper. "We had words—he struck me. In a fit of fury, I—I—choked him."

"Much?" inquired the bewildered woman.

"*Much?*" repeated Mr. Cox, frantically. "I've killed him and hidden the body. Now I must escape and fly the country."

The bewilderment on Mrs. Cox's face increased; she was trying to reconcile her husband's statement with a vision of a trim little figure which she had seen ten minutes before with its head tilted backwards studying the signpost, and which she was now quite certain was Mr. Piper.

"Are you sure he's dead?" she inquired.

"Dead as a door nail," replied Mr. Cox, promptly. "I'd no idea he was such a delicate little man. What am I to do? Every moment adds to my danger. I must fly. How much money have you got?"

The question explained everything. Mrs. Cox closed her lips with a snap and shook her head.

"Don't play the fool," said her husband, wildly; "my neck's in danger."

"I haven't got anything," asseverated Mrs. Cox. "It's no good looking like that, Henry, I can't make money."

Mr. Cox's reply was interrupted by a loud knock at the hall door, which he was pleased to associate with the police. It gave him a fine opportunity for melodrama, in the midst of which his wife, rightly guessing that Mrs. Berry had returned according to arrangement, went to the door to admit her. The visitor was only busy two minutes on the door-mat, but in that time Mrs. Cox was able in low whispers to apprise her of the state of affairs.

"That's my uncle all over," said Mrs. Berry, fiercely; "that's just the mean trick I should have expected of him. You leave 'em to me, my dear."

She followed her friend into the drawing-room, and having shaken hands with Mr. Cox, drew her handkerchief from her pocket and applied it to her eyes.

"She's told me all about it," she said, nodding at Mrs. Cox, "and it's worse than you think, much worse. It isn't a broker's man—it's my poor uncle, Joseph Piper."

"Your *uncle!*" repeated Mr. Cox, reeling back; "the broker's man your *uncle?*"

Mrs. Berry sniffed. "It was a little joke on our part," she admitted, sinking into a chair and holding her handkerchief to her face. "Poor uncle; but I dare say he's happier where he is."

With its head tilted back, studying Mr. Cox wiped his brow, and then, leaning his elbow on the mantelpiece, stared at her in well-simulated amazement.

"See what your joking has led to," he said, at last. "I have got to be a wanderer over the face of the earth, all on account of your jokes."

"It was an accident," murmured Mrs. Berry, "and nobody knows he was here, and I'm sure, poor dear, he hadn't got much to live for."

"It's very kind of you to look at it in that way, Susan, I'm sure," said Mrs. Cox.

"I was never one to make mischief," said Mrs. Berry. "It's no good crying over spilt milk. If uncle's killed, he's killed, and there's an end of it But I don't think it's quite safe for Mr. Cox to stay here."

"Just what I say," said that gentleman, eagerly; "but I've got no money."

"You get away," said Mrs. Berry, with a warning glance at her friend, and nodding to emphasise her words; "leave us some address to write to, and we must try and scrape twenty or thirty pounds to send you."

"Thirty?" said Mr. Cox, hardly able to believe his ears.

Mrs. Berry nodded. "You'll have to make that do to go on with," she said, pondering. "'And as soon as you get it you had better get as far away as possible before poor uncle is discovered. Where are we to send the money?"

Mr. Cox affected to consider.

"The White Horse, Newstead," he said at length, in a whisper; "better write it down."

Mrs. Berry obeyed; and this business being completed, Mr. Cox, after trying in vain to obtain a shilling or two cash in hand, bade them a pathetic farewell and went off down the path, for some reason best known to himself, on tiptoe.

For the first two days Messrs. Cox and Piper waited with exemplary patience for the remittance, the demands of the landlord, a man of coarse fibre, being met in the meantime by the latter gentleman from his own slender resources. They were both reasonable men, and knew from experience the difficulty of raising money at short notice; but on the fourth day, their funds being nearly exhausted, an urgent telegram was dispatched to Mrs. Cox.

Mr. Cox was alone when the reply came, and Mr. Piper, returning to the inn-parlour, was amazed and distressed at his friend's appearance.

Twice he had to address him before he seemed to be aware of his presence, and then Mr. Cox, breathing hard and staring at him strangely, handed him the message.

"Eh?" said Mr. Piper, in amaze, as he read slowly: "'*No—need—send—money—Uncle—Joseph—has—come—back.*—Berry,' What does it mean? Is she mad?"

Mr. Cox shook his head, and taking the paper from him, held it at arm's length and regarded it at an angle.

"How can you be there when you're supposed to be dead?" he said, at length.

"How can I be there when I'm here?" rejoined Mr. Piper, no less reasonably.

Both gentlemen lapsed into a wondering silence, devoted to the attempted solution of their own riddles. Finally, Mr. Cox, seized with a bright idea that the telegram had got altered in transmission, went off to the post-office and dispatched another, which went straight to the heart of things:

"*Don't—understand—is—Uncle—Joseph—alive?*"

A reply was brought to the inn-parlour an hour later on. Mr. Cox opened it, gave one glance at it, and then with a suffocating cry handed it to the other. Mr. Piper took it gingerly, and his eyebrows almost disappeared as he read:

"Yes—smoking—in—drawing-room."

His first strong impression was that it was a case for the Psychical Research Society, but this romantic view faded in favour of a simple solution, propounded by Mr. Cox with much crispness, that Mrs. Berry was leaving the realms of fact for those of romance. His actual words were shorter, but the meaning is the same.

"I'll go home and ask to see you," he said, fiercely; "that'll bring things to a head, I should think."

"And she'll say I've gone back to London, perhaps," said Mr. Piper, gifted with sudden clearness of vision. "You can't show her up unless you take me with you, and that'll show us up. That's her artfulness; that's Susan all over."

"She's a wicked, untruthful woman," gasped Mr. Cox.

"I never did like Susan," said Mr. Piper, with acerbity, "never."

Mr. Cox said he could easily understand it, and then, as a forlorn hope, sat down and wrote a long letter to his wife, in which, after dwelling at great length on the lamentable circumstances surrounding the sudden demise of Mr. Piper, he bade her thank Mrs. Berry for her well-meant efforts to ease his mind, and asked for the immediate dispatch of the money promised.

A reply came the following evening from Mrs. Berry herself. It was a long letter, and not only long, but badly written and crossed. It began with the weather, asked after Mr. Cox's health, and referred to the writer's; described with much minuteness a strange headache which had attacked Mrs. Cox, together with a long list of the remedies prescribed and the effects of each, and wound up in an out-of-the-way corner, in a vein of cheery optimism which reduced both readers to the verge of madness.

Dear Uncle Joseph has quite recovered, and, in spite of a little nervousness—he was always rather timid—at meeting you again, has consented to go to the White Horse to satisfy you that he is alive. I dare say he will be with you as soon as this letter—perhaps help you to read it.

Mr. Cox laid the letter down with extreme care, and, coughing gently, glanced in a sheepish fashion at the goggle-eyed Mr. Piper.

For some time neither of them spoke. Mr. Cox was the first to break the silence and—when he had finished—Mr. Piper said "Hush."

"Besides, it does no good," he added.

"It does *me* good," said Mr. Cox, recommencing.

Mr. Piper held up his hand with a startled gesture for silence. The words died away on his friend's lips as a familiar voice was heard in the passage, and the next moment Mrs. Berry entered the room and stood regarding them.

"I ran down by the same train to make sure you came, uncle," she remarked. "How long have you been here?"

Mr. Piper moistened his lips and gazed wildly at Mr. Cox for guidance.

"'Bout—'bout five minutes," he stammered.

"We were so glad dear uncle wasn't hurt much," continued Mrs. Berry, smiling, and shaking her head at Mr. Cox; "but the idea of your burying him in the geranium-bed; we haven't got him clean yet."

Mr. Piper, giving utterance to uncouth noises, quitted the room hastily, but Mr. Cox sat still and stared at her dumbly.

"Weren't you surprised to see him?" inquired his tormentor.

"Not after your letter," said Mr. Cox, finding his voice at last, and speaking with an attempt at chilly dignity. "Nothing could surprise me much after that."

Mrs. Berry smiled again.

"Ah, I've got another little surprise for you," she said, briskly. "Mrs. Cox was so upset at the idea of being alone while you were a wanderer over the face of the earth, that she and I have gone into partnership. We have had a proper deed drawn up, so that now there are two of us to look after things. Eh? What did you say?"

"I was just thinking," said Mr. Cox.

In the Library

The fire had burnt low in the library, for the night was wet and warm. It was now little more than a grey shell, and looked desolate. Trayton Burleigh, still hot, rose from his armchair, and turning out one of the gas-jets, took a cigar from a box on a side-table and resumed his seat again.

The apartment, which was on the third floor at the back of the house, was a combination of library, study, and smoke-room, and was the daily despair of the old housekeeper who, with the assistance of one servant, managed the house. It was a bachelor establishment, and had been left to Trayton Burleigh and James Fletcher by a distant connection of both men some ten years before.

Trayton Burleigh sat back in his chair watching the smoke of his cigar through half-closed eyes. Occasionally he opened them a little wider and glanced round the comfortable, well-furnished room, or stared with a cold gleam of hatred at Fletcher as he sat sucking stolidly at his brier pipe. It was a comfortable room and a valuable house, half of which belonged to Trayton Burleigh; and yet he was to leave it in the morning and become a rogue and a wanderer over the face of the earth. James Fletcher had said so. James Fletcher, with the pipe still between his teeth and speaking from one corner of his mouth only, had pronounced his sentence.

"It hasn't occurred to you, I suppose," said Burleigh, speaking suddenly, "that I might refuse your terms."

"No," said Fletcher, simply.

Burleigh took a great mouthful of smoke and let it roll slowly out.

"I am to go out and leave you in possession?" he continued. "You will stay here sole proprietor of the house; you will stay at the office sole owner and representative of the firm? You are a good hand at a deal, James Fletcher."

"I am an honest man," said Fletcher, "and to raise sufficient money to make your defalcations good will not by any means leave me the gainer, as you very well know."

"There is no necessity to borrow," began Burleigh, eagerly. "We can pay the interest easily, and in course of time make the principal good without a soul being the wiser."

"That you suggested before," said Fletcher, "and my answer is the same. I will be no man's confederate in dishonesty; I will raise every penny at all costs, and save the name of the firm—and yours with it— but I will never have you darken the office again, or sit in this house after tonight."

"You won't," cried Burleigh, starting up in a frenzy of rage.

"I won't," said Fletcher. "You can choose the alternative: disgrace and penal servitude. Don't stand over me; you won't frighten me, I can assure you. Sit down."

"You have arranged so many things in your kindness," said Burleigh, slowly, resuming his seat again, "have you arranged how I am to live?"

"You have two strong hands, and health," replied Fletcher. "I will give you the two hundred pounds I mentioned, and after that you must look out for yourself. You can take it now."

He took a leather case from his breast pocket, and drew out a roll of notes. Burleigh, watching him calmly, stretched out his hand and took them from the table. Then he gave way to a sudden access of rage, and crumpling them in his hand, threw them into a corner of the room. Fletcher smoked on.

"Mrs. Marl is out?" said Burleigh, suddenly.

Fletcher nodded.

"She will be away the night," he said, slowly; "and Jane too; they have gone together somewhere, but they will be back at half-past eight in the morning."

"You are going to let me have one more breakfast in the old place, then," said Burleigh. "Half-past eight, half-past——"

He rose from his chair again. This time Fletcher took his pipe from his mouth and watched him closely. Burleigh stooped, and picking up the notes, placed them in his pocket.

"If I am to be turned adrift, it shall not be to leave you here," he said, in a thick voice.

He crossed over and shut the door; as he turned back Fletcher rose from his chair and stood confronting him. Burleigh put his hand to the wall, and drawing a small Japanese sword from its sheath of carved ivory, stepped slowly toward him.

"I give you one chance, Fletcher," he said, grimly. "You are a man of your word. Hush this up and let things be as they were before, and you are safe."

"Put that down," said Fletcher, sharply.

"By ——, I mean what I say!" cried the other.

"I mean what I said!" answered Fletcher.

He looked round at the last moment for a weapon, then he turned suddenly at a sharp sudden pain, and saw Burleigh's clenched fist nearly touching his breast-bone. The hand came away from his breast again, and something with it. It went a long way off. Trayton Burleigh suddenly went to a great distance and the room darkened. It got quite dark, and Fletcher, with an attempt to raise his hands, let them fall to his side instead, and fell in a heap to the floor.

He was so still that Burleigh could hardly realize that it was all over, and stood stupidly waiting for him to rise again. Then he took out his handkerchief as though to wipe the sword, and thinking better of it, put it back into his pocket again, and threw the weapon on to the floor.

The body of Fletcher lay where it had fallen, the white face turned up to the gas. In life he had been a commonplace-looking man, not to say vulgar; now Burleigh, with a feeling of nausea, drew back toward the door, until the body was hidden by the table, and relieved from the sight, he could think more clearly. He looked down carefully and examined his clothes and his boots. Then he crossed the room again, and with his face averted, turned out the gas. Something seemed to stir in the darkness, and with a faint cry he blundered toward the door before he had realized that it was the clock. It struck twelve.

He stood at the head of the stairs trying to recover himself; trying to think. The gas on the landing below, the stairs and the furniture, all looked so prosaic and familiar that he could not realize what had occurred. He walked slowly down and turned the light out. The darkness of the upper part of the house was now almost appalling, and in a sudden panic he ran down stairs into the lighted hall, and snatching a hat from the stand, went to the door and walked down to the gate.

Except for one window the neighbouring houses were in darkness, and the lamps shone up a silent street. There was a little rain in the air, and the muddy road was full of pebbles. He stood at the gate trying to screw up his courage to enter the house again. Then he noticed a figure coming slowly up the road and keeping close to the palings.

The full realisation of what he had done broke in upon him when he found himself turning to fly from the approach of the constable. The wet cape glistening in the lamplight, the slow, heavy step, made him tremble. Suppose the thing upstairs was not quite dead and should cry out? Suppose the constable should think it strange for him to be standing there and follow him in? He assumed a careless attitude, which did not feel careless, and as the man passed bade him goodnight, and made a remark as to the weather.

Ere the sound of the other's footsteps had gone quite out of hearing, he turned and entered the house again before the sense of companionship should have quite departed. The first flight of stairs was lighted by the gas in the hall, and he went up slowly. Then he struck a match and went up steadily, past the library door, and with firm fingers turned on the gas in his bedroom and lit it. He opened the window a little way, and sitting down on his bed, tried to think.

He had got eight hours. Eight hours and two hundred pounds in small notes. He opened his safe and took out all the loose cash it contained, and walking about the room, gathered up and placed in his pockets such articles of jewellery as he possessed.

The first horror had now to some extent passed, and was succeeded by the fear of death.

With this fear on him he sat down again and tried to think out the first moves in that game of skill of which his life was the stake. He had often read of people of hasty temper, evading the police for a time, and eventually falling into their hands for lack of the most elementary common sense. He had heard it said that they always made some stupid blunder, left behind them some damning clue. He took his revolver from a drawer and saw that it was loaded. If the worst came to the worst, he would die quickly.

Eight hours' start; two hundred odd pounds. He would take lodgings at first in some populous district, and let the hair on his face grow. When the hue-and-cry had ceased, he would go abroad and start life again. He would go out of a night and post letters to himself, or better still, postcards, which his landlady would read. Postcards from cheery friends, from a sister, from a brother. During the day he would stay in and write, as became a man who described himself as a journalist.

Or suppose he went to the sea? Who would look for him in flannels, bathing and boating with ordinary happy mortals? He sat and pondered. One might mean life, and the other death. Which?

His face burned as he thought of the responsibility of the choice.

So many people went to the sea at that time of year that he would surely pass unnoticed. But at the sea one might meet acquaintances. He got up and nervously paced the room again. It was not so simple, now that it meant so much, as he had thought.

The sharp little clock on the mantel-piece rang out "one," followed immediately by the deeper note of that in the library. He thought of the clock, it seemed the only live thing in that room, and shuddered. He wondered whether the thing lying by the far side of the table heard it. He wondered——

He started and held his breath with fear. Somewhere down stairs a board creaked loudly, then another. He went to the door, and opening it a little way, but without looking out, listened. The house was so still that he could hear the ticking of the old clock in the kitchen below. He opened the door a little wider and peeped out. As he did so there was a sudden sharp outcry on the stairs, and he drew back into the room and stood trembling before he had quite realized that the noise had been made by the cat. The cry was unmistakable; but what had disturbed it?

There was silence again, and he drew near the door once more. He became certain that something was moving stealthily on the stairs. He heard the boards creak again, and once the rails of the balustrade rattled. The silence and suspense were frightful. Suppose that the something which had been Fletcher waited for him in the darkness outside?

He fought his fears down, and opening the door, determined to see what was beyond. The light from his room streamed out on to the landing, and he peered about fearfully. Was it fancy, or did the door of Fletcher's room opposite close as he looked? Was it fancy, or did the handle of the door really turn?

In perfect silence, and watching the door as he moved, to see that nothing came out and followed him, he proceeded slowly down the dark stairs. Then his jaw fell, and he turned sick and faint again. The library door, which he distinctly remembered closing, and which, moreover, he had seen was closed when he went upstairs to his room, now stood open some four or five inches. He fancied that there was a rustling inside, but his brain refused to be certain. Then plainly and unmistakably he heard a chair pushed against the wall.

He crept to the door, hoping to pass it before the thing inside became aware of his presence. Something crept stealthily about the room. With a sudden impulse he caught the handle of the door, and, closing it violently, turned the key in the lock, and ran madly down the stairs.

A fearful cry sounded from the room, and a heavy hand beat upon the panels of the door. The house rang with the blows, but above them sounded the loud hoarse cries of human fear. Burleigh, half-way down to the hall, stopped with his hand on the balustrade and listened. The beating ceased, and a man's voice cried out loudly for God's sake to let him out.

At once Burleigh saw what had happened and what it might mean for him. He had left the hall door open after his visit to the front, and some wandering bird of the night had entered the house. No need for him to go now. No need to hide either from the hangman's rope or the felon's cell. The fool above had saved him. He turned and ran upstairs again just as the prisoner in his furious efforts to escape wrenched the handle from the door.

"Who's there?" he cried, loudly.

"Let me out!" cried a frantic voice. "For God's sake, open the door! There's something here."

"Stay where you are!" shouted Burleigh, sternly. "Stay where you are! If you come out, I'll shoot you like a dog!"

The only response was a smashing blow on the lock of the door. Burleigh raised his pistol, and aiming at the height of a man's chest, fired through the panel.

The report and the crashing of the wood made one noise, succeeded by an unearthly stillness, then the noise of a window hastily opened. Burleigh fled hastily down the stairs, and flinging wide the hall door, shouted loudly for assistance.

It happened that a sergeant and the constable on the beat had just met in the road. They came toward the house at a run. Burleigh, with incoherent explanations, ran upstairs before them, and halted outside the library door. The prisoner was still inside, still trying to demolish the lock of the sturdy oaken door. Burleigh tried to turn the key, but the lock was too damaged to admit of its moving. The sergeant drew back, and, shoulder foremost, hurled himself at the door and burst it open.

He stumbled into the room, followed by the constable, and two shafts of light from the lanterns at their belts danced round the room. A man lurking behind the door made a dash for it, and the next instant the three men were locked together.

Burleigh, standing in the doorway, looked on coldly, reserving himself for the scene which was to follow. Except for the stumbling of the men and the sharp catch of the prisoner's breath, there was no noise. A helmet fell off and bounced and rolled along the floor. The men fell; there was a sobbing snarl and a sharp click. A tall figure rose from the floor; the other, on his knees, still held the man down. The standing figure felt in his pocket, and, striking a match, lit the gas.

The light fell on the flushed face and fair beard of the sergeant. He was bare-headed, and his hair dishevelled. Burleigh entered the room and gazed eagerly at the half-insensible man on the floor–a short, thick-set fellow with a white, dirty face and a black moustache. His lip was cut and bled down his neck. Burleigh glanced furtively at the table. The cloth had come off in the struggle, and was now in the place where he had left Fletcher.

"Hot work, sir," said the sergeant, with a smile. "It's fortunate we were handy."

The prisoner raised a heavy head and looked up with unmistakable terror in his eyes.

"All right, sir," he said, trembling, as the constable increased the pressure of his knee. "I 'ain't been in the house ten minutes altogether. By ——, I've not."

The sergeant regarded him curiously.

"It don't signify," he said, slowly; "ten minutes or ten seconds won't make any difference."

The man shook and began to whimper.

"It was 'ere when I come," he said, eagerly; "take that down, sir. I've only just come, and it was 'ere when I come. I tried to get away then, but I was locked in."

"What was?" demanded the sergeant.

"That," he said, desperately.

The sergeant, following the direction of the terror-stricken black eyes, stooped by the table. Then, with a sharp exclamation, he dragged away the cloth. Burleigh, with a sharp cry of horror, reeled back against the wall.

"All right, sir," said the sergeant, catching him; "all right. Turn your head away."

He pushed him into a chair, and crossing the room, poured out a glass of whiskey and brought it to him. The glass rattled against his teeth, but he drank it greedily, and then groaned faintly. The sergeant waited patiently. There was no hurry.

"Who is it, sir?" he asked at length.

"My friend—Fletcher," said Burleigh, with an effort. "We lived together." He turned to the prisoner.

"You damned villain!"

"He was dead when I come in the room, gentlemen," said the prisoner, strenuously. "He was on the floor dead, and when I see 'im, I tried to get out. S' 'elp me he was. You heard me call out, sir. I shouldn't ha' called out if I'd killed him."

"All right," said the sergeant, gruffly; "you'd better hold your tongue, you know."

"You keep quiet," urged the constable.

The sergeant knelt down and raised the dead man's head.

"I 'ad nothing to do with it," repeated the man on the floor. "I 'ad nothing to do with it. I never thought of such a thing. I've only been in the place ten minutes; put that down, sir."

The sergeant groped with his left hand, and picking up the Japanese sword, held it at him.

"I've never seen it before," said the prisoner, struggling.

"It used to hang on the wall," said Burleigh. "He must have snatched it down. It was on the wall when I left Fletcher a little while ago."

"How long?" inquired the sergeant.

"Perhaps an hour, perhaps half an hour," was the reply. "I went to my bedroom."

The man on the floor twisted his head and regarded him narrowly.

"You done it!" he cried, fiercely. "You done it, and you want me to swing for it."

"That'll do," said the indignant constable.

The sergeant let his burden gently to the floor again.

"You hold your tongue, you devil!" he said, menacingly.

He crossed to the table and poured a little spirit into a glass and took it in his hand. Then he put it down again and crossed to Burleigh.

"Feeling better, sir?" he asked.

The other nodded faintly.

"You won't want this thing anymore," said the sergeant.

He pointed to the pistol which the other still held, and taking it from him gently, put it into his pocket.

"You've hurt your wrist, sir," he said, anxiously.

Burleigh raised one hand sharply, and then the other.

"This one, I think," said the sergeant. "I saw it just now."

He took the other's wrists in his hand, and suddenly holding them in the grip of a vice, whipped out something from his pocket—something hard and cold, which snapped suddenly on Burleigh's wrists, and held them fast.

"That's right," said the sergeant; "keep quiet."

The constable turned round in amazement; Burleigh sprang toward him furiously.

"Take these things off!" he choked. "Have you gone mad? Take them off!"

"All in good time," said the sergeant.

"Take them off!" cried Burleigh again.

For answer the sergeant took him in a powerful grip, and staring steadily at his white face and gleaming eyes, forced him to the other end of the room and pushed him into a chair.

"Collins," he said, sharply.

"Sir?" said the astonished subordinate.

"Run to the doctor at the corner hard as you can run!" said the other. "This man is not dead!"

As the man left the room the sergeant took up the glass of spirits he had poured out, and kneeling down by Fletcher again, raised his head and tried to pour a little down his throat. Burleigh, sitting in his corner, watched like one in a trance. He saw the constable return with the breathless surgeon, saw the three men bending over Fletcher, and then saw the eyes of the dying man open and the lips of the dying man move. He was conscious that the sergeant made some notes in a pocket-book, and that all three men eyed him closely. The sergeant stepped toward him and placed his hand on his shoulder, and obedient to the touch, he arose and went with him out into the night.

His Brother's Keeper

1

Anthony Keller, white and dazed, came stumbling out into the small hall and closed the door of his study noiselessly behind him. Only half an hour ago he had entered the room with Henry Martle, and now Martle would never leave it again until he was carried out of it.

He took out his watch and put it back again without looking at it. He sank into a chair and, trying to still his quivering legs, strove to think. The clock behind the closed door struck nine. He had ten hours, ten hours before the woman who attended to his small house came to start the next day's work.

Ten hours! His mind refused to act. There was so much to be done, so much to be thought of. God! If only he could have the last ten minutes over again and live it differently. If Martle only had not happened to say that it was a sudden visit and that nobody knew of it.

He went into the back room and, going to the sideboard, gulped down half a tumbler of raw whisky. It seemed to him inconceivable that the room should look the same. This pleasant room, with etchings on the walls, and his book, face downwards, just as he had left it to answer Martle's knock. He could hear the knock now, and—

The empty tumbler smashed his hand, and he caught his breath in a sob. Somebody else was knocking. He stood for a moment quivering, and then, wiping some of the blood from his hand, kicked the pieces of glass aside and stood irresolute. The knocking came again, so loud and insistent that for one horrible moment he fancied it might arouse the thing in the next rom. Then he walked to the door and opened it. A short, sturdy man, greeting him noisily stepped into the hall.

"Thought you were dead," he said breezily. "Hello!"

"Cut myself with a broken glass," said Keller, in a constrained voice.

"Look here, that wants binding up," said his friend. "Got a clean handkerchief?"

He moved towards the door, and was about to turn the handle when Keller flung himself upon him and dragged him back. "Not there," he said thickly. "Not there."

"What the devil's the matter?" inquired the visitor, staring.

Keller's mouth worked. "Somebody in there," he muttered;— "somebody in there. Come here."

He pushed him into the back room and in a dazed fashion motioned him to a chair.

"Thanks, rather not," said the other stiffly. "I just came in to smoke a pipe. I didn't know you had visitors. Anyway, I shouldn't eat them. Goodnight."

Keller stood staring at him. His friend stared back, then suddenly his eyes twinkled and he smiled roguishly.

"What have you got in there?" he demanded, jerking his thumb towards the study.

Keller shrank back. "Nothing," he stammered. "Nothing—no—"

"Ho, ho!" said the other. "All right. Don't worry. Mum's the word. You quiet ones are always the worst. Be good."

He gave him a playful dig in the ribs and went out chuckling. Keller, hardly breathing, watched him to the gate and, closing the gate softly, bolted it and returned to the back room.

He steadied his nerves with some more whisky, and strove to steel himself to the task before him. He had got to conquer his horror and remorse, to overcome his dread of the thing in the next room, and put it where no man should ever see it. He, Anthony Keller, a quiet, ordinary citizen, had got to do this thing.

The little clock in the next room struck ten. Nine hours left. With a soft tread he went out at the back door and unlocking the bicycle-shed peered in. Plenty of room.

He left the door open and, returning to the house, went to the door of the study. Twice he turned the handle—and softly closed the door again. Suppose when he looked in at Martle, Martle should turn and look at him? He turned the handle suddenly and threw the door open.

Martle was quiet enough. Quiet and peaceful, and perhaps, a little pitiful. Keller's fear passed, but envy took its place. Martle had got the best of it, after all. No horror-haunted life for him, no unavailing despair and fear of the unknown. Keller, looking down at the white face and battered head, thought of the years before himself. Or would it be weeks? With a gasp he came back to the need for action, and taking Martle by the shoulders drew him, with heels dragging and scraping, to the shed.

He locked the door and put the key in his pocket. Then he drew a bucket of water from the scullery tap and found some towels. His injured hand was still bleeding, but he regarded it with a sort of cunning satisfaction. It would account for much.

It was a long job, but it was finished at last. He sat down and thought, and then searched round and round the room for the overlooked thing which might be his undoing.

It was nearly midnight, and necessary, unless he wanted to attract the attention of any passing constable, to extinguish or lower the companionable lights. He turned them out swiftly, and, with trembling haste, passed upstairs to his room.

The thought of bed was impossible. He lowered the gas and dropping into a chair, sat down to wait for day. Erect in the chair, his hands gripping the arms, he sat tense and listening. The quiet house was full of rustlings. Suppose the suddenly released spirit of Martle was wandering around the house!

He rose and paced up and down the room, pausing every now and then to listen. He could have sworn that there was something fumbling blindly at the other side of the door, and once, turning sharply, thought that he saw the handle move. Sometimes sitting and sometimes walking, the hours passed until in the distance a cock smelt the dawn, and a little later the occasional note of a bird announced the approach of day.

2

In the bright light of day his courage returned, and dismissing all else from his mind, he thought only of how to escape the consequences of his crime. Inch by inch he examined the room and the hall. Then he went into the garden, and going round the shed, satisfied himself that no crack or hole existed that might reveal his secret. He walked the length of the garden and looked about him. The nearest house was a hundred yards away, and the bottom of the garden screened by trees. Near the angle of the fence he would dig a shallow trench and over it, pile up a rockery of bricks and stone and earth. Once started he could take his time about it, and every day would make him more and more secure. There was an air of solidity and permanency about a rockery that nothing else could give.

He was back in the house when the charwoman arrived, and in a few words told her of his accident of the night before. "I cleaned up the—mess as well as I could," he concluded.

Mrs. Howe nodded. "I'll have a go at it while you're having your breakfast," she remarked.

"Good job for you, sir, that you ain't one o' them as faints at the sight of blood."

She brought coffee and bacon into the little back dining-room, and Keller, as he sat drinking his coffee and trying to eat, heard her at work in the study. He pushed away his plate at last, and filling a pipe from which all flavour had departed sat smoking and thinking.

He was interrupted by Mrs. Howe. She stood in the doorway with a question which numbed his brain, and for a time arrested speech.

"Eh?" he said at last.

"Key of the bicycle-shed," repeated the woman, staring at him. "You had a couple o' my dusters to clean your bicycle with."

Keller felt in his pockets, thinking, "H'mm!" he said at last. "I'm afraid I've mislaid it. I'll look for it presently."

Mrs. Howe nodded. "You do look bad," she said, with an air of concern. "P'r'haps you hurt yourself more than what you think."

Keller forced a smile and shook his head, sinking back in his chair as she vanished, and trying to control his quivering limbs.

For a long time, he sat inert, listening duly to the movements of Mrs. Howe as she bustled to and fro. He heard her washing the step at the back door, and, after that, a rasping, grating noise to which at first, he paid but little heed. Then there was a faint, musical chinking as of keys knocking together. Keys!

He sprang from his chair like a madman, and dashed to the door. Mrs. Howe, with a bunch of odd keys tied to a string, had inserted one in the lock of the bicycle-shed, and was striving to turn it.

"Stop!" cried Keller, in a dreadful voice.

"—*Stop!*"

He snatched the keys from her, and flinging them from him, stood mouthing dumbly at her. The fear in her eyes recalled him to his senses.

"Spoil the lock," he muttered, "spoil the lock. Sorry I didn't mean to shout. No sleep all night. Neuralgia; 'fraid my nerves are wrong."

The woman's face relaxed and her eyes softened.

"—I saw you weren't yourself as soon as I saw you this morning," she exclaimed.

She went back into the house, but he thought she eyed him curiously as she passed. She resumed her work, but in a subdued fashion, and, two or three times that morning meeting his eyes, nervously turned away her own. He realised at last, that he was behaving in an unusual fashion altogether. In and out of the house, and, in the garden, never far from the shed.

By lunchtime he had regained control of himself. He opened a bottle of beer, and congratulating Mrs. Howe upon the grilling of the chops, went on to speak of her husband and the search for work which had been his only occupation since his marriage ten years before.

Some of the fear went out of the woman's eyes—but not all, and it was with obvious relief she left the room.

For some time after lunch Keller stayed in the dining-room, and that in itself was unusual. Two or three times he got up and resolved, for the sake of appearances, to take a short walk, but the shed held him. He dare not leave it unguarded. With a great effort he summoned up sufficient resolution to take him to the bottom of the garden and start his gruesome task.

He dug roughly, avoiding the shape which might have aroused comment from any chance visitor. The ground was soft and, in spite of his injured hand, he made good progress, breaking off at frequent intervals to listen or to move aside and obtain an unobstructed view of the shed.

With a short break for tea he went on with his task until he was called in to his simple meal at seven. The manual labour had done him god and his appearance was almost normal. To Mrs. Howe he made a casual reference to his afternoon's work and questioned where to obtain the best rock-plants.

With her departure after she had cleared away, fear descended upon him again. The house became uncanny, and the shed a place of unspeakable horror. Suppose his nerve failed and he found himself unable to open it! For an hour he paced up and down in the long twilight, waiting for the dark.

It came at last, and, fighting down his fears and nausea, he drew the garden-barrow up to the shed, and took the key from his pocket. He walked to the front gate and looked up and down the silent road. Then he came back and, inserting the key in the lock, opened the door, and, in the light of an electric torch, stood looking down at what he had placed there the night before.

With his ears alert for the slightest sound, he took the inhabitant of the shed by the shoulders, and dragging it outside, strove to lift it into the barrow. He succeeded at last, and, with the rigid body balanced precariously and the dead face looking up into his, seized the handles and slowly and silently took Martle to the place prepared for him.

He did not leave him for a long time. Not until the earth was piled high above him in a circular mound and a score or two of bricks formed the first beginnings of a rockery. Then he walked slowly up the garden, and, after attending to the shed, locked it up and went indoors.

The disposal of the body gave a certain measure of relief. He would live, with time for repentance, and, perhaps, for forgetting. He washed in the scullery, and then, fearing the shadows upstairs, drew the heavy curtains in the dining-room to shut in the light and settled himself in an easy chair. He drank until his senses were deadened; his nerves quietened, his aching limbs relaxed, and he fell into a heavy sleep.

3

He awoke at six, and staggering to his feet, drew back the curtains and turned out the gas. Then he went upstairs, and after disarranging his bed went to the bathroom. The cold water and a shave, together with a change of linen, did him good. He opened doors and windows, and let the clean sweet air blow through the house. The house which he must continue to inhabit because he dare not leave it. Other people might not share his taste for rockeries.

To the watchful eye of Mrs. Howe he appeared to be almost himself again. The key of the shed had turned up, and he smiled as he presented her with her "precious dusters." Then he rode off on his bicycle to order slabs of stone and plants from the nearest nurseryman.

He worked more and more leisurely as the days passed, and the rockery grew larger and more solid. Every added stone and plant seemed to increase his security. He ate well, and, to his surprise, slept well; but every morning misery opened his eyes for him.

The garden was no longer a place of quiet recreation; the house, which was part of the legacy that had so delighted him only a year before, was a prison in which he must serve a lifelong sentence. He could neither let it nor sell it; other people might alter the garden—and dig. Since the fatal evening he had not looked at a newspaper for fear of reading of Martle's disappearance, and in all that time had not spoken to a friend.

Martle was very quiet. There were no shadows in the house, no furtive noises, no dim shape pattering about the garden by night. Memory was the only thing that assailed him; but it suffered.

Then the dream came. A dream confused and grotesque, as most dreams are. He dreamt that he was standing by the rockery, in the twilight, when he thought he saw one of the stones move. Other stones followed suit. A big slab near the top came slithering down, and it was apparent that the whole pile of earth and stone was being shaken by some internal force. Then he remembered that he was buried there, and had no business to be standing outside. He must get back. Martle had put him there, and for some reason which he was quite unable to remember he was afraid of Martle. He procured his tools and set to work. It was a long and tedious job and made more difficult by the fact that he was not allowed to make a noise. He dug and dug, but the grave had disappeared. Then suddenly something took hold of him and held him down; down. He could neither move nor cry out.

He awoke with a scream and for a minute or two lay trembling and shaking. Thank God, it was only a dream. The room was full of sunlight, and he could hear Mrs. Howe moving about downstairs. Life was good and might yet hold something in store for him.

He lay still for ten minutes, and was about to rise when he heard Mrs. Howe running upstairs. Even before her sudden and heavy rapping on the door he scented disaster.

"—Mr. Keller! Mr. Keller!"

"Well?" he said heavily.

"—Your rockery!" gasped the charwoman. "Your beautiful rockery! All gone."

"—Gone?" shouted Keller, springing out of bed and snatching his dressing gown from the door.

"Pulled all to pieces," said Mrs. Howe, as he opened the door. "You never see such a mess. All over the place, as if a madman had done it."

In a mechanical fashion he thrust his feet into slippers and went downstairs. He hurried down the garden, and waving the woman back, stood looking at the ruin. Stones and earth were indeed all over the place, but the spot that mattered was untouched. He stood gazing and trembling. Who could have done it? Why was it done?

He thought of his dream and the truth burst upon him. No need for his aching back and limbs to remind him. No need to remember the sleep-walking feats of his youth. He knew the culprit now.

"Shall I go for the police?" inquired the voice of Mrs. Howe.

Keller turned a stony face upon her. "No," he said slowly. "I—I'll speak to them about it myself."

He took up the spade and began the task of reconstruction. He worked for an hour, and then went in to dress and breakfast. For the rest of the day he worked slowly and steadily, so that by evening most of the damage had been repaired. Then he went indoors to face the long night.

Sleep, man's best friend, had become his unrelenting enemy. He made himself coffee on the gas-stove and fought his drowsiness cup by cup. He read and smoked and walked about the room. Bits of his dream that he had forgotten came back to him and stayed with him. And ever at the back of his mind was the certainty that he was doomed.

There was only one hope left to him. He would go away for a time. Far enough away to render a visit home in his sleep impossible. And perhaps the change of scene would strengthen him and help his frayed nerves. Afterwards it might be possible to let the house for a time on condition that the garden was not interfered with. It was one risk against another.

He went down the garden as soon as it was light and completed his work. Then he went indoors to breakfast and to announce his plans for a sudden departure to Mrs. Howe, his white and twitching face amply corroborating his tale of neuralgia and want of sleep.

"Things'll be all right," said the woman. "I'll ask the police to keep an eye on the house of a night. I did speak to one last night about them brutes as destroyed the rockery. If they try it again, they may get a surprise."

Keller quivered but made no sign. He went upstairs and packed his bag, and two hours later was in the train on his way to Exeter, where he proposed to stay the night. After that, Cornwall, perhaps.

He secured a room at an hotel and went for a stroll to pass the time before dinner. How happy the people in the streets seemed to be, even the poorest! All free and all sure of their freedom. They could eat and sleep and enjoy the countless trivial things that make up life. Of battle and murder and sudden death they had no thought.

The light and bustle of the dining-room gave him a little comfort. After his lonely nights it was good to know that there were people all around him, that the house would be full of them whilst he slept. He felt that he was beginning a fresh existence. In future he would live amongst a crowd.

It was late when he went upstairs, but he lay awake for a few minutes. A faint sound or two reached him from downstairs, and the movements of somebody in the next room gave him a comfortable feeling of security. With a sigh of content, he fell asleep.

He was awakened by a knocking; a knocking which sounded just above the head of his bed and died away almost before he had brushed the sleep from his eyes. He looked around fearfully, and then, lighting his candle, lay listening. The noise was not repeated. He had been dreaming, but he could not remember the substance of his dream. It had been unpleasant, but vague. More than unpleasant, terrifying. Somebody had been shouting at him. *Shouting!*

He fell back with a groan. The faint hopes of the night before died within him. He had been shouting and the strange noise came from the occupant of the next room. What had he said? And what had his neighbour heard?

He slept no more. From somewhere below he heard a clock toll the hours, and tossing in his bed, wondered how many more remained to him.

Day came at last and he descended to breakfast. The hour was early and only two other tables were occupied, from one of which, between mouthfuls, a bluff-looking elderly man eyed him curiously. He caught Keller's eye at last and spoke.

"Better?" he inquired.

Keller tried to force his quivering lips to a smile.

"Stood it as long as I could," said the other; "then I knocked. I thought perhaps you were delirious. Same words over and over again; sounded like 'Mockery' and 'Mortal.'

"'Mockery' and 'Mortal' you must have used them a hundred times."

Keller finished his coffee, and, lighting a cigarette, went and sat in the lounge. He had made his bid for freedom and failed. He looked up the times of the trains to town and rang for his bill.

4

He was back in the silent house, upon which, in the fading light of the summer evening, a great stillness seemed to have descended. The atmosphere of horror had gone and left only a sense of abiding peace. All fear had left him, and pain and remorse had gone with it. Serene and tranquil he went into the fatal room, and, opening the window, sat by it, watching the succession of shadowy tableaux that had been his life. Some of it good and some of it bad, but most of it neither good nor bad. A very ordinary life until fate linked it for all time with that of Martle's. He was a living man bound to a corpse with bonds that could never be severed.

It grew dark and he lit the gas and took a volume of poems from the shelves. Never before had he read with such insight and appreciation. In some odd fashion all his senses seemed to have been sharpened and refined.

He read for an hour, and then, replacing the book, went slowly upstairs. For a long time, he lay in bed thinking and trying to analyse the calm and indifference which had overtaken him and, with the problem still unsolved, fell asleep.

For a time, he dreamt, but of pleasant, happy things. He seemed to be filled with a greater content than he had ever known before, a content which did not leave him even when these dreams faded and he found himself back in the old one.

This time, however, it was different. He was still digging, but not in a state of frenzy and horror. He dug because something told him it was his duty to dig, and only by digging could he make reparation. And it was a matter of no surprise to him that Martle stood close by looking on. Not the Martle he had known, nor a bloody and decaying Martle, but one of grave and noble aspect. And there was a look of understanding on his face that nearly made Keller weep.

He went on digging with a sense of companionship such as he had never known before. Then suddenly, without warning, the sun blazed out of the darkness and struck him full in the face. The light was unbearable, and with a wild cry he dropped his spade and clapped his hands over his eyes. The light went, and a voice spoke to him out of the darkness.

He opened his eyes on a dim figure standing a yard or two away.

"Hope I didn't frighten you sir," said the voice. "I called to you once or twice and then I guessed you were doing this in your sleep."

"—In my sleep," repeated Keller. "Yes."

"—And a pretty mess you've made of it," said the constable, with a genial chuckle. "Lord! To think of you working at it every day and then pulling it down every night. Shouted at you I did, but you wouldn't wake."

He turned on the flashlight that had dazzled Keller, and surveyed the ruins. Keller stood by motionless—and waiting.

"Looks like an earthquake," muttered the constable. He paused and kept the light directed upon one spot. Then he stooped down and scratched away the earth with his fingers, and tugged. He stood up suddenly and turned the light on Keller, while with the other he fumbled in his pocket. He spoke in a voice cold and official.

"Are you coming quietly?" he asked.

Keller stepped towards him with both hands outstretched.

"I am coming quietly," he said, in a low voice. "Thank God!"

Over the Side

Of all classes of men, those who follow the sea are probably the most prone to superstition. Afloat upon the black waste of waters, at the mercy of wind and sea, with vast depths and strange creatures below them, a belief in the supernatural is easier than ashore, under the cheerful gas-lamps. Strange stories of the sea are plentiful, and an incident which happened within my own experience has made me somewhat chary of dubbing a man fool or coward because he has encountered something he cannot explain. There are stories of the supernatural with prosaic sequels; there are others to which the sequel has never been published.

I was fifteen years old at the time, and as my father, who had a strong objection to the sea, would not apprentice me to it, I shipped before the mast on a sturdy little brig called the *Endeavour*, bound for Riga. She was a small craft, but the skipper was as fine a seaman as one could wish for, and, in fair weather, an easy man to sail under. Most boys have a rough time of it when they first go to sea, but, with a strong sense of what was good for me, I had attached myself to a brawny, good-natured infant, named Bill Smith, and it was soon understood that whoever hit me struck Bill by proxy. Not that the crew were particularly brutal, but a sound cuffing occasionally is held by most seamen to be beneficial to a lad's health and morals.

The only really spiteful fellow among them was a man named Jem Dadd. He was a morose, sallow-looking man, of about forty, with a strong taste for the supernatural, and a stronger taste still for frightening his fellows with it. I have seen Bill almost afraid to go on deck of a night for his trick at the wheel, after a few of his reminiscences. Rats were a favourite topic with him, and he would never allow one to be killed if he could help it, for he claimed for them that they were the souls of drowned sailors, hence their love of ships and their habit of leaving them when they became unseaworthy. He was a firm believer in the transmigration of souls, some idea of which he had, no doubt, picked up in Eastern ports, and gave his shivering auditors to understand that his arrangements for his own immediate future were already perfected.

We were six or seven days out when a strange thing happened. Dadd had the second watch one night, and Bill was to relieve him. They were not very strict aboard the brig in fair weather, and when a man's time was up, he just made the wheel fast, and, running for'ard, shouted down the fo'c's'le. On this night I happened to awake suddenly, in time to see Bill slip out of his bunk and stand by me, rubbing his red eyelids with his knuckles.

"Dadd's giving me a long time," he whispered, seeing that I was awake; "it's a whole hour after his time."

He pattered up on deck, and I was just turning over, thankful that I was too young to have a watch to keep, when he came softly down again, and, taking me by the shoulders, shook me roughly.

"Jack," he whispered. "Jack."

I raised myself on my elbows, and, in the light of the smoking lamp, saw that he was shaking all over.

"Come on deck," he said, thickly.

I put on my clothes, and followed him quietly to the sweet, cool air above. It was a beautiful clear night, but, from his manner, I looked nervously around for some cause of alarm. I saw nothing. The deck was deserted, except for the solitary figure at the wheel.

"Look at him," whispered Bill, bending a contorted face to mine.

I walked aft a few steps, and Bill followed slowly. Then I saw that Jem Dadd was leaning forward clumsily on the wheel, with his hands clenched on the spokes.

"He's asleep," said I, stopping short.

Bill breathed hard. "He's in a queer sleep," said he; "kind o' trance more like. Go closer."

I took fast hold of Bill's sleeve, and we both went. The light of the stars was sufficient to show that Dadd's face was very white, and that his dim, black eyes were wide open, and staring in a very strange and dreadful manner straight before him.

"Dadd," said I, softly, "Dadd!"

There was no reply, and, with a view of arousing him, I tapped one sinewy hand as it gripped the wheel, and even tried to loosen it.

He remained immovable, and, suddenly with a great cry, my courage deserted me, and Bill and I fairly bolted down into the cabin and woke the skipper.

Then we saw how it was with Jem, and two strong seamen forcibly loosened the grip of those rigid fingers, and, laying him on the deck, covered him with a piece of canvas. The rest of the night two men stayed at the wheel, and, gazing fearfully at the outline of the canvas, longed for dawn.

It came at last, and, breakfast over, the body was sewn up in canvas, and the skipper held a short service compiled from a Bible which belonged to the mate, and what he remembered of the Burial Service proper. Then the corpse went overboard with a splash, and the men, after standing awkwardly together for a few minutes, slowly dispersed to their duties.

For the rest of that day we were all very quiet and restrained; pity for the dead man being mingled with a dread of taking the wheel when night came.

"The wheel's haunted," said the cook, solemnly; "mark my words, there's more of you will be took the same way Dadd was."

The cook, like myself, had no watch to keep.

The men bore up pretty well until night came on again, and then they unanimously resolved to have a double watch. The cook, sorely against his will, was impressed into the service, and I, glad to oblige my patron, agreed to stay up with Bill.

Some of the pleasure had vanished by the time night came, and I seemed only just to have closed my eyes when Bill came, and, with a rough shake or two, informed me that the time had come. Any hope that I might have had of escaping the ordeal was at once dispelled by his expectant demeanour, and the helpful way in which he assisted me with my clothes, and, yawning terribly, I followed him on deck.

The night was not so clear as the preceding one, and the air was chilly, with a little moisture in it. I buttoned up my jacket, and thrust my hands in my pockets.

"Everything quiet?" asked Bill as he stepped up and took the wheel.

"Ay, ay," said Roberts, "quiet as the grave," and, followed by his willing mate, he went below.

I sat on the deck by Bill's side as, with a light touch on the wheel, he kept the brig to her course. It was weary work sitting there, doing nothing, and thinking of the warm berth below, and I believe that I should have fallen asleep, but that my watchful companion stirred me with his foot whenever he saw me nodding.

I suppose I must have sat there, shivering and yawning, for about an hour, when, tired of inactivity, I got up and went and leaned over the side of the vessel. The sound of the water gurgling and lapping by was so soothing that I began to doze.

I was recalled to my senses by a smothered cry from Bill, and, running to him, I found him staring to port in an intense and uncomfortable fashion. At my approach, he took one hand from the wheel, and gripped my arm so tightly that I was like to have screamed with the pain of it.

"Jack," said he, in a shaky voice, "while you was away something popped its head up, and looked over the ship's side."

"You've been dreaming," said I, in a voice which was a very fair imitation of Bill's own.

"Dreaming," repeated Bill, "dreaming! Ah, *look there!*"

He pointed with outstretched finger, and my heart seemed to stop beating as I saw a man's head appear above the side. For a brief space it peered at us in silence, and then a dark figure sprang like a cat on to the deck, and stood crouching a short distance away.

A mist came before my eyes, and my tongue failed me, but Bill let off a roar, such as I have never heard before or since. It was answered from below, both aft and for'ard, and the men came running up on deck just as they left their beds.

"What's up?" shouted the skipper, glancing aloft.

For answer, Bill pointed to the intruder, and the men, who had just caught sight of him, came up and formed a compact knot by the wheel.

"Come over the side, it did," panted Bill, "come over like a ghost out of the sea."

The skipper took one of the small lamps from the binnacle, and, holding it aloft, walked boldly up to the cause of alarm. In the little patch of light, we saw a ghastly black-bearded man, dripping with water, regarding us with unwinking eyes, which glowed red in the light of the lamp.

"Where did you come from?" asked the skipper.

The figure shook its head.

"Where did you come from?" he repeated, walking up, and laying his hand on the other's shoulder.

Then the intruder spoke, but in a strange fashion and in strange words. We leaned forward to listen, but, even when he repeated them, we could make nothing of them.

"He's a furriner," said Roberts.

"Blest if I've ever 'eard the lingo afore," said Bill. "Does anybody rekernize it?"

Nobody did, and the skipper, after another attempt, gave it up, and, falling back upon the universal language of signs, pointed first to the man and then to the sea. The other understood him, and, in a heavy, slovenly fashion, portrayed a man drifting in an open boat, and clutching and clambering up the side of a passing ship. As his meaning dawned upon us, we rushed to the stern, and, leaning over, peered into the gloom, but the night was dark, and we saw nothing.

"Well," said the skipper, turning to Bill, with a mighty yawn, "take him below, and give him some grub, and the next time a gentleman calls on you, don't make such a confounded row about it."

He went below, followed by the mate, and after some slight hesitation, Roberts stepped up to the intruder, and signed to him to follow. He came stolidly enough, leaving a trail of water on the deck, and, after changing into the dry things we gave him, fell to, but without much appearance of hunger, upon some salt beef and biscuits, regarding us between bites with black, lack-lustre eyes.

"He seems as though he's a-walking in his sleep," said the cook.

"He ain't very hungry," said one of the men; "he seems to mumble his food."

"Hungry!" repeated Bill, who had just left the wheel. "Course he ain't famished. He had his tea last night."

The men stared at him in bewilderment.

"Don't you see?" said Bill, still in a hoarse whisper; "ain't you ever seen them eyes afore? Don't you know what he used to say about dying? It's Jem Dadd come back to us. Jem Dadd got another man's body, as he always said he would."

"Rot!" said Roberts, trying to speak bravely, but he got up, and, with the others, huddled together at the end of the fo'c's'le, and stared in a bewildered fashion at the sodden face and short, squat figure of our visitor. For his part, having finished his meal, he pushed his plate from him, and, leaning back on the locker, looked at the empty bunks.

Roberts caught his eye, and, with a nod and a wave of his hand, indicated the bunks. The fellow rose from the locker, and, amid a breathless silence, climbed into one of them—Jem Dadd's!

He slept in the dead sailor's bed that night, the only man in the fo'c's'le who did sleep properly, and turned out heavily and lumpishly in the morning for breakfast.

133

The skipper had him on deck after the meal, but could make nothing of him. To all his questions he replied in the strange tongue of the night before, and, though our fellows had been to many ports, and knew a word or two of several languages, none of them recognised it. The skipper gave it up at last, and, left to himself, he stared about him for some time, regardless of our interest in his movements, and then, leaning heavily against the side of the ship, stayed there so long that we thought he must have fallen asleep.

"He's half-dead *now!*" whispered Roberts.

"Hush!" said Bill, "mebbe he's been in the water a week or two, and can't quite make it out. See how he's looking at it now."

He stayed on deck all day in the sun, but, as night came on, returned to the warmth of the fo'c's'le. The food we gave him remained untouched, and he took little or no notice of us, though I fancied that he saw the fear we had of him. He slept again in the dead man's bunk, and when morning came still lay there.

Until dinner-time, nobody interfered with him, and then Roberts, pushed forward by the others, approached him with some food. He motioned, it away with a dirty, bloated hand, and, making signs for water, drank it eagerly.

For two days he stayed there quietly, the black eyes always open, the stubby fingers always on the move. On the third morning Bill, who had conquered his fear sufficiently to give him water occasionally, called softly to us.

"Come and look at him," said he. "What's the matter with him?"

"He's dying!" said the cook, with a shudder.

"He can't be going to die *yet!*" said Bill, blankly.

As he spoke the man's eyes seemed to get softer and more life-like, and he looked at us piteously and helplessly. From face to face he gazed in mute inquiry, and then, striking his chest feebly with his fist, uttered two words.

We looked at each other blankly, and he repeated them eagerly, and again touched his chest.

"It's his name," said the cook, and we all repeated them.

He smiled in an exhausted fashion, and then, rallying his energies, held up a forefinger; as we stared at this new riddle, he lowered it, and held up all four fingers, doubled.

"Come away," quavered the cook; "he's putting a spell on us."

We drew back at that, and back farther still, as he repeated the motions. Then Bill's face cleared suddenly, and he stepped towards him.

"He means his wife and younkers!" he shouted eagerly. "This ain't no Jem Dadd!"

It was good then to see how our fellows drew round the dying sailor, and strove to cheer him. Bill, to show he understood the finger business, nodded cheerily, and held his hand at four different heights from the floor. The last was very low, so low that the man set his lips together, and strove to turn his heavy head from us.

"Poor devil!" said Bill, "he wants us to tell his wife and children what's become of him. He must ha' been dying when he come aboard. What was his name, again?"

But the name was not easy to English lips, and we had already forgotten it.

"Ask him again," said the cook, "and write it down. Who's got a pen?"

He went to look for one as Bill turned to the sailor to get him to repeat it. Then he turned round again, and eyed us blankly, for, by this time, the owner had himself forgotten it.

The Three Sisters

Thirty years ago, on a wet autumn evening the household of Mallett's Lodge was gathered round the deathbed of Ursula Mallow, the eldest of the three sisters who inhabited it. The dingy moth-eaten curtains of the old wooden bedstead were drawn apart, the light of a smoking oil-lamp falling upon the hopeless countenance of the dying woman as she turned her dull eyes upon her sisters. The room was in silence except for an occasional sob from the youngest sister, Eunice. Outside the rain fell steadily over the steaming marshes.

"Nothing is to be changed, Tabitha," gasped Ursula to the other sister, who bore a striking likeness to her although her expression was harder and colder; "this room is to be locked up and never opened."

"Very well," said Tabitha brusquely, "though I don't see how it can matter to you then."

"It does matter," said her sister with startling energy. "How do you know; how do I know that I may not sometimes visit it? I have lived in this house so long I am certain that I shall see it again. I *will* come back. Come back to watch over you both and see that no harm befalls you."

"You are talking wildly," said Tabitha, by no means moved at her sister's solicitude for her welfare. "Your mind is wandering; you know that I have no faith in such things."

Ursula sighed, and beckoning to Eunice, who was weeping silently at the bedside, placed her feeble arms around her neck and kissed her.

"Do not weep, dear," she said feebly. "Perhaps it is best so. A lonely woman's life is scarce worth living. We have no hopes, no aspirations; other women have had happy husbands and children, but we in this forgotten place have grown old together. I go first, but you must soon follow."

Tabitha, comfortably conscious of only forty years and an iron

137

frame, shrugged her shoulders and smiled grimly.

"I go first," repeated Ursula in a new and strange voice as her heavy eyes slowly closed, "but I will come for each of you in turn, when your lease of life runs out. At that moment I will be with you to lead your steps whither I now go."

As she spoke the flickering lamp went out suddenly as though extinguished by a rapid hand, and the room was left in utter darkness. A strange suffocating noise issued from the bed, and when the trembling women had relighted the lamp, all that was left of Ursula Mallow was ready for the grave.

That night the survivors passed together. The dead woman had been a firm believer in the existence of that shadowy borderland which is said to form an unhallowed link between the living and the dead, and even the stolid Tabitha, slightly unnerved by the events of the night, was not free from certain apprehensions that she might have been right.

With the bright morning their fears disappeared. The sun stole in at the window, and seeing the poor earth-worn face on the pillow so touched it and glorified it that only its goodness and weakness were seen, and the beholders came to wonder how they could ever have felt any dread of aught so calm and peaceful. A day or two passed, and the body was transferred to a massive coffin long regarded as the finest piece of work of its kind ever turned out of the village carpenter's workshop. Then a slow and melancholy cortege headed by four bearers wound its solemn way across the marshes to the family vault in the grey old church, and all that was left of Ursula was placed by the father and mother who had taken that self-same journey some thirty years before.

To Eunice as they toiled slowly home the day seemed strange and Sabbath-like, the flat prospect of marsh wilder and more forlorn than usual, the roar of the sea more depressing. Tabitha had no such fancies. The bulk of the dead woman's property had been left to Eunice, and her avaricious soul was sorely troubled and her proper sisterly feelings of regret for the deceased sadly interfered with in consequence.

"What are you going to do with all that money, Eunice?" she asked as they sat at their quiet tea.

"I shall leave it as it stands," said Eunice slowly. "We have both got sufficient to live upon, and I shall devote the income from it to supporting some beds in a children's hospital."

"If Ursula had wished it to go to a hospital," said Tabitha in her deep tones, "she would have left the money to it herself. I wonder you do not respect her wishes more."

"What else can I do with it then?" inquired Eunice.

"Save it," said the other with gleaming eyes, "save it."

Eunice shook her head.

"No," said she, "it shall go to the sick children, but the principal I will not touch, and if I die before you it shall become yours and you can do what you like with it."

"Very well," said Tabitha, smothering her anger by a strong effort; "I don't believe that was what Ursula meant you to do with it, and I don't believe she will rest quietly in the grave while you squander the money she stored so carefully."

"What do you mean?" asked Eunice with pale lips. "You are trying to frighten me; I thought that you did not believe in such things."

Tabitha made no answer, and to avoid the anxious inquiring gaze of her sister, drew her chair to the fire, and folding her gaunt arms, composed herself for a nap.

For some time, life went on quietly in the old house. The room of the dead woman, in accordance with her last desire, was kept firmly locked, its dirty windows forming a strange contrast to the prim cleanliness of the others. Tabitha, never very talkative, became more taciturn than ever, and stalked about the house and the neglected garden like an unquiet spirit, her brow roughened into the deep wrinkles suggestive of much thought. As the winter came on, bringing with it the long dark evenings, the old house became more lonely than ever, and an air of mystery and dread seemed to hang over it and brood in its empty rooms and dark corridors.

The deep silence of night was broken by strange noises for which neither the wind nor the rats could be held accountable. Old Martha, seated in her distant kitchen, heard strange sounds upon the stairs, and once, upon hurrying to them, fancied that she saw a dark figure squatting upon the landing, though a subsequent search with candle and spectacles failed to discover anything. Eunice was disturbed by several vague incidents, and, as she suffered from a complaint of the heart, rendered very ill by them. Even Tabitha admitted a strangeness about the house, but, confident in her piety and virtue, took no heed of it, her mind being fully employed in another direction.

Since the death of her sister all restraint upon her was removed, and she yielded herself up entirely to the stern and hard rules enforced by avarice upon its devotees. Her housekeeping expenses were kept rigidly separate from those of Eunice and her food limited to the coarsest dishes, while in the matter of clothes, the old servant was by far the better dressed. Seated alone in her bedroom this uncouth, hard-featured creature revelled in her possessions, grudging even the expense of the candle-end which enabled her to behold them. So completely did this passion change her that both Eunice and Martha became afraid of her, and lay awake in their beds, night after night, trembling at the chinking of the coins at her unholy vigils.

One day Eunice ventured to remonstrate. "Why don't you bank your money, Tabitha?" she said; "it is surely not safe to keep such large sums in such a lonely house."

"Large sums!" repeated the exasperated Tabitha, "large sums! what nonsense is this? You know well that I have barely sufficient to keep me."

"It's a great temptation to housebreakers," said her sister, not pressing the point. "I made sure last night that I heard somebody in the house."

"Did you?" said Tabitha, grasping her arm, a horrible look on her face. "So, did I. I thought they went to Ursula's room, and I got out of bed and went on the stairs to listen."

"Well?" said Eunice faintly, fascinated by the look on her sister's face.

"There was something there," said Tabitha slowly. "I'll swear it, for I stood on the landing by her door and listened; something scuffling on the floor round and round the room. At first, I thought it was the cat, but when I went up there this morning the door was still locked, and the cat was in the kitchen."

"Oh, let us leave this dreadful house," moaned Eunice.

"What!" said her sister grimly; "afraid of poor Ursula? Why should you be? Your own sister who nursed you when you were a babe, and who perhaps even now comes and watches over your slumbers."

"Oh!" said Eunice, pressing her hand to her side, "if I saw her, I should die. I should think that she had come for me as she said she would. O God! have mercy on me, I am dying."

She reeled as she spoke, and before Tabitha could save her, sank senseless to the floor.

"Get some water," cried Tabitha, as old Martha came hurrying up the stairs, "Eunice has fainted."

The old woman, with a timid glance at her, retired, reappearing shortly afterwards with the water, with which she proceeded to restore her much-loved mistress to her senses. Tabitha, as soon as this was accomplished, stalked off to her room, leaving her sister and Martha sitting drearily enough in the small parlour, watching the fire and conversing in whispers.

It was clear to the old servant that this state of things could not last much longer, and she repeatedly urged her mistress to leave a house so lonely and so mysterious. To her great delight Eunice at length consented, despite the fierce opposition of her sister, and at the mere idea of leaving gained greatly in health and spirits. A small but comfortable house was hired in Morville, and arrangements made for a speedy change.

It was the last night in the old house, and all the wild spirits of the marshes, the wind and the sea seemed to have joined forces for one supreme effort. When the wind dropped, as it did at brief intervals, the sea was heard moaning on the distant beach, strangely mingled with the desolate warning of the bell-buoy as it rocked to the waves. Then the wind rose again, and the noise of the sea was lost in the fierce gusts which, finding no obstacle on the open marshes, swept with their full fury upon the house by the creek. The strange voices of the air shrieked in its chimneys, windows rattled, doors slammed, and even, the very curtains seemed to live and move.

Eunice was in bed, awake. A small nightlight in a saucer of oil shed a sickly glare upon the worm-eaten old furniture, distorting the most innocent articles into ghastly shapes. A wilder gust than usual almost deprived her of the protection afforded by that poor light, and she lay listening fearfully to the creakings and other noises on the stairs, bitterly regretting that she had not asked Martha to sleep with her. But it was not too late even now. She slipped hastily to the floor, crossed to the huge wardrobe, and was in the very act of taking her dressing-gown from its peg when an unmistakable footfall was heard on the stairs. The robe dropped from her shaking fingers, and with a quickly beating heart she regained her bed.

The sounds ceased and a deep silence followed, which she herself was unable to break although she strove hard to do so. A wild gust of wind shook the windows and nearly extinguished the light, and when its flame had regained its accustomed steadiness, she saw that the door was slowly opening, while the huge shadow of a hand blotted the papered wall. Still her tongue refused its office. The door flew open with a crash, a cloaked figure entered and, throwing aside its coverings, she saw with a horror past all expression the napkin-bound face of the dead Ursula smiling terribly at her. In her last extremity she raised her faded eyes above for succour, and then as the figure noiselessly advanced and laid its cold hand upon her brow, the soul of Eunice Mallow left its body with a wild shriek and made its way to the Eternal.

Martha, roused by the cry, and shivering with dread, rushed to the door and gazed in terror at the figure which stood leaning over the bedside. As she watched, it slowly removed the cowl and the napkin and exposed the fell face of Tabitha, so strangely contorted between fear and triumph that she hardly recognized it.

"Who's there?" cried Tabitha in a terrible voice as she saw the old woman's shadow on the wall.

"I thought I heard a cry," said Martha, entering. "Did anybody call?"

"Yes, Eunice," said the other, regarding her closely. "I, too, heard the cry, and hurried to her. What makes her so strange? Is she in a trance?"

"Ay," said the old woman, falling on her knees by the bed and sobbing bitterly, "the trance of death. Ah, my dear, my poor lonely girl, that this should be the end of it! She has died of fright," said the old woman, pointing to the eyes, which even yet retained their horror. "She has seen something *devilish*."

Tabitha's gaze fell. "She has always suffered with her heart," she muttered; "the night has frightened her; it frightened me."

She stood upright by the foot of the bed as Martha drew the sheet over the face of the dead woman.

"First Ursula, then Eunice," said Tabitha, drawing a deep breath. "I can't stay here. I'll dress and wait for the morning."

She left the room as she spoke, and with bent head proceeded to her own. Martha remained by the bedside, and gently closing the staring eyes, fell on her knees, and prayed long and earnestly for the departed soul. Overcome with grief and fear she remained with bowed head until a sudden sharp cry from Tabitha brought her to her feet.

"Well," said the old woman, going to the door.

"Where are you?" cried Tabitha, somewhat reassured by her voice.

"In Miss Eunice's bedroom. Do you want anything?"

"Come down at once. Quick! I am unwell."

Her voice rose suddenly to a scream. "Quick! For God's sake! Quick, or I shall go mad. There is some strange woman in the house."

The old woman stumbled hastily down the dark stairs. "What is the matter?" she cried, entering the room. "Who is it? What do you mean?"

"I saw it," said Tabitha, grasping her convulsively by the shoulder. "I was coming to you when I saw the figure of a woman in front of me going up the stairs. Is it—can it be Ursula come for the soul of Eunice, as she said she would?"

"Or for yours?" said Martha, the words coming from her in some odd fashion, despite herself.

Tabitha, with a ghastly look, fell cowering by her side, clutching tremulously at her clothes. "Light the lamps," she cried hysterically. "Light a fire, make a noise; oh, this dreadful darkness! Will it never be day!"

"Soon, soon," said Martha, overcoming her repugnance and trying to pacify her. "When the day comes you will laugh at these fears."

"I murdered her," screamed the miserable woman, "I killed her with fright. Why did she not give me the money? 'Twas no use to her. Ah! *Look there!*"

Martha, with a horrible fear, followed her glance to the door, but saw nothing.

"It's Ursula," said Tabitha from between her teeth. "Keep her off! Keep her off!"

The old woman, who by some unknown sense seemed to feel the presence of a third person in the room, moved a step forward and stood before her. As she did so Tabitha waved her arms as though to free herself from the touch of a detaining hand, half rose to her feet, and without a word fell dead before her.

At this the old woman's courage forsook her, and with a great cry she rushed from the room, eager to escape from this house of death and mystery. The bolts of the great door were stiff with age, and strange voices seemed to ring in her ears as she strove wildly to unfasten them. Her brain whirled. She thought that the dead in their distant rooms called to her, and that a devil stood on the step outside laughing and holding the door against her. Then with a supreme effort she flung it open, and heedless of her night-clothes passed into the bitter night. The path across the marshes was lost in the darkness, but she found it; the planks over the ditches slippery and narrow, but she crossed them in safety, until at last, her feet bleeding and her breath coming in great gasps, she entered the village and sank down more dead than alive on a cottage doorstep.

The Brown Man's Servant

The shop of Solomon Hyams stood in a small thoroughfare branching off the Commercial Road. In its windows unredeemed pledges of all kinds, from old-time watches to seamen's boots, appealed to all tastes and requirements. Bundles of cigars, candidly described as "wonderful," were marked at absurdly low figures, while silver watches endeavoured to excuse the clumsiness of their make by describing themselves as "strong workmen's." The side entrance, up a narrow alley, was surmounted by the usual three brass balls, and here Mr. Hyams' clients were wont to call. They entered as optimists, smiled confidently upon Mr. Hyams, argued, protested shrilly, and left the establishment pessimists of a most pronounced and virulent type.

None of these things, however, disturbed the pawnbroker. The drunken client who endeavoured to bail out his Sunday clothes with a tram ticket was accommodated with a chair, while the assistant went to hunt up his friends and contract for a speedy removal; the old woman who, with a view of obtaining a higher advance than usual, poured a tale of grievous woe into the hardened ears of Mr. Hyams, found herself left to the same invaluable assistant, and, realizing her failure, would at once become cheerful and take what was offered. Mr. Hyams' methods of business were quiet and unostentatious, and rumour had it that he might retire at any time and live in luxury.

It was a cold, cheerless afternoon in November as Mr. Hyams, who had occasional hazy ideas of hygiene, stood at his door taking the air. It was an atmosphere laden with soot and redolent of many blended odours, but after the fusty smell of the shop it was almost health-giving. In the large public-house opposite, with its dirty windows and faded signboards, the gas was already being lit, which should change it from its daylight dreariness to a resort of light and life.

Mr. Hyams, who was never in a hurry to light up his own premises, many of his clients preferring the romantic light which comes between day and night for their visits, was about to leave the chilly air for the warmth inside, when his attention was attracted by a seaman of sturdy aspect stopping and looking in at his window. Mr. Hyams rubbed his hands softly. There was an air of comfort and prosperity about this seaman, and the pawnbroker had many small articles in his window, utterly useless to the man, which he would have liked to have sold him.

The man came from the window, made as though to pass, and then paused irresolute before the pawn-broker.

"You want a watch?" said the latter genially. "Come inside."

Mr. Hyams went behind his counter and waited.

"I don't want to buy nothing, and I don't want to pawn nothing," said the sailor. "What do you think o' that?"

Mr. Hyams, who objected to riddles, especially those which seemed to be against business, eyed him unfavourably from beneath his shaggy eyebrows.

"We might have a little quiet talk together," said the seaman, "you an' me; we might do a little bit o' business together, you an' me. In the parler, shall we say, over a glass o' something hot?"

Mr. Hyams hesitated. He was not averse to a little business of an illicit nature, but there rose up vividly before him the picture of another sailor who had made much the same sort of proposal, and, after four glasses of rum, had merely suggested to him that he should lend him twenty pounds on the security of an I.O.U. It was long since, but the memory of it still rankled.

"What sort of business is it?" he inquired.

"Business that's too big for you, p'raps," said the sailor with a lordly air. "I'll try a bigger place. What's that lantern-faced swab shoving his ugly mug into the daylight for?"

"Get off," said the pawnbroker to the assistant, who was quietly and unobtrusively making a third.

"Mind the shop. This gentleman and I have business in the parlour. Come this way, sir."

He raised the flap of the counter, and led the way to a small, untidy room at the back of the shop. A copper kettle was boiling on the fire, and the table was already laid for tea. The pawnbroker, motioning his visitor to a dingy leather armchair, went to a cupboard and produced a bottle of rum, three parts full, and a couple of glasses.

"Tea for me," said the seaman, eyeing the bottle wistfully.

The pawnbroker pricked up his ears. "Nonsense," he said, with an attempt at heartiness, "a jolly fellow like you don't want tea. Have some o' this."

"Tea, confound yer!" said the other. "When I say tea, I mean tea."

The pawnbroker, repressing his choler, replaced the bottle, and, seating himself at the table, reached over for the kettle, and made the tea. It was really a pleasing picture of domestic life, and would have looked well in a lantern slide at a temperance lecture, the long, gaunt Jew and the burly seaman hobnobbing over the blameless teapot. But Mr. Hyams grew restless. He was intent upon business; but the other, so far as his inroads on the teapot and the eatables gave any indication, seemed to be bent only upon pleasure. Once again, the picture of the former sailor rose before Mr. Hyams' eyes, and he scowled fiercely as the seaman pushed his cup up for the fourth time.

"And now for a smoke," said his visitor, as he settled back in his chair. "A good 'un, mind. Lord, this is comfort! It's the first bit o' comfort I've 'ad since I come ashore five days ago."

The pawnbroker grunted, and producing a couple of black, greasy-looking cigars, gave one to his guest. They both fell to smoking, the former ill at ease, the latter with his feet spread out on the small fender, making the very utmost of his bit of comfort.

"Are you a man as is fond of asking questions?" he said at length.

"No," said the pawnbroker, shutting his lips illustratively.

"Suppose," said the sailor, leaning forward intently—"suppose a man came to you an' ses—there's that confounded assistant of yours peeping through the door."

The pawnbroker got up almost as exasperated as the seaman, and, after rating his assistant through the half-open door, closed it with a bang, and pulled down a small blind over the glass.

"Suppose a man came to you," resumed the sailor, after the pawnbroker had seated himself again, "and asked you for five hundred pounds for something. Have you got it?"

"Not here," said the pawnbroker suspiciously. "I don't keep any money on the premises."

"You could get it, though?" suggested the other.

"We'll see," said the pawnbroker; "five hundred pounds is a fortune—five hundred pounds, why it takes years of work—five hundred pounds—"

"I don't want no blessed psalms," said the seaman abruptly; "but, look here, suppose I wanted five hundred pounds for something, and you wouldn't give it. How am I to know you wouldn't give information to the police if I didn't take what you offered me for it?"

The pawnbroker threw up his huge palms in virtuous horror.

"I'd mark you for it if you did," said the seaman menacingly, through his teeth. "It 'ud be the worst day's work you ever did. Will you take it or leave it at my price, an' if you won't give it, leave me to go as I came?"

"I will," said the pawnbroker solemnly.

The seaman laid his cigar in the tray, where it expired in a little puddle of tea, and, undoing his coat, cautiously took from his waist a canvas belt. In a hesitating fashion he dangled the belt in his hands, looking from the Jew to the door, and from the door back to the Jew again. Then from a pocket in the belt he took something wrapped in a small piece of dirty flannel, and, unrolling it, deposited on the table a huge diamond, whose smouldering fires flashed back in many colours the light from the gas.

The Jew, with an exclamation, reached forward to handle it, but the sailor thrust him back.

"Hands off," he said grimly. "None of your ringing the changes on me."

He tipped it over with his fingernail on the table from side to side, the other, with his head bent down, closely inspecting it. Then, as a great indulgence, he laid it on the Jew's open palm for a few seconds.

"Five hundred pounds," he said, taking it in his own hands again.

The pawnbroker laughed. It was a laugh which he kept for business purposes, and would have formed a valuable addition to the goodwill of the shop.

"I'll give you fifty," he said, after he had regained his composure.

The seaman replaced the gem in its wrapper again.

"Well, I'll give you seventy, and risk whether I lose over it," continued the pawnbroker.

"Five hundred's my price," said the seaman calmly, as he placed the belt about his waist and began to buckle it up.

"Seventy-five," said the pawnbroker persuasively.

"Look here," said the seaman, regarding him sternly, "you drop it. I'm not going to haggle with you. I'm not going to haggle with any man. I ain't no judge o' diamonds, but I've 'ad cause to know as this is something special. See here."

He rolled back the coat sleeve from his brawny arm, and revealed a long, newly healed scar.

"I risked my life for that stone," he said slowly. "I value my life at five hundred pounds. It's likely worth more than as many thousands, and you know it. However, goodnight to you, mate. How much for the tea?"

He put his hand contemptuously in his trouser pocket, and pulled out some small change.

"There's the risk of getting rid of the stone," said the pawnbroker, pushing aside the proffered coin. "Where did it come from? Has it got a history?"

"Not in Europe it ain't," said the seaman. "So far as I know, you an' me an' one other are the only white men as know of it. That's all I'm going to tell you."

"Do you mind waiting while I go and fetch a friend of mine to see it?" inquired the pawnbroker. "You needn't be afraid," he added hastily. "He's a respectable man and as close as the grave."

"I'm not afraid," said the seaman quietly. "But no larks, mind. I'm not a nice man to play them on. I'm pretty strong, an' I've got something else besides."

He settled himself in the armchair again, and accepting another cigar, watched his host as he took his hat from the sideboard.

"I'll be back as soon as I can," said the latter somewhat anxiously. "You won't go before I come?"

"Not me," said the seaman bluntly. "When I say a thing, I stick to it. I don't haggle, and haggle, and—" he paused a moment for a word, "and haggle," he concluded.

Left to himself, he smoked on contentedly, blandly undisturbed by the fact that the assistant looked in at the door occasionally, to see that things were all right. It was quite a new departure for Mr. Hyams to leave his parlour to a stranger, and the assistant felt a sense of responsibility so great that it was a positive relief to him when his master returned, accompanied by another man.

"This is my friend," said Mr. Hyams, as they entered the parlour and closed the door. "You might let him see the stone."

The seaman took off his belt again, and placing the diamond in his hand held it before the stranger who, making no attempt to take it, turned it over with his finger and examined it critically.

"Are you going to sea again just yet?" he inquired softly.

"Thursday night," said the seaman, "Five hundred is my price; p'raps he told you. I'm not going to haggle."

"Just so, just so," said the other quietly. "It's worth five hundred."

"Spoke like a man," said the seaman warmly.

"I like to deal with a man who knows his own mind," said the stranger, "it saves trouble. But if we buy it for that amount you must do one thing for us. Keep quiet and don't touch a drop of liquor until you sail, and not a word to anybody."

"You needn't be afraid o' the licker," said the sailor grimly. "I shan't touch that for my own sake."

"He's a teetotaller," explained the pawnbroker.

"He's not," said the seaman indignantly.

"Why won't you drink, then?" asked the other man.

"Fancy," said the seaman dryly, and closed his mouth.

Without another word the stranger turned to the pawnbroker, who, taking a pocket-book from his coat, counted out the amount in notes. These, after the sailor had examined them in every possible manner, he rolled up and put in his pocket, then without a word he took out the diamond again and laid it silently on the table. Mr. Hyams, his fingers trembling with eagerness, took it up and examined it delightedly.

"You've got it a bargain," said the seaman. "Goodnight, gentlemen. I hope, for your sakes, nobody'll know I've parted with it. Keep your eyes open, and trust nobody. When you see black, smell mischief. I'm glad to get rid of it."

He threw his head back, and, expanding his chest as though he already breathed more freely, nodded to both men, and, walking through the shop, passed out into the street and disappeared.

Long after he had gone, the pawnbroker and his friend, Levi, sat with the door locked and the diamond before them, eagerly inspecting it.

"It's a great risk," said the pawnbroker. "A stone like that generally makes some noise."

"Anything good is risky," said the other somewhat contemptuously. "You don't expect to get a windfall like that without any drawback, do you?"

He took the stone in his hand again, and eyed it lovingly. "It's from the East somewhere," he said quietly. "It's badly cut, but it's a diamond of diamonds, a king of gems."

"I don't want any trouble with the police," said the pawnbroker, as he took it from him.

"You are talking now as though you have just made a small advance on a stolen overcoat," said his friend impatiently. "A risk like that—and you have done it before now—is a foolish one to run; the game is not worth the candle. But this—why it warms one's blood to look at it."

"Well, I'll leave it with you," said the pawnbroker. "If you do well with it I ought not to want to work anymore."

The other placed it in an inside pocket, while the owner watched him anxiously.

"Don't let any accident happen to you tonight, Levi," he said nervously.

"Thanks for your concern," said Levi grimacing. "I shall probably be careful for my own sake."

He buttoned up his coat, and, drinking a glass of hot whisky, went out whistling. He had just reached the door when the pawnbroker called him back.

"If you like to take a cab, Levi," he said, in a low voice so that the assistant should not hear, "I'll pay for it."

"I'll take an omnibus," said Levi, smiling quietly. "You're getting extravagant, Hyams. Besides, fancy the humour of sitting next to a pickpocket with this on me."

He waved a cheery farewell, and the pawnbroker, watching him from the door, scowled angrily as he saw his light-hearted friend hail an omnibus at the corner and board it. Then he went back to the shop, and his everyday business of making advances on flat-irons and other realisable assets of the neighbourhood.

At ten o'clock he closed for the night, the assistant hurriedly pulling down the shutters that his time for recreation might not be unduly curtailed. He slept off the premises, and the pawnbroker, after his departure, made a slight supper, and sat revolving the affairs of the day over another of his black cigars until nearly midnight. Then, well contented with himself, he went up the bare, dirty stairs to his room and went to bed, and, despite the excitement of the evening, was soon in a loud slumber, from which he was aroused by a distant and sustained knocking.

CHAPTER 2

At first the noise mingled with his dreams, and helped to form them. He was down a mine, and grimy workers with strong picks were knocking diamonds from the walls, diamonds so large that he became despondent at the comparative smallness of his own. Then he awoke suddenly and sat up with a start, rubbing his eyes. The din was infernal to a man who liked to do a quiet business in an unobtrusive way. It was a knocking which he usually associated with the police, and it came from his side door. With a sense of evil strong upon him, the Jew sprang from his bed, and, slipping the catch, noiselessly opened the window and thrust his head out. In the light of a lamp which projected from the brick wall at the other end of the alley he saw a figure below.

"Hulloa!" said the Jew harshly.

His voice was drowned in the noise.

"What do you want?" he yelled. "Hulloa, there! What do you want, I say?"

The knocking ceased, and the figure, stepping back a little, looked up at the window.

"Come down and open the door," said a voice which the pawnbroker recognised as the sailor's.

"Go away," he said, in a low, stern voice. "Do you want to rouse the neighbourhood?"

"Come down and let me in," said the other. "It's for your own good. You're a dead man if you don't."

Impressed by his manner the Jew, after bidding him shortly not to make any more noise, lit his candle, and, dressing hurriedly, took the light in his hand and went grumbling downstairs into the shop.

"Now, what do you want?" he said through the door.

"Let me in and I'll tell you," said the other, "or I'll bawl it through the keyhole, if you like."

The Jew, placing the candle on the counter, drew back the heavy bolts and cautiously opened the door. The seaman stepped in, and, as the other closed the door, vaulted on to the counter and sat there with his legs dangling.

"That's right," he said, nodding approvingly in the direction of the Jew's right hand. "I hope you know how to use it."

"What do you want?" demanded the other irritably, putting his hand behind him. "What time o' night do you call this for turning respectable men out of their beds?"

"I didn't come for the pleasure o' seeing your pretty face again, you can bet," said the seaman carelessly. "It's good nature what's brought me here. What have you done with that diamond?"

"That's my business," said the other. "What do you want?"

"I told you I sailed in five days," said the seaman. "Well, I got another ship this evening instead, and I sail at 6 a.m. Things are getting just a bit too thick for me, an' I thought out o' pure good nature I'd step round and put you on your guard."

"Why didn't you do so at first?" said the Jew, eyeing him suspiciously.

"Well, I didn't want to spoil a bargain," said the seaman carelessly. "Maybe, you wouldn't have bought the stone if I had told you. Mind that thing don't go off; I don't want to rob you. Point it the other way."

"There was four of us in that deal," he continued, after the other had complied with his request. "Me an' Jack Ball and Nosey Wheeler and a Burmese chap; the last I see o' Jack Ball he was quiet and peaceful, with a knife sticking in his chest. If I hadn't been a very careful man, I'd have had one sticking in mine. If you ain't a very careful man, and do what I tell you, you'll have one sticking in yours."

"Speak a little more plainly," said the Jew. "Come into the parlour, I don't want the police to see a light in the shop."

"We stole it," said the seaman, as he followed the other into the little back parlour, "the four of us, from—"

"I don't want to know anything about that," interrupted the other hastily.

The sailor grinned approvingly, and continued: "Then me an' Jack being stronger than them, we took it from them two, but they got level with poor Jack. I shipped before the mast on a barque, and they came over by steamer an' waited for me."

"Well, you're not afraid of them?" said the Jew interrogatively. "Besides, a word to the police—"

"Telling 'em all about the diamond," said the seaman. "Oh, yes. Well, you can do that now if you feel so inclined. They know all about that, bless you, and, if they were had, they'd blab about the diamond."

"Have they been dogging you?" inquired the pawnbroker.

"Dogging me!" said the seaman. "Dogging's no word for it. Wherever I've been they've been my shadders. They want to hurt me, but they're careful about being hurt themselves. That's where I have the pull of them. They want the stone back first, and revenge afterwards, so I thought I'd put you on your guard, for they pretty well guess who's got the thing now. You'll know Wheeler by his nose, which is broken."

"I'm not afraid of them," said the Jew, "but thank you for telling me. Did they follow you here?"

"They're outside, I've no doubt," said the other; "but they come along like human cats—leastways, the Burmah chap does. You want eyes in the back of your head for them almost. The Burmese is an old man and soft as velvet, and Jack Ball just afore he died was going to tell me something about him. I don't know what it was; but, pore Jack, he was a superstitious sort o' chap, and I know it was something horrible. He was as brave as a lion, was Jack, but he was afraid o' that little shrivelled-up Burmese. They'll follow me to the ship tonight. If they'll only come close enough, and there's nobody nigh, I'll do Jack a good turn."

"Stay here till the morning," said the Jew.

The seaman shook his head. "I don't want to miss my ship," said he; "but remember what I've told you, and mind, they're villains, both of them, and if you are not very careful, they'll have you, sooner or later. Goodnight!"

He buttoned up his coat, and leading the way to the door, followed by the Jew with the candle, opened it noiselessly, and peered carefully out right and left. The alley was empty.

"Take this," said the Jew, proffering his pistol.

"I've got one," said the seaman. "Goodnight!"

He strode boldly up the alley, his footsteps sounding loudly in the silence of the night. The Jew watched him to the corner, and then, closing the door, secured it with extra care, and went back to his bed-room, where he lay meditating upon the warning which had just been given to him until he fell asleep.

Before going downstairs next morning he placed the revolver in his pocket, not necessarily for use, but as a demonstration of the lengths to which he was prepared to go. His manner with two or three inoffensive gentlemen of colour was also somewhat strained. Especially was this the case with a worthy Lascar, who, knowing no English, gesticulated cheerfully in front of him with a long dagger which he wanted to pawn.

The morning passed without anything happening, and it was near-ly dinner-time before anything occurred to justify the sailor's warning. Then, happening to glance at the window, he saw between the articles which were hanging there a villainous face, the principal feature of which being strangely bent at once recalled the warning of the sailor. As he looked the face disappeared, and a moment later its owner, after furtively looking in at the side door, entered quietly.

"Morning, boss," said he.

The pawnbroker nodded and waited.

"I want to have a little talk with you, boss," said the man, after waiting for him to speak.

"All right, go on," said the other.

"What about 'im?" said the man, indicating the assistant with a nod.

"Well, what about him?" inquired the Jew.

"What I've got to say is private," said the man.

The Jew raised his eyebrows.

"You can go in and get your dinner, Bob," he said. "Now, what do you want?" he continued. "Hurry up, because I'm busy."

"I come from a pal o' mine," said the man, speaking in a low voice, "him what was 'ere last night. He couldn't come himself, so he sent me. He wants it back."

"Wants what back?" asked the Jew.

"The diamond," said the other.

"Diamond? What on earth are you talking about?" demanded the pawnbroker.

"You needn't try to come it on me," said the other fiercely. "We want that diamond back, and, mind you, we'll have it."

"You clear out," said the Jew. "I don't allow people to come threatening me. Out you go."

"We'll do more than threaten you," said the man, the veins in his forehead swelling with rage. "You've got that diamond. You got it for five 'undred pound. We'll give you that back for it, and you may think yourself lucky to get it."

"You've been drinking," said the Jew, "or somebody's been fooling you."

"Look here," said the man with a snarl, "drop it. I'm dealing fair an' square by you. I don't want to hurt a hair of your head. I'm a peaceable man, but I want my own, and, what's more, I can get it. I got the shell, and I can get the kernel. Do you know what I mean by that?"

"I don't know, and I don't care," said the Jew. He moved off a little way, and, taking some tarnished spoons from a box, began to rub them with a piece of leather.

"I daresay you can take a hint as well as anybody else," said the other. "Have you seen that before?"

He threw something on the counter, and the Jew started, despite himself, as he glanced up. It was the sailor's belt.

"That's a hint," said the man with a leer, "and a very fair one."

The Jew looked at him steadily, and saw that he was white and nervous; his whole aspect that of a man who was running a great risk for a great stake.

"I suppose," he said at length, speaking very slowly, "that you want me to understand that you have murdered the owner of this."

"Understand what you like," said the other with sullen ferocity. "Will you let us have that back again?"

"No," said the Jew explosively. "I have no fear of a dog like you; if it was worth the trouble I'd send for the police and hand you over to them."

"Call them," said the other; "do; I'll wait. But mark my words, if you don't give us the stone back, you're a dead man. I've got a pal what half that diamond belongs to. He's from the East, and a bad man to cross. He has only got to wish it, and you're a dead man without his raising a finger at you. I've come here to do you a good turn; if he comes here it's all up with you."

"Well, you go back to him," jeered the Jew; "a clever man like that can get the diamond without going near it seemingly. You're wasting your time here, and it's a pity; you must have got a lot of friends."

"Well, I've warned you," said the other, "you'll have one more warning. If you won't be wise you must keep the diamond, but it won't be much good to you. It's a good stone, but, speaking for myself I'd sooner be alive without it than dead with it."

He gave the Jew a menacing glance and departed, and the assistant having by this time finished his dinner, the pawnbroker went to his own with an appetite by no means improved by his late interview.

CHAPTER 3

The cat, with its fore-paws tucked beneath it, was dozing on the counter. Business had been slack that morning, and it had only been pushed off three times. It had staked out a claim on that counter some five years before, and if anything was required to convince it of the value of the possession it was the fact that it was being constantly pushed off. To a firm-minded cat this alone gave the counter a value difficult to overestimate, and sometimes an obsequious customer fell into raptures over its beauty. This was soothing, and the animal allowed customers of this type to scratch it gently behind the ear.

The cat was for the time the only occupant of the shop. The assistant was out, and the pawnbroker sat in the small room beyond, with the door half open, reading a newspaper. He had read the financial columns, glanced at the foreign intelligence, and was just about to turn to the leader when his eye was caught by the headline, "Murder in White-chapel."

He folded the paper back, and, with a chilly feeling creeping over him, perused the account. In the usual thrilling style, it recorded the finding of the body of a man, evidently a sailor, behind a hoarding placed in front of some shops in course of erection. There was no clue to the victim, who had evidently been stabbed from behind in the street, and then dragged or carried to the place in which the body had been discovered.

The pockets had been emptied, and the police who regarded the crime as an ordinary one of murder and robbery, entertained the usual hopes of shortly arresting the assassins.

The pawnbroker put the paper down, and drummed on the table with his fingers. The description of the body left no room for doubt that the victim of the tragedy and the man who had sold him the diamond were identical. He began to realise the responsibilities of the bargain, and the daring of his visitor of the day before, in venturing before him almost red-handed, gave him an unpleasant idea of the lengths to which he was prepared to go. In a pleasanter direction it gave him another idea; it was strong confirmation of Levi's valuation of the stone.

"I shall see my friend again," said the Jew to himself, as he looked up from the paper. "Let him make an attempt on me and we'll see."

He threw the paper down, and, settling back in his chair, fell into a pleasing reverie. He saw his release from sordid toil close at hand. He would travel and enjoy his life. Pity the diamond hadn't come twenty years before. As for the sailor, well, poor fellow, why didn't he stay when he was asked?

The cat, still dozing, became aware of a strong strange odour. In a lazy fashion it opened one eye, and discovered that an old, shrivelled up little man, with a brown face, was standing by the counter. It watched him lazily, but warily, out of a half-closed eye, and then, finding that he appeared to be quite harmless, closed it again.

The intruder was not an impatient type of customer. He stood for some time gazing round him; then a thought struck him, and he approached the cat and stroked it with a masterly hand. Never, in the course of its life, had the animal met such a born stroker. Every touch was a caress, and a gentle thrum, thrum rose from its interior in response.

Something went wrong with the stroker. He hurt. The cat started up suddenly and jumped behind the counter. The dark gentleman smiled an evil smile, and, after waiting a little longer, tapped on the counter.

The pawnbroker came from the little room beyond, with the newspaper in his hand, and his brow darkened as he saw the customer. He was of a harsh and dominant nature, and he foresaw more distasteful threats.

"Well, what do you want?" he demanded abruptly.

"Morning, sir," said the brown man in perfect English; "fine day."

"The day's well enough," said the Jew.

"I want a little talk with you," said the other suavely, "a little, quiet, reasonable talk."

"You'd better make it short," said the Jew. "My time is valuable."

The brown man smiled, and raised his hand with a deprecatory gesture. "Many things are valuable," said he, "but time is the most valuable of all. And time to us means life."

The Jew saw the covert threat, and grew more irritable still.

"Get to your business," he said sharply.

The brown man leant on the counter, and regarded him with a pair of fierce, brown eyes, which age had not dimmed.

"You are a reasonable man," he said slowly, "a good merchant. I can see it. But sometimes a good merchant makes a bad bargain. In that case what does the good merchant do?"

"Get out of here," said the Jew angrily.

"He makes the best of it," continued the other calmly, "and he is a lucky man if he is not too late to repair the mischief. *You are not too late.*"

The Jew laughed boisterously.

"There was a sailor once made a bad bargain," said the brown man, still in the same even tones, "and he died—of grief."

He grinned at this pleasantry until his face looked like a cracked mask.

"I read in this paper of a sailor being killed," said the Jew, holding it up. "Have you ever heard of the police, of prison, and of the hangman?"

"All of them," said the other softly.

"I might be able to put the hangman on the track of the sailor's murderer," continued the Jew grimly.

The brown man smiled and shook his head. "You are too good a merchant," he said; "besides, it would be very difficult."

"It would be a pleasure to me," said the Jew.

"Let us talk business like men, not nonsense like children," said the brown man suddenly. "You talk of hangmen. I talk of death. Well, listen. Two nights ago, you bought a diamond from a sailor for five hundred pounds. Unless you give me that diamond back for the same money, I will kill you."

"What?" snarled the Jew, drawing his gaunt figure to its full height. "You, you miserable mummy?"

"I will kill you," repeated the brown man calmly. "I will send death to you—death in a horrible shape. I will send a devil, a little artful, teasing devil, to worry you and kill you. In the darkness he will come and spring out on you. You had better give back the diamond, and live. If you give it back, I promise you your life."

He paused, and the Jew noticed that his face had changed, and in place of the sardonic good-humour which had before possessed it, was now distorted by a devilish malice. His eyes gleamed coldly, and he snapped them quickly as he spoke.

"Well, what do you say?" he demanded.

"This," said the Jew.

He leant over the counter, and, taking the brown man's skinny throat in his great hand, flung him reeling back to the partition, which shook with his weight. Then he burst into a laugh as the being who had just been threatening him with a terrible and mysterious death changed into a little weak old man, coughing and spitting as he clutched at his throat and fought for breath.

"What about your servant, the devil?" asked the Jew maliciously.

"He serves when I am absent," said the brown man faintly. "Even now I give you one more chance. I will let you see the young fellow in your shop die first. But no, he has not offended. I will kill—"

He paused, and his eye fell on the cat, which at that moment sprang up and took its old place on the counter. "I will kill your cat," said the brown man. "I will send the devil to worry it. Watch the cat, and as its death is so shall yours be—unless—"

"Unless?" said the Jew, regarding him mockingly.

"Unless tonight before ten o'clock you mark on your door-post two crosses in chalk," said the other. "Do that and live. Watch your cat."

He pointed his lean, brown finger at the animal, and, still feeling at his throat, stepped softly to the door and passed out.

With the entrance of other customers, the pawnbroker forgot the annoyance to which he had been subjected, and attended to their wants in a spirit made liberal by the near prospect of fortune. It was certain that the stone must be of great value. With that and the money he had made by his business, he would give up work and settle down to a life of pleasant ease. So liberal was he that an elderly Irishwoman forgot their slight differences in creeds and blessed him fervently with all the saints in the calendar.

His assistant being back in his place in the shop, the pawnbroker returned to the little sitting-room, and once more carefully looked through the account of the sailor's murder. Then he sat still trying to work out a problem; to hand the murderers over to the police without his connection with the stolen diamond being made public, and after considerable deliberation, convinced himself that the feat was impossible. He was interrupted by a slight scuffling noise in the shop, and the cat came bolting into the room, and, after running round the table, went out at the door and fled upstairs. The assistant came into the room.

"What are you worrying the thing for?" demanded his master.

"I'm not worrying it," said the assistant in an aggrieved voice. "It's been moving about up and down the shop, and then it suddenly started like that. It's got a fit, I suppose."

He went back to the shop, and the Jew sat in his chair half ashamed of his nervous credulity, listening to the animal, which was rushing about in the rooms upstairs.

"Go and see what's the matter with the thing, Bob," he cried.

The assistant obeyed, returning hastily in a minute or two, and closing the door behind him.

"Well, what's the matter?" demanded his master.

"The brute's gone mad," said the assistant, whose face was white. "It's flying about upstairs like a wild thing. Mind it don't get in, it's as bad as a mad dog."

"Oh, rubbish," said the Jew. "Cats are often like that."

"Well, I've never seen one like it before," said the other, "and, what's more, I'm not going to see that again."

The animal came downstairs, scuffling along the passage, hit the door with its head, and then dashed upstairs again.

"It must have been poisoned, or else it's mad," said the assistant. "What's it been eating, I wonder?"

The pawnbroker made no reply. The suggestion of poisoning was a welcome one. It was preferable to the sinister hintings of the brown man. But even if it had been poisoned it was a very singular coincidence, unless indeed the Burmese had himself poisoned it. He tried to think whether it could have been possible for his visitor to have administered poison undetected.

"It's quiet now," said the assistant, and he opened the door a little way.

"It's all right," said the pawnbroker, half ashamed of his fears, "get back to the shop."

The assistant complied, and the Jew, after sitting down a little while to persuade himself that he really had no particular interest in the matter, rose and went slowly upstairs. The staircase was badly lighted, and half way up he stumbled on something soft.

He gave a hasty exclamation and, stooping down, saw that he had trodden on the dead cat.

CHAPTER 4.

At ten o'clock that night the pawnbroker sat with his friend Levi discussing a bottle of champagne, which the open-eyed assistant had procured from the public-house opposite.

"You're a lucky man, Hyams," said his friend, as he raised his glass to his lips. "Thirty thousand pounds! It's a fortune, a small fortune," he added correctively.

"I shall give this place up," said the pawnbroker, "and go away for a time. I'm not safe here."

"Safe?" queried Levi, raising his eyebrows.

The pawnbroker related his adventures with his visitors.

"I can't understand that cat business," said Levi when he had finished. "It's quite farcical; he must have poisoned it."

"He wasn't near it," said the pawnbroker, "it was at the other end of the counter."

"Oh, hang it," said Levi, the more irritably because he could not think of any solution to the mystery. "You don't believe in occult powers and all that sort of thing. This is the neighbourhood of the Commercial Road; time, nineteenth century. The thing's got on your nerves. Keep your eyes open, and stay indoors; they can't hurt you here. Why not tell the police?"

"I don't want any questions," said the pawnbroker.

"I mean, just tell them that one or two suspicious characters have been hanging round lately," said the other. "If this precious couple see that they are watched they'll probably bolt. There's nothing like a uniform to scare that sort."

"I won't have anything to do with the police," said the pawnbroker firmly.

"Well, let Bob sleep on the premises," suggested his friend.

"I think I will tomorrow," said the other. "I'll have a bed fixed up for him."

"Why not tonight?" asked Levi.

"He's gone," said the pawnbroker briefly. "Didn't you hear him shut up?"

"He was in the shop five minutes ago," said Levi.

"He left at ten," said the pawnbroker.

"I'll swear I heard somebody only a minute or two back," said Levi, staring.

"Nerves, as you remarked a little while ago," said his friend, with a grin.

"Well, I thought I heard him," said Levi. "You might just secure the door anyway."

The pawnbroker went to the door and made it fast, giving a careless glance round the dimly lighted shop as he did so.

"Perhaps you could stay tonight yourself," he said, as he returned to the sitting-room.

"I can't possibly, tonight," said the other. "By the way, you might lend me a pistol of some kind. With all these cut-throats hanging round, visiting you is a somewhat perilous pleasure. They might take it into their heads to kill me to see whether I have got the stone."

"Take your pick," said the pawnbroker, going to the shop and returning with two or three second-hand revolvers and some cartridges.

"I never fired one in my life," said Levi dubiously, "but I believe the chief thing is to make a bang. Which'll make the loudest?"

On his friend's recommendation he selected a revolver of the service pattern, and, after one or two suggestions from the pawnbroker, expressed himself as qualified to shoot anything between a chimney-pot and a paving-stone.

"Make your room-door fast tonight, and tomorrow let Bob have a bed there," he said earnestly, as he rose to go. "By the way, why not make those chalk marks on the door just for the night? You can laugh at them tomorrow. Sort of suggestion of the Passover about it, isn't there?"

"I'm not going to mark my door for all the assassins that ever breathed," said the Jew fiercely, as he rose to see the other out.

"Well, I think you're safe enough in the house," said Levi. "Beastly dreary the shop looks. To a man of imagination like myself it's quite easy to fancy that there is one of your brown friend's pet devils crouching under the counter ready to spring."

The pawnbroker grunted and opened the door.

"Poof, fog," said Levi, as a cloud streamed in. "Bad night for pistol practice. I shan't be able to hit anything."

The two men stood in the doorway for a minute, trying to peer through the fog. A heavy, measured tread sounded in the alley; a huge figure loomed up, and, to the relief of Levi, a constable halted before them.

"Thick night, sir," said he to the pawnbroker.

"Very," was the reply. "Just keep your eye on my place tonight, constable. There have been one or two suspicious-looking characters hanging about here lately."

"I will, sir," said the constable, and moved off in company with Levi.

The pawnbroker closed the door hastily behind them and bolted it securely. His friend's jest about the devil under the counter occurred to him as he eyed it, and for the first time in his life, the lonely silence of the shop became oppressive. He half thought of opening the door again and calling them back, but by this time they were out of earshot, and he had a very strong idea that there might be somebody lurking in the fog outside.

"Bah!" said he aloud, "thirty thousand pounds."

He turned the gas-jet on full—a man that had just made that sum could afford to burn a little gas—and, first satisfying himself by looking under the counter and round the shop, re-entered the sitting room.

Despite his efforts, he could not get rid of the sense of loneliness and danger which possessed him. The clock had stopped, and the only sound audible was the snapping of the extinguished coals in the grate. He crossed over to the mantelpiece, and, taking out his watch, wound the clock up. Then he heard something else.

With great care he laid the key softly on the mantelpiece and listened intently. The clock was now aggressively audible, so that he opened the case again, and putting his finger against the pendulum, stopped it. Then he drew his revolver and cocked it, and, with his set face turned towards the door, and his lips parted, waited.

At first—nothing. Then all the noises which a lonely man hears in a house at night. The stairs creaked, something moved in the walls. He crossed noiselessly to the door and opened it. At the head of the staircase he fancied the darkness moved.

"Who's there?" he cried in a strong voice.

Then he stepped back into the room and lit his lamp. "I'll get to bed," he said grimly; "I've got the horrors."

He left the gas burning, and with the lamp in his left hand and the pistol in his right slowly ascended the stairs. The first landing was clear. He opened the doors of each room, and, holding the lamp aloft, peered in. Then he mounted higher, and looked in the rooms, crammed from floor to ceiling with pledges, ticketed and placed on shelves. In one room he thought he saw something crouching in a corner. He entered boldly, and as he passed along one side of a row of shelves could have sworn that he heard a stealthy footfall on the other. He rushed back to the door, and hung listening over the shaky balusters.

Nothing stirred, and, satisfied that he must have been mistaken, he gave up the search and went to his bedroom. He set the lamp down on the drawers, and turned to close the door, when he distinctly heard a noise in the shop below. He snatched up the lamp again and ran hastily downstairs, pausing halfway on the lowest flight as he saw a dark figure spread-eagled against the side door, standing on tiptoe to draw back the bolt.

At the noise of his approach, it turned its head hastily, and revealed the face of the brown man; the bolt shot back, and at the same moment the Jew raised his pistol and fired twice.

From beneath the little cloud of smoke, as it rose, he saw that the door stood open and that the figure had vanished. He ran hastily down to the door, and, with the pistol raised, stood listening, trying to peer through the fog.

An unearthly stillness followed the deafening noise of the shots. The fog poured in at the doorway as he stood there hoping that the noise had reached the ears of some chance passer-by. He stood so for a few minutes, and then, closing the door again, resolutely turned back and went upstairs.

His first proceeding upon entering his room was to carefully look beneath and behind the heavy, dusty pieces of furniture, and, satisfied that no foe lurked there, he closed the door and locked it. Then he opened the window gently, and listened. The court below was perfectly still. He closed the window, and, taking off his coat, barricaded the door with all the heaviest furniture in the room. With a feeling of perfect security, he complacently regarded his handiwork, and then, sitting on the edge of the bed, began to undress. He turned the lamp down a little, and reloading the empty chambers of his revolver, placed it by the side of the lamp on the drawers. Then, as he turned back the clothes, he fancied that something moved beneath them. As he paused, it dropped lightly from the other side of the bed to the floor.

At first, he sat, with knitted brows, trying to see what it was. He had only had a glimpse of it, but he certainly had an idea that it was alive. A rat perhaps. He got off the bed again with an oath, and, taking the lamp in his hand, peered cautiously about the floor. Twice he walked round the room in this fashion. Then he stooped down, and, raising the dirty bed hangings, peered beneath.

He almost touched the wicked little head of the brown man's devil, and with a stifled cry, sprang hastily backward. The lamp shattered against the corner of the drawers, and, falling in a shower of broken glass and oil about his stockinged feet, left him in darkness. He threw the fragment of glass stand which remained in his hand from him, and, quick as thought, gained the bed again, and crouched there, breathing heavily.

He tried to think where he had put the matches, and remembered there were some on the widow-sill. The room was so dark that he could not see the foot of the bed, and in his fatuity, he had barricaded himself in the room with the loathsome reptile which was to work the brown man's vengeance.

For some time, he lay listening intently. Once or twice he fancied that he heard the rustle of the snake over the dingy carpet, and he wondered whether it would attempt to climb on to the bed. He stood up, and tried to get his revolver from the drawers. It was out of reach, and as the bed creaked beneath his weight, a faint hiss sounded from the floor, and he sat still again, hardly daring to breathe.

The cold rawness of the room chilled him. He cautiously drew the bedclothes towards him, and rolled himself up in them, leaving only his head and arms exposed. In this position he began to feel more secure, until the thought struck him that the snake might be inside them. He fought against this idea, and tried to force his nerves into steadiness. Then his fears suggested that two might have been placed in the bed. At this his fears got the upper hand, and it seemed to him that something stirred in the clothes. He drew his body from them slowly and stealthily, and taking them in his arms, flung them violently to the other end of the room. On his hands and knees, he now travelled over the bare bed, feeling. There was nothing there.

In this state of suspense and dread time seemed to stop. Several times he thought that the thing had got on the bed, and to stay there in suspense in the darkness was impossible. He felt it over again and again. At last, unable to endure it any longer, he resolved to obtain the matches, and stepped cautiously off the bed; but no sooner had his feet touched the floor than his courage forsook him, and he sprang hurriedly back to his refuge again.

After that, in a spirit of dogged fatalism, he sat still and waited. To his disordered mind it seemed that footsteps were moving about the house, but they had no terrors for him. To grapple with a man for life and death would be play; to kill him, joy unspeakable. He sat still, listening. He heard rats in the walls and a babel of jeering voices on the staircase. The whole blackness of the room with the devilish, writhing thing on the floor became invested with supernatural significance. Then, dimly at first, and hardly comprehending the joy of it, he saw the window. A little later he saw the outlines of the things in the room. The night had passed and he was alive!

He raised his half-frozen body to its full height, and, expanding his chest, planted his feet firmly on the bed, stretching his long body to the utmost. He clenched his fist, and felt strong. The bed was unoccupied except by himself. He bent down and scrutinised the floor for his enemy, and set his teeth as he thought how he would tear it and mangle it. It was light enough, but first he would put on his boots. He leant over cautiously, and lifting one on to the bed, put it on. Then he bent down and took up the other, and, swift as lightning, something issued from it, and, coiling round his wrist, ran up the sleeve of his shirt.

With starting eyeballs, the Jew held his breath, and, stiffened into stone, waited helplessly. The tightness round his arm relaxed as the snake drew the whole of its body under the sleeve and wound round his arm. He felt its head moving. It came wriggling across his chest, and with a mad cry, the wretched man clutched at the front of his shirt with both hands and strove to tear it off. He felt the snake in his hands, and for a moment hoped. Then the creature got its head free, and struck him smartly in the throat.

The Jew's hold relaxed, and the snake fell at his feet. He bent down and seized it, careless now that it bit his hand, and, with bloodshot eyes, dashed it repeatedly on the rail of the bed. Then he flung it to the floor, and, raising his heel, smashed its head to pulp.

His fury passed, he strove to think, but his brain was in a whirl. He had heard of sucking the wound, but one puncture was in his throat, and he laughed discordantly. He had heard that death had been prevented by drinking heavily of spirits. He would do that first, and then obtain medical assistance.

He ran to the door, and began to drag the furniture away. In his haste the revolver fell from the drawers to the floor. He looked at it steadily for a moment and then, taking it up, handled it wistfully. He began to think more clearly, although a numbing sensation was already stealing over him.

"Thirty thousand pounds!" he said slowly, and tapped his cheek lightly with the cold barrel.

Then he slipped it in his mouth, and, pulling the trigger, crashed heavily to the floor.

The Ghost of Jerry Bundler

Cast at The Haymarket Theatre.
Sept. 9, 1902.

Hirst	Mr. Cyril Maude.
Penfold	Mr. George Trollope.
Malcolm	Mr. Lewis Broughton.
Somers	Mr. Marsh Allen.
Beldon	Mr. H. Norton.
Dr. Leek	Mr. Wilfred Forster.
George (a waiter)	Mr. Charles Rock.

Note.—Penfold, Malcolm, and Beldon represent different types of Commercial Travellers.

Original Cast.

Penfold	Mr. Holman Clarke.
Malcolm	Mr. Holmes Gore.
Hirst	Mr. Cyril Maude.
Somers	Mr. Frank Gillmore.
Doctor Leek	Mr. C. M. Hallard.
Beldon	Mr. Cecil Ramsay.
George (a waiter)	Mr. Mark Kinghorne.

First produced, St. James's Theatre, London, June 20, 1899.

Revived. Her Majesty's Theatre, June 20, 1902. Same cast as above except Mr. Frank Gillmore, whose part was played by Mr. Charles Rock. The Herman Merivale Benefit Matinee.

Haymarket Theatre. Sept. 9, 1902. Ran 100 performances.

Avenue Theatre. Dec. 20, 1902. Ran 38 performances.

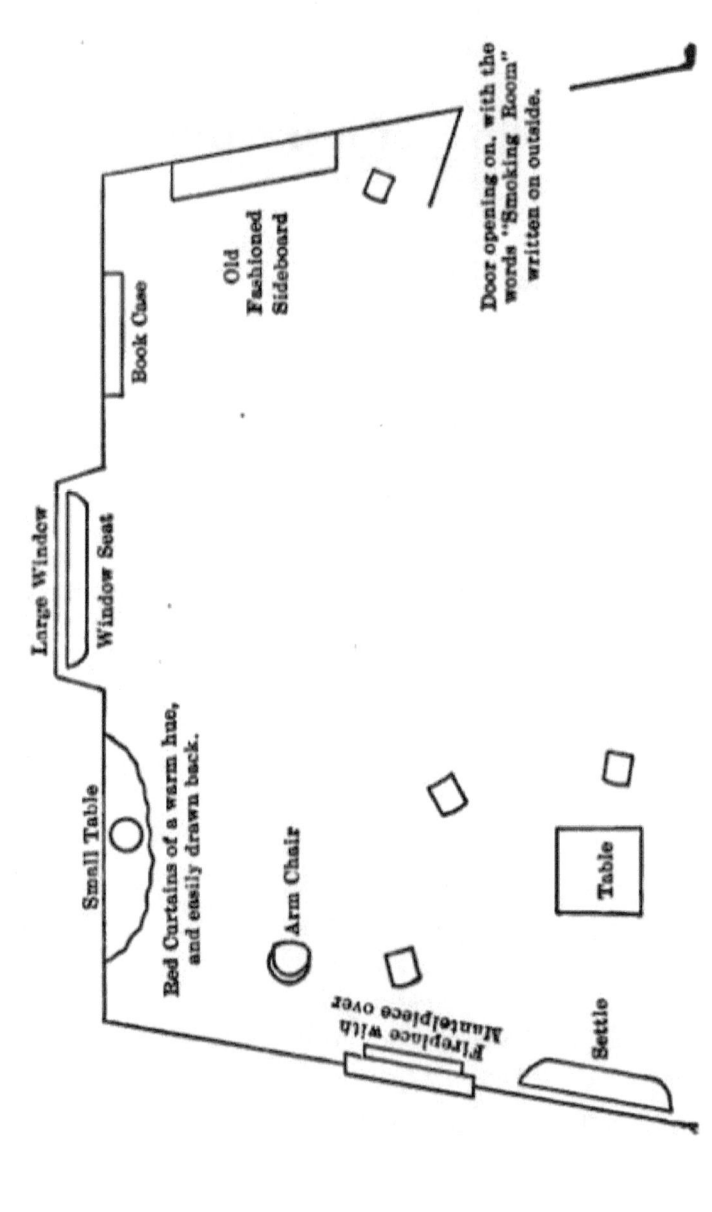

Large Window

Window Seat

Book Case

Old Fashioned Sideboard

Door opening on, with the words "Smoking Room" written on outside.

Small Table

Bed Curtains of a warm hue, and easily drawn back.

Arm Chair

Fireplace with Mantelpiece over

Table

Settle

Scene.—*The Commercial Room in an old-fashioned hotel in a small country town. An air of old-fashioned comfort is in evidence everywhere. Old sporting prints on the walls.*

On the table up C. are half a dozen candlesticks, old-fashioned shape with snuffer attached. Two pairs of carpet slippers are set up within fender. Red curtains to window recess. Shutters or blinds to windows. Armchair and about six other chairs in the room. One old-fashioned settle. One small table. Clock. Decanter of water, half a dozen toddy tumblers. Matches, etc. The only light is a ruddy glow from the fire. Kettle on hob. Moonlight from R. of window when shutter is opened. Practical chandelier from ceiling or lights at side of mantelpiece. Doctor's coat and muffler on chair up L., his cap on mantelpiece.

All lights out, dark stage. Opening music. Curtain rise—ticking of clock heard. Wind, then church clock chimes, the lights come very slowly up, when the red glow is seen in the fireplace the low murmurs of the characters heard, and gradually get louder as lights come up to when Somers' *voice tops all.*

(The stage occupied by all characters except George *the waiter. Discovered,* Penfold, *sitting in armchair L. of fire, above it.* Doctor Leek *standing above fire and leaning on mantel-shelf.* Hirst *sitting on settle below fire and nearest to audience.* Somers *seated on settle with him but above him.* Malcolm *and* Beldon *on chairs R. C., facing fire. All are smoking, and drink from their respective glasses from time to time.* Somers *has just finished a story as curtain rises.)*

Omnes. Oh, I say, that sounds impossible, etc.

Somers. Haunted or not haunted, the fact remains that no one stays in the house long. It's been let to several tenants since the time of the murder, but they never completed their tenancy. The last tenant held out for a month, but at last he gave up like the rest, and cleared out, although he had done the place up thoroughly, and must have been pounds out of pocket by the transaction.

Malcolm. Well, it's a capital ghost story, I admit, that is, as a story, but I for one can't swallow it.

Hirst. I don't know, it is not nearly so improbable as some I have heard. Of course, it's an old idea that spirits like to get into the company of human beings. A man told me once, that he travelled down by the Great Western, with a ghost as fellow passenger, and hadn't the slightest suspicion of it, until the inspector came for tickets. My friend said, the way that ghost tried to keep up appearances, by feeling in all its pockets, and even looking on the floor for its ticket, was quite touching. Ultimately it gave it up, and with a loud groan vanished through the ventilator.

(Somers, Malcolm *and* Leek *laugh heartily.*)

Beldon. Oh, I say come now, that'll do.

Penfold *(seriously).* Personally, I don't think it's a subject for jesting. I have never seen an apparition myself, but I have known people who have, and I consider that they form a very interesting link between us and the afterlife. There's a ghost story connected with this house, you know.

Omnes. Eh! Oh? Really!

Malcolm *(rising and going to mantelpiece, takes up his glass of toddy).* Well, I have used this house for some years now. I travel for Blennet and Burgess—wool—and come here regularly three times a year, and I've never heard of it. *(Sits down again on his chair, holding glass in his hand.)*

Leek. And I've been here pretty often too, though I have only been in practice here for a couple of years, and I have never heard it mentioned, and I must say I don't believe in anything of the sort. In my opinion ghosts are the invention of weak-minded idiots.

Penfold. Weak-minded idiots or not, there is a ghost story connected with this house, but it dates a long time back.

(George, *the waiter, enters* D. L. *with tray and serviette.*)

Oh, here's George, he'll bear me out. You've heard of Jerry Bundler, George?

George (C.). Well, I've just 'eard odds and ends, sir, but I never put much count to 'em. There was one chap 'ere, who was under me when fust I come, he said he seed it, and the Guv'nor sacked him there and then. *(Goes to table by window, puts tray down, takes up glass and wipes it slowly.)*

(Men *laugh.*)

Penfold. Well, my father was a native of this town, and he knew the story well. He was a truthful man and a steady churchgoer. But I have heard him declare that once in his life he saw the ghost of Jerry Bundler in this house; let me see, George, you don't remember my old dad, do you?

(George *puts down glasses over table.*)

172

George. No, sir. I come here forty years ago next Easter, but I fancy he was before my time.

Penfold.Yes, though not by long. He died when I was twenty, and I shall be sixty-two next month, but that's neither here nor there.

(George *goes up to table C. tidying up and listening.*)

Leek.Who was this Jerry Bundler?

Penfold. A London thief, pickpocket, highwayman—anything he could turn his dishonest hand to, and he was run to earth in this house some eighty years ago.

(George *puts glass down and stands listening.*)

He took his last supper in this room.

(Penfold *leans forward.* Beldon *looks round to L. nervously.*)

That night soon after he had gone to bed, a couple of Bow Street runners, the predecessors of our present detective force turned up here. They had followed him from London, but had lost scent a bit, so didn't arrive till late. A word to the landlord, whose description of the stranger who had retired to rest, pointed to the fact that he was the man they were after, of course enlisted his aid and that of the male servants and stable hands. The officers crept quietly up to Jerry's bed-room and tried the door, it wouldn't budge. It was of heavy oak and bolted from within.

(Omnes *lean forward, showing interest.*)

Leaving his comrade and a couple of grooms to guard the bed-room door, the other officer went into the yard, and, procuring a short ladder, by this means reached the window of the room in which Jerry was sleeping. The Inn servants and stable hands saw him get on to the sill and try to open the window. Suddenly there was a crash of glass, and with a cry, he fell in a heap on to the stones at their feet. Then in the moonlight, they saw the face of the highwayman peering over the sill.

(Omnes *move uneasily.*)

They sent for the blacksmith, and with his sledge-hammer he battered in the strong oak panels, and the first thing that met their eyes was the body of Jerry Bundler dangling from the top of the four-post bed by his own handkerchief.

(Omnes *sit back, draw their breath, and are generally uneasy. Slight pause.*)

Somers. I say, which bedroom was it? (*Earnestly*).

Penfold. That I can't tell you, but the story goes that Jerry still haunts this house, and my father used to declare positively that the last time he slept here, the ghost of Jerry Bundler lowered itself from the top of his four-post bed and tried to strangle him.

Beldon (*jumps up, gets behind his chair, twists chair round; nervously*). O, I say, that'll do. I wish you'd thought to ask your father which bedroom it was.

Penfold. What for?

Beldon. Well, I should take jolly good care not to sleep in it, that's all. (*Goes to back.*)

(Penfold *rising, goes to fire, and knocks out his pipe, Leek gets by armchair.*)

Penfold. There's nothing to fear. I don't believe for a moment that ghosts could really hurt one. (George *lights candle at table.*) In fact, my father used to say that it was only the unpleasantness of the thing that upset him, and that, for all practical purposes, Jerry's fingers might have been made of cotton wool for all the harm they could do.

(George *hands candle, gets to door and holds it open.*)

Beldon. That's all very fine, a ghost story is a ghost story, but when a gentleman tells a tale of a ghost that haunts the house in which one is going to sleep, I call it most ungentlemanly.

(Beldon *places his chair to* L. *of table* R. Penfold *goes up to* C. Leek *sits in armchair.* Beldon *goes to fireplace.*)

Penfold. Pooh! Nonsense. (*At table up* C.*).*

(*During his speech George lights one of the candles.*)

Ghosts can't hurt you. For my own part, I should rather like to see one.

Omnes. Oh, come now—— etc.

Penfold. Well, I'll bid you goodnight, gentlemen.

(*He goes towards door* L. George *opens it for him; he passes out as they all say.*)

Omnes. Goodnight.

(Hirst *rises, crosses to* L. C.*)*

Beldon (*up* R., *calling after him*). And I hope Jerry'll pay you a visit.

Malcolm (*rises, goes to fire*). Well, I'm going to have another whisky if you gentlemen will join me. I think it'll do us all good after that tale. George, take the orders.

(George comes down with salver to table R., *gathers up glasses.)*

Somers. Not quite so much hot water in mine.

Malcolm. I'll have the same again, George.

Beldon. A leetle bit of lemon in mine, George.

Leek. Whisky and soda for me, please.

Hirst. Whisky!

(George goes to table R., *collects glasses, crosses to door* L. *speaks.)*

George *(to* Malcolm*)*. Shall I light the gas, Mr. Malcolm? *(At door.)*

Malcolm. No, the fire's very comfortable, unless any of you gentlemen prefer the gas.

Omnes. No, not at all—etc.

Malcolm. Never mind, George. *(This to* George *as no one wants the gas.)* The firelight is pleasanter.

(Exit George *for orders* L.*)*
*(*Beldon *gets* C.*)*

Malcolm *(at fire)*. Does any gentleman know another——?

Somers *(seated* R.*)*. Well, I remember hearing——

Beldon *(up* C.*)*. Oh, I say—that'll do.

(Omnes laugh.)

Leek. Yes, I think you all look as if you'd heard enough ghost stories to do you the rest of your lives. And you're not all as anxious to see the real article as the old gentleman who's just gone.

Hirst *(looking to* L.*)*. Old humbug! I should like to put him to the test. *(*C.*)* *(Bus.)* I say, suppose I dress up as Jerry Bundler and go and give him a chance of displaying his courage? I bet I'd make the old party sit up.

Malcolm. Capital!

Beldon. A good idea.

Leek. I shouldn't, if I were you.

Hirst. Just for the joke, gentlemen *(*C.*)*.

Somers. No, no—drop it, Hirst.

Hirst. Only for the joke. Look here, I've got some things that'll do very well. We're going to have some amateur theatricals at my house. We're doing a couple of scenes from *The Rivals*, Somers, *(pointing to* Somers*)* and I have been up to town to get the costumes, wigs,

175

etc., today. I've got them upstairs—knee-breeches, stockings, buckled shoes, and all that sort of thing. It's a rare chance. If you wait a bit, I'll give you a full dress rehearsal, entitled *Jerry Bundler, or the Nocturnal Stranger. (At door L.).*

Leek *(sneeringly).* You won't frighten us, will you?

Hirst. I don't know so much about that—it's a question of acting, that's all.

Malcolm. I'll bet you a level sov, you don't frighten me.

Hirst *(quietly).* A level sov. *(Pauses.)* Done. I'll take the bet to frighten you first, and the old boy afterwards. These gentlemen shall be the judges. *(Points to* Leek *and* Beldon.*)*

Beldon *(up C.).* You won't frighten us because we're prepared for you, but you'd better leave the old man alone. It's dangerous play. *(Appeals to* Leek*)*.

Hirst. Well, I'll try you first. *(Moves to door and pauses.)* No gas, mind.

Omnes. No! no!

Hirst *(laughs).* I'll give you a run for your money.

(George *enters, holds door open.*)
(*Exit* Hirst.)

(George *passes drinks round. Five drinks.* Somers *takes the one ordered for* Hirst *and puts it on the table R.* Beldon *sits R. C.* George *crosses to table, puts two drinks down, goes to fire and gives drinks, then up to table, puts tray down, takes up glass and begins to wipe it, gets down L. for lines.)*

Leek *(to* Malcolm*).* I think you'll win your bet, sir, but I vote we give him a chance. Suppose we have cigars round, and if he's not back by the time we've finished them I must be off, as I have a quarter of an hour's walk before me. *(Looks at watch.)* He's a friend of yours, isn't he?

Somers. Yes, I have known him a good many years now, and I must say he's a rum chap; just crazy about acting and practical joking, though I've often told him he carries the latter too far at times. In this case it doesn't matter, but I won't let him try it on the *old gentleman*. You see we know what he's going to do, and are prepared, but he doesn't, and it might lead to illness or worse; the old chap's sixty-two and such a shock might have serious consequences. But Hirst won't mind giving up that part of it, so long as he gets an opportunity of

176

acting to us.

Leek *(knocks pipe on grate)*. Well, I hope he'll hurry up. It's getting pretty late. *(To* Somers.*)*

Malcolm. Well, gentlemen, your health!

Somers. Good luck.

Leek. Hurrah!

Beldon. Chin-chin!

Leek. By the way, how is it you happen to be here tonight?

Somers. Oh, we missed the connection at Tolleston Junction and as the accommodation at the Railway Arms there was rather meagre, the Station Master advised us to drive on here, put up for the night, and catch the Great Northern express from Exton in the morning. *(Rises, crosses to* L.*)* Oh, George, that reminds me—you might see that 'Boots' calls us at 7 sharp.

(Beldon *rises, goes up to them to fire.)*

George. Certainly, sir. What are your numbers?

Somers. 13 and 14.

George. I'll put it on the slate, special, sir. *(Goes to door* L.*)*

Leek. I beg pardon, gentlemen, I forgot the cigars; George, bring some cigars back with you.

Beldon. A very mild one for me.

George. Very well, sir. *(Takes up tray from sideboard.)*

(*Exit* L.*)*

(Somers *sits* R. C.*)*

Malcolm. I think you were very wise coming on here. *(Sits on settle* R.*)* I stayed at the Railway Arms, Tolleston, once—never again though. Is your friend clever at acting?

Somers. I don't think he's clever enough to frighten you. I'm to spend Christmas at his place, and he's asked me to assist at the theatricals he spoke of. Nothing would satisfy him till I consented, and I must honestly say I am very sorry I ever did, for I expect I shall be pretty bad. I know I have scarcely slept a wink these last few nights, trying to get the words into my head.

(George *enters backwards, pale and trembling.)*

Malcolm. Why! Look—what the devil's the matter with George? *(Crosses to* George.*)*

177

George. I've seen it, gentlemen. *(Down stage* L. C.*)*

Omnes. Seen who?

(Beldon down R. *edge of table* R. Leek *up* R. C. Somers *up* R.*)*

George. The ghost. Jer—Bun—

Malcolm. Why, you're frightened, George.

George. Yes, sir. It was the suddenness of it, and besides I didn't look for seeing it in the bar. There was only a glimmer of light there, and it was sitting on the floor. I nearly touched it.

Malcolm *(goes to door, looks off, then returns—to others).* It must be Hirst up to his tricks. George was out of the room when he suggested it. *(To* George.*)* Pull yourself together, man.

George. Yes, sir—but it took me unawares. I'd never have gone to the bar by myself if I'd known it was there, and I don't believe you would, either, sir.

Malcolm. Nonsense, I'll go and fetch him in. *(Crosses to* L.*)*

George *(clutching him by the sleeve).* You don't know what it's like, sir. It ain't fit to look at by yourself, it ain't indeed. It's got the awfullest deathlike face, and short cropped red hair—it's—

(Smothered cry is heard.)

What's that? *(Backs to* C *and leans on chair.)*

(All start, and a quick pattering of footsteps is heard rapidly approaching the room. The door flies open and Hirst *flings himself gasping and shivering into* Malcolm's *arms. The door remains open. He has only his trousers and shirt on, his face very white with fear and his own hair all standing on end.* Leek *lights the gas, then goes to* R. *of* Hirst.*)*

Omnes. What's the matter?

Malcolm. Why, it's Hirst.

(Shakes him roughly by the shoulder.)

What's up?

Hirst. I've seen—oh, Lord! I'll never play the fool again. *(Goes* C.*)*

Others. Seen what?

Hirst. Him—it—the ghost—anything.

Malcolm *(uneasily).* Rot!

Hirst. I was coming down the stairs to get something I'd forgotten, when I felt a tap—*(He breaks off suddenly gazing through open door.)* I thought I saw it again—Look—at the foot of the stairs, can't you see anything? *(Shaking Leek.)*

Leek *(crosses to door peering down passage).* No, there's nothing there. *(Stays up L.)*

(Hirst gives a sigh of relief.)

Malcolm *(L. C.).* Go on—you felt a tap——

Hirst *(C.).* I turned and saw it—a little wicked head with short red hair—and a white dead face—horrible.

(Clock chimes three-quarters.)
(They assist him into chair L. of table R.)

George *(up C.).* That's what I saw in the bar—'orrid—it was devilish. *(Coming C.)*

(Malcolm crosses to L. Hirst shudders.)

Malcolm. Well, it's a most unaccountable thing. It's the last time I come to this house. *(Goes to R. of Leek.)*

George. I leave tomorrow. I wouldn't go down to that bar alone—no, not for fifty pounds. *(Goes up R. to armchair.)*

Somers *(crosses to door R. then returns to R. C.).* It's talking about the thing that's caused it, I expect. We've had it in our minds, and we've been practically forming a spiritualistic circle without knowing it. *(Goes to back of table R.)*

Beldon *(crosses to R. C.).* Hang the old gentleman. Upon my soul I'm half afraid to go to bed.

Malcolm. Doctor, it's odd they should both think they saw something.

(They both drop down L. C.)

George *(up C.).* I saw it as plainly as I see you, sir. P'raps if you keep your eyes turned up the passage, you'll see it for yourself. *(Points.)*

(They all look. Beldon goes to Somers.)

Beldon. There—what was that?

Malcolm. Who'll go with me to the bar!

Leek. I will. *(Goes to door.)*

Beldon *(gulps).* So—will I. *(Crosses to door L. They go to the door. To Malcolm.)* After you. *(They slowly pass into the passage. George watching them. All exit except Hirst and Somers.)*

Somers. How do you feel now, old man?

Hirst (*changing his frightened manner to one of assurance*). Splendid!

Somers. But——(*a step back.*)

Hirst. I tell you I feel splendid.

Somers. But the ghost——(*Steps back to C.*)

Hirst. Well, upon my word, Somers—you're not as sharp as I thought you.

Somers. What do you mean?

Hirst. Why, that I was the ghost George saw. (*Crosses to L. C.*) By Jove, he *was* in a funk! I followed him to the door and overheard his description of what he'd seen, then I burst in myself and pretended I'd seen it too. I'm going to win that, bet——(*Voices heard. Crosses to R.*) Look out, they're coming back. (*Sits.*)

Somers. Yes, but——

Hirst. Don't give me away—hush!

(*Re-enter* Malcolm, Leek, Beldon *and* George L.)
(Beldon *and* George *go up to back C.*)

Hirst. Did you see it? (*In his frightened manner.*)

Malcolm (*C.*) I don't know—I thought I saw something, but it might have been fancy. I'm in the mood to see anything just now. (*To* Hirst.*) How are you feeling now, sir?

Hirst. Oh, I feel a bit better now. I daresay you think I'm easily scared—but you didn't see it.

Malcolm. Well, I'm not quite sure. (*Goes to fire.*)

Leek. You've had a bit of a shock. Best thing you can do is to go to bed.

Hirst (*finishing his drink*). Very well. Will you, (*rises*) share my room with me, Somers?

(George *lights two candles.*)

Somers (*crosses to L. C.*). I will with pleasure. (*Gets up to table C. and gets a candle*). Provided you don't mind sleeping with the gas full on all night. (*Goes to door L.*)

Leek (*to* Hirst*). You'll be all right in the morning.

Hirst. Goodnight, all. (*As he crosses to door.*)

Omnes. Goodnight.

(All *talking at fire, not looking to* L. *as* Hirst *and* Somers *exeunt.*

Hirst *chuckles and gives* Somers *a sly dig.)*

Somers. Goodnight.

Malcolm *(at fireplace)*. Well, I suppose the bet's off, though as far as I can see I won it. I never saw a man so scared in all my life. Sort of poetic justice about it. *(Leek with revolver in his hand, is just putting it into his pocket. Seeing him.)* Why, what's that you've got there?

Leek. A revolver. *(At fire.)* You see I do a lot of night driving, visiting patients in outlying districts—they're a tough lot round here, and one never knows what might happen, so I have been accustomed to carry it. I just pulled it out so as to have it handy. I meant to have a pot at that ghost if I had seen him. There's no law against it, is there? I never heard of a close time for ghosts.

Beldon.—Oh, I say, never mind ghosts. Will *you* share my room? *(To* Malcolm.*)*

(George comes down a little, holding candle.)

Malcolm. With pleasure. I'm not exactly frightened, but I'd sooner have company, and I daresay George here would be glad to be allowed to make up a bed on the floor.

Beldon. Certainly.

Malcolm. Well, that's settled. A majority of three to one ought to stop any ghost. Will that arrangement suit you, George?

George. Thank you, sir. And if you gentlemen would kindly come down to the bar with me while I put out the gas. I could never be sufficiently grateful, and when *(at door)* we come back we can let the Doctor out at the front door. Will that do, sir?

Leek. All right; I'll be getting my coat on. *(George gets to door. They exit at door L.* Leek *picks up his coat off chair up L., puts it on and then turns up trousers. Footsteps heard in flies, then goes to the window R., pulls curtain aside and opens the shutters of the window nearest the fire. A flood of moonlight streams in from R. Clock strikes twelve.)* By Jove, what a lovely night. That poor devil did get a fright, and no mistake. *(Crossing down to fireplace for his cap which is on the mantelpiece.* Malcolm, Beldon *and* George *return—the door closes after them.)* Well, no sign of it, eh?

Malcolm. No, we've seen nothing this time. Here, give me the candle, George, while you turn out the gas.

Leek. All right, George, I'll put this one out. *(Turns out gas below fire.)*

(Malcolm and Beldon *are up at sideboard,* George *having put the other gas out, goes up to them and is just lighting the candles for them. The* Doctor *is filling his pipe at mantel-shelf, and stooping to get a light with a paper spill.* Leek *whistles and lights spill. The handle of the door is heard moving.* Omnes *stand motionless—*Malcolm *and* Beldon *very frightened. They all watch. The room is lit only by the firelight which is very much fainter than it was at the beginning of the play, by the candle which* George *holds, and by the flood of moonlight from the window.)*

(The door slowly opens, a hand is seen, then a figure appears in dark breeches, white stockings, buckled shoes, white shirt, very neat in every detail, with a long white or spotted handkerchief tied round the neck, the long end hanging down in front. The face cadaverous, with sunken eyes and a leering smile, and close-cropped red hair. The figure blinks at the candle, then slowly raises its hands and unties the handkerchief, its head falls on to one shoulder, it holds handkerchief out at arm's length and advances towards Malcolm.*)*

Table

GEORGE

LEEK　　　BELDON　　MALCOLM

Chair

Fire　　　　　　　　　　　　　　　　　HIRST

(Just as the figure reaches the place where the moonbeams touch the floor, Leek *fires—he has very quietly and unobtrusively drawn his revolver.* George *drops the candle and the figure, writhing, drops to the floor. It coughs once a choking cough.* Malcolm *goes slowly forward, touches it with his foot, and kneels by figure, lifts figure up, gazes at it, and pulls the red wig off, discovering* Hirst. Malcolm *gasps out "Doctor."* Leek *places the revolver on chair, kneels behind* Hirst. Malcolm *is L. C., kneeling. At this moment* Somers *enters very brightly with lighted candle.)*

Somers. Well, did Hirst win his bet? *(Seeing* Hirst *on floor, he realises the matter).* My God, you didn't—I told him not to. I told him not to!! I told him—*(falls fainting into arms of* George.*)*

Curtain.
PICTURE.

BELDON　　　　　GEORGE

LEEK　　　HIRST　　MALCOLM　　SOMERS

(kneeling)　*(seated*　*(kneeling)*　*(at door L.)*

on floor)

182

Note. *When played at The Haymarket the piece finished with a differ-ent ending as given below.* Mr. Cyril Maude *fearing the above tragic termination would be too serious.*

From Somers' *entrance.*

Somers *enters with lighted candle, and exclaims very brightly.*

Somers. Well, did Hirst win his bet?

Slight pause.

Hirst *(suddenly sitting up).* Yes. *(Turning to* Dr. Leek.*)* You're a damned bad shot, Doctor. *(Then to* Malcolm.*)* And I'll trouble you for that sovereign.

The remaining characters express astonishment.

Curtain

The Lost Ship

On a fine spring morning in the early part of the present century, Tetby, a small port on the east coast, was keeping high holiday. Tradesmen left their shops, and labourers their work, and flocked down to join the maritime element collected on the quay.

In the usual way Tetby was a quiet, dull little place, clustering in a tiny heap of town on one side of the river, and perching in scattered red-tiled cottages on the cliffs of the other.

Now, however, people were grouped upon the stone quay, with its litter of fish-baskets and coils of rope, waiting expectantly, for today the largest ship ever built in Tetby, by Tetby hands, was to start upon her first voyage.

As they waited, discussing past Tetby ships, their builders, their voyages, and their fate, a small piece of white sail showed on the noble barque from her moorings up the river. The groups on the quay grew animated as more sail was set, and in a slow and stately fashion the new ship drew near. As the light breeze took her sails she came faster, sitting the water like a duck, her lofty masts tapering away to the sky as they broke through the white clouds of canvas. She passed within ten fathoms of the quay, and the men cheered and the women held their children up to wave farewell, for she was manned from captain to cabin boy by Tetby men, and bound for the distant southern seas.

Outside the harbour she altered her course somewhat and bent, like a thing of life, to the wind blowing outside. The crew sprang into the rigging and waved their caps, and kissed their grimy hands to receding Tetby. They were answered by rousing cheers from the shore, hoarse and masculine, to drown the lachrymose attempts of the women.

They watched her until their eyes were dim, and she was a mere white triangular speck on the horizon. Then, like a melting snowflake, she vanished into air, and the Tetby folk, some envying the bold mariners, and others thankful that their lives were cast upon the safe and pleasant shore, slowly dispersed to their homes.

Months passed, and the quiet routine of Tetby went on undisturbed. Other craft came into port and, discharging and loading in an easy, comfortable fashion, sailed again. The keel of another ship was being laid in the shipyard, and slowly the time came round when the return of *Tetby's Pride*, for so she was named, might be reasonably looked for.

It was feared that she might arrive in the night—the cold and cheerless night, when wife and child were abed, and even if roused to go down on to the quay would see no more of her than her side-lights staining the water, and her dark form stealing cautiously up the river. They would have her come by day. To see her first on that horizon, into which she had dipped and vanished. To see her come closer and closer, the good stout ship seasoned by southern seas and southern suns, with the crew crowding the sides to gaze at Tetby, and see how the children had grown.

But she came not. Day after day the watchers waited for her in vain. It was whispered at length that she was overdue, and later on, but only by those who had neither kith nor kin aboard of her, that she was missing.

Long after all hope had gone wives and mothers, after the manner of their kind, watched and waited on the cheerless quay. One by one they stayed away, and forgot the dead to attend to the living. Babes grew into sturdy, ruddy-faced boys and girls, boys and girls into young men and women, but no news of the missing ship, no word from the missing men. Slowly year succeeded year, and the lost ship became a legend. The man who had built her was old and grey, and time had smoothed away the sorrows of the bereaved.

It was on a dark, blustering September night that an old woman sat by her fire knitting. The fire was low, for it was more for the sake of company than warmth, and it formed an agreeable contrast to the wind which whistled round the house, bearing on its wings the sound of the waves as they came crashing ashore.

"God help those at sea tonight," said the old woman devoutly, as a stronger gust than usual shook the house.

She put her knitting in her lap and clasped her hands, and at that moment the cottage door opened. The lamp flared and smoked up the chimney with the draught, and then went out. As the old woman rose from her seat the door closed.

"Who's there?" she cried nervously.

Her eyes were dim and the darkness sudden, but she fancied she saw something standing by the door, and snatching a spill from the mantelpiece she thrust it into the fire, and relit the lamp.

A man stood on the threshold, a man of middle age, with white drawn face and scrubby beard. His clothes were in rags, his hair unkempt, and his light grey eyes sunken and tired.

The old woman looked at him, and waited for him to speak. When he did so he took a step towards her, and said—

"Mother!"

With a great cry she threw herself upon his neck and strained him to her withered bosom, and kissed him. She could not believe her eyes, her senses, but clasped him convulsively, and bade him speak again, and wept, and thanked God, and laughed all in a breath.

Then she remembered herself, and led him tottering to the old Windsor chair, thrust him in it, and quivering with excitement took food and drink from the cupboard and placed them before him. He ate hungrily, the old woman watching him, and standing by his side to keep his glass filled with the home-brewed beer. At times he would have spoken, but she motioned him to silence and bade him eat, the tears coursing down her aged cheeks as she looked at his white famished face.

At length he laid down his knife and fork, and drinking off the ale, intimated that he had finished.

"My boy, my boy," said the old woman in a broken voice, "I thought you had gone down with *Tetby's Pride* long years ago."

He shook his head heavily.

"The captain and crew, and the good ship," asked his mother. "Where are they?"

"Captain—and—crew," said the son, in a strange hesitating fashion; "it is a long story—the ale has made me heavy. They are—"

He left off abruptly and closed his eyes.

"Where are they?" asked his mother. "What happened?"

He opened his eyes slowly.

"I—am—tired—dead tired. I have not—slept. I'll tell—you—morning."

He nodded again, and the old woman shook him gently.

"Go to bed then. Your old bed, Jem. It's as you left it, and it's made and the sheets aired. It's been ready for you ever since."

He rose to his feet, and stood swaying to and fro. His mother opened a door in the wall, and taking the lamp lighted him up the steep wooden staircase to the room he knew so well. Then he took her in his arms in a feeble hug, and kissing her on the forehead sat down wearily on the bed.

The old woman returned to her kitchen, and falling upon her knees remained for some time in a state of grateful, pious ecstasy. When she arose, she thought of those other women, and, snatching a shawl from its peg behind the door, ran up the deserted street with her tidings.

In a very short time the town was astir. Like a breath of hope the whisper flew from house to house. Doors closed for the night were thrown open, and wondering children questioned their weeping mothers. Blurred images of husbands and fathers long since given over for dead stood out clear and distinct, smiling with bright faces upon their dear ones.

At the cottage door two or three people had already collected, and others were coming up the street in an unwonted bustle.

They found their way barred by an old woman—a resolute old woman, her face still working with the great joy which had come into her old life, but who refused them admittance until her son had slept. Their thirst for news was uncontrollable, but with a swelling in her throat she realised that her share in *Tetby's Pride* was safe.

Women who had waited, and got patient at last after years of waiting, could not endure these additional few hours. Despair was endurable, but suspense! "Ah, God! Was their man alive? What did he look like? Had he aged much?"

"He was so fatigued he could scarce speak," said she. She had questioned him, but he was unable to reply. Give him but till the dawn, and they should know all.

So, they waited, for to go home and sleep was impossible. Occasionally they moved a little way up the street, but never very far, and gathering in small knots excitedly discussed the great event It came to be understood that the rest of the crew had been cast away on an uninhabited island, it could be nothing else, and would doubtlessly soon be with them; all except one or two perhaps, who were old men when the ship sailed, and had probably died in the meantime. One said this in the hearing of an old woman whose husband, if alive, would be in extreme old age, but she smiled peacefully, albeit her lip trembled, and said she only expected to hear of him, that was all.

The suspense became almost unendurable. "Would this man never awake? Would it never be dawn?"The children were chilled with the wind, but their elders would scarcely have felt an Arctic frost. With growing impatience they waited, glancing at times at two women who held themselves somewhat aloof from the others; two women who had married again, and whose second husbands waited, awkwardly enough, with them.

Slowly the weary windy night wore away, the old woman, deaf to their appeals, still keeping her door fast. The dawn was not yet, though the oft-consulted watches announced it near at hand. It was very close now, and the watchers collected by the door. It was undeniable that things were seen a little more distinctly. One could see better the grey, eager faces of his neighbours.

They knocked upon the door, and the old woman's eyes filled as she opened it and saw those faces. Unasked and unchided they invaded the cottage and crowded round the door.

"I will go up and fetch him," said the old woman.

If each could have heard the beating of the others' hearts, the noise would have been deafening, but as it was there was complete silence, except for some overwrought woman's sob.

The old woman opened the door leading to the room above, and with the slow, deliberate steps of age ascended the stairs, and those below heard her calling softly to her son.

Two or three minutes passed and she was heard descending the stairs again—alone. The smile, the pity, had left her face, and she seemed dazed and strange.

"I cannot wake him," she said piteously. "He sleeps so sound. He is fatigued. I have shaken him, but he still sleeps."

As she stopped, and looked appealingly round, the other old woman took her hand, and pressing it led her to a chair. Two of the men sprang quickly up the stairs. They were absent but a short while, and then they came down like men bewildered and distraught. No need to speak. A low wail of utter misery rose from the women, and was caught up and repeated by the crowd outside, for the only man who could have set their hearts at rest had escaped the perils of the deep, and died quietly in his bed.

The Rival Beauties

"If you hadn't asked me," said the night watchman, "I should never have told you; but, seeing as you've put the question point blank, I will tell you my experience of it. You're the first person I've ever opened my lips to upon the subject, for it was so eggstraordinary that all our chaps swore as they'd keep it to theirselves for fear of being disbelieved and jeered at.

"It happened in '84, on board the steamer *George Washington*, bound from Liverpool to New York. The first eight days passed without anything unusual happening, but on the ninth I was standing aft with the first mate, hauling in the log, when we hears a yell from aloft, an' a chap what we called Stuttering Sam come down as if he was possessed, and rushed up to the mate with his eyes nearly starting out of his 'ed.

"'There's the s-s-s-s-s-sis-sis-sip!' ses he.

"'The what?' ses the mate.

"'The s-s-sea-sea-sssssip!'

"'Look here, my lad,' ses the mate, taking out a pocket-hankerchief an' wiping his face, 'you just tarn your 'ed away till you get your breath. It's like opening a bottle o' soda water to stand talking to you. Now, what is it?'

"'It's the ssssssis-sea-sea-sea-sarpint!' ses Sam, with a bust.

"'Rather a long un by your account of it,' ses the mate, with a grin.

"'What's the matter?' ses the skipper, who just came up.

"'This man has seen the sea-sarpint, sir, that's all,' ses the mate.

"'Y-y-yes,' said Sam, with a sort o' sob.

"'Well, there ain't much doing just now,' ses the skipper, 'so you'd better get a slice o' bread and feed it.'

"The mate bust out larfing, an' I could see by the way the skipper smiled he was rather tickled at it himself.

"The skipper an' the mate was still larfing very hearty when we heard a dreadful 'owl from the bridge, an' one o' the chaps suddenly leaves the wheel, jumps on to the deck, and bolts below as though he was mad. T'other one follows 'm a'most d'reckly, and the second mate caught hold o' the wheel as he left it, and called out something we couldn't catch to the skipper.

"'What the d——'s the matter?' yells the skipper.

"The mate pointed to starboard, but as 'is 'and was shaking so that one minute it was pointing to the sky an' the next to the bottom o' the sea, it wasn't much of a guide to us. Even when he got it steady, we couldn't see anything, till all of a sudden, about two miles off, something like a telegraph pole stuck up out of the water for a few seconds, and then ducked down again and made straight for the ship.

"Sam was the fust to speak, and, without wasting time stuttering or stammering, he said he'd go down and see about that bit o' bread, an' he went afore the skipper or the mate could stop 'im.

"In less than 'arf a minute there was only the three officers an' me on deck. The second mate was holding the wheel, the skipper was holding his breath, and the first mate was holding me. It was one o' the most exciting times I ever had.

"'Better fire the gun at it,' ses the skipper, in a trembling voice, looking at the little brass cannon we had for signalling.

"'Better not give him any cause for offence,' ses the mate, shaking his head.

"'I wonder whether it eats men,' ses the skipper. 'Perhaps it'll come for some of us.'

"'There ain't many on deck for it to choose from,' ses the mate, looking at 'im significant like.

"'That's true,' ses the skipper, very thoughtful; 'I'll go an' send all hands on deck. As captain, it's my duty not to leave the ship till the *last*, if I can anyways help it.'

"How he got them on deck has always been a wonder to me, but he did it. He was a brutal sort o' a man at the best o' times, an' he carried on so much that I s'pose they thought even the sarpint couldn't be worse. Anyway, up they came, an' we all stood in a crowd watching the sarpint as it came closer and closer.

"We reckoned it to be about a hundred yards long, an' it was about the most awful-looking creetur you could ever imagine. If you took all the ugliest things in the earth and mixed 'em up—gorillas an' the like—you'd only make a hangel compared to what that was. It just hung off our quarter, keeping up with us, and every now and then it would open its mouth and let us see about four yards down its throat.

"'It seems peaceable,' whispers the fust mate, arter awhile.

"'P'raps it ain't hungry,' ses the skipper. 'We'd better not let it get peckish. Try it with a loaf o' bread.'

"The cook went below and fetched up half-a-dozen, an' one o' the chaps, plucking up courage, slung it over the side, an' afore you could say 'Jack Robinson' the sarpint had woffled it up an' was looking for more. It stuck its head up and came close to the side just like the swans in Victoria Park, an' it kept that game up until it had 'ad ten loaves an' a hunk o' pork.

"'I'm afraid we're encouraging it,' ses the skipper, looking at it as it swam alongside with an eye as big as a saucer cocked on the ship.

"'P'raps it'll go away soon if we don't take no more notice of it,' ses the mate. 'Just pretend it isn't here.'

"Well, we did pretend as well as we could; but everybody hugged the port side o' the ship, and was ready to bolt down below at the shortest notice; and at last, when the beast got craning its neck up over the side as though it was looking for something, we gave it some more grub. We thought if we didn't give it, he might take it, and take it off the wrong shelf, so to speak. But, as the mate said, it was encouraging it, and long arter it was dark we could hear it snorting and splashing behind us, until at last it 'ad such an effect on us the mate sent one o' the chaps down to rouse the skipper.

"'I don't think it'll do no 'arm,' ses the skipper, peering over the side, and speaking as though he knew all about sea-sarpints and their ways.

"'S'pose it puts its 'ead over the side and takes one o' the men,' ses the mate.

"'Let me know at once,' ses the skipper firmly; an' he went below agin and left us.

"Well, I was jolly glad when eight bells struck, an' I went below; an' if ever I hoped anything I hoped that when I go up that ugly brute would have gone, but, instead o' that, when I went on deck it was playing alongside like a kitten a'most, an' one o' the chaps told me as the skipper had been feeding it agin.

"'It's a wonderful animal,' ses the skipper, 'an' there's none of you now but has seen the sea-sarpint; but I forbid any man here to say a word about it when we get ashore.'

"'Why not, sir?' ses the second mate.

"'Becos you wouldn't be believed,' said the skipper sternly. 'You might all go ashore and kiss the Book an' make affidavits an' not a soul 'ud believe you. The comic papers 'ud make fun of it, and the respectable papers 'ud say it was seaweed or gulls.'

"Why not take it to New York with us?' ses the fust mate suddenly.

"'What?' ses the skipper.

"'Feed it every day,' ses the mate, getting excited, 'and bait a couple of shark hooks and keep 'em ready, together with some wire rope. Git 'im to foller us as far as he will, and then hook him. We might git him in alive and show him at a sovereign a head. Anyway, we can take in his carcase if we manage it properly.'

"'By Jove! if we only could,' ses the skipper, getting excited too.

"'We can try,' ses the mate. 'Why, we could have noosed it this mornin' if we had liked; and if it breaks the lines we must blow its head to pieces with the gun.'

"It seemed a most eggstraordinary thing to try and catch it that way; but the beast was so tame, and stuck so close to us, that it wasn't quite so ridikilous as it seemed at fust.

"Arter a couple o' days nobody minded the animal a bit, for it was about the most nervous thing of its size you ever saw. It hadn't got the soul of a mouse; and one day when the second mate, just for a lark, took the line of the foghorn in his hand and tooted it a bit, it flung up its 'ead in a scared sort o' way, and, after backing a bit, turned clean round and bolted.

"I thought the skipper 'ud have gone mad. He chucked over loaves o' bread, bits o' beef and pork, an' scores o' biskits, and by-and-bye, when the brute plucked up heart an' came arter us again, he fairly beamed with joy. Then he gave orders that nobody was to touch the horn for any reason whatever, not even if there was a fog, or chance of collision, or anything of the kind; an' he also gave orders that the bells wasn't to be struck, but that the bosen was just to shove 'is 'ead in the fo'c's'le and call 'em out instead.

"Arter three days had passed, and the thing was still follering us, everybody made certain of taking it to New York, an' I b'leeve if it hadn't been for Joe Cooper the question about the sea-sarpint would ha' been settled long ago. He was a most eggstraordinary ugly chap was Joe. He had a perfic cartoon of a face, an' he was so delikit-minded and sensitive about it that if a chap only stopped in the street and whistled as he passed him, or pointed him out to a friend, he didn't like it. He told me once when I was symperthizing with him, that the only time a woman ever spoke civilly to him was one night down Poplar way in a fog, an' he was so 'appy about it that they both walked into the canal afore he knew where they was.

"On the fourth morning, when we was only about three days from Sandy Hook, the skipper got out o' bed wrong side, an' when he went on deck he was ready to snap at anybody, an' as luck would have it, as he walked a bit forrard, he sees Joe a-sticking his phiz over the side looking at the sarpint.

"'What the d— are you doing?' shouts the skipper, 'What do you mean by it?'

"'Mean by what, sir?' asks Joe.

"'Putting your black ugly face over the side o' the ship an' frightening my sea-sarpint!' bellows the skipper, 'You know how easy it's skeered.'

"'Frightening the sea-sarpint?' ses Joe, trembling all over, an' turning very white.

"'If I see that face o' yours over the side agin, my lad,' ses the skipper very fierce, 'I'll give it a black eye. Now cut!'

"Joe cut, an' the skipper, having worked off some of his ill-temper, went aft again and began to chat with the mate quite pleasant like. I was down below at the time, an' didn't know anything about it for hours arter, and then I heard it from one o' the firemen. He comes up to me very mysterious like, an' ses, 'Bill,' he ses, 'you're a pal o' Joe's; come down here an' see what you can make of 'im.'

"Not knowing what he meant, I follered 'im below to the engine-room, an' there was Joe sitting on a bucket staring wildly in front of 'im, and two or three of 'em standing round looking at''im with their 'eads on one side.

"'He's been like that for three hours,' ses the second engineer in a whisper, 'dazed like.'

"As he spoke Joe gave a little shudder; 'Frighten the sea-sarpint!' ses he, 'O Lord!'

"'It's turned his brain,' ses one o' the firemen, 'he keeps saying nothing but that.'

"'If we could only make 'im cry,' ses the second engineer, who had a brother what was a medical student, 'it might save his reason. But how to do it, that's the question.'

"'Speak kind to 'im, sir,' ses the fireman. 'I'll have a try if you don't mind.' He cleared his throat first, an' then he walks over to Joe and puts his hand on his shoulder an' ses very soft an' pitiful like:

"'Don't take on, Joe, don't take on, there's many a ugly mug 'ides a good 'art,'

"Afore he could think o' anything else to say, Joe ups with his fist an' gives 'im one in the ribs as nearly broke 'em. Then he turns away 'is 'ead an' shivers again, an' the old dazed look come back.

"'Joe,' I ses, shaking him, 'Joe!'

"'Frightened the sea-sarpint!' whispers Joe, staring.

"'Joe,' I ses, 'Joe. You know me, I'm your pal, Bill.'

"'Ay, ay,' ses Joe, coming round a bit.

"'Come away,' I ses, 'come an' git to bed, that's the best place for you.'

"I took 'im by the sleeve, and he gets up quiet an' obedient and follers me like a little child. I got 'im straight into 'is bunk, an' arter a time he fell into a soft slumber, an' I thought the worst had passed, but I was mistaken. He got up in three hours' time an' seemed all right, 'cept that he walked about as though he was thinking very hard about something, an' before I could make out what it was, he had a fit.

"He was in that fit ten minutes, an' he was no sooner out o' that one than he was in another. In twenty-four hours, he had six full-sized fits, and I'll allow I was fairly puzzled. What pleasure he could find in tumbling down hard and stiff an' kicking at everybody an' everything I couldn't see. He'd be standing quiet and peaceable like one minute, and the next he'd catch hold o' the nearest thing to him and have a bad fit, and lie on his back and kick us while we was trying to force open his hands to pat 'em.

"The other chaps said the skipper's insult had turned his brain, but I wasn't quite so soft, an' one time when he was alone, I put it to him.

"'Joe, old man,' I ses, 'you an' me's been very good pals.'

"'Ay, ay,' ses he, suspicious like.

"'Joe,' I whispers, 'what's yer little game?'

"'Wodyermean?' ses he, very short.

"'I mean the fits,' ses I, looking at 'im very steady, 'It's no good looking hinnercent like that, 'cos I see yer chewing soap with my own eyes.'

"'Soap,' ses Joe, in a nasty sneering way, 'you wouldn't reckernise a piece if you saw it.'

"Arter that I could see there was nothing to be got out of 'im, an' I just kept my eyes open and watched. The skipper didn't worry about his fits, 'cept that he said he wasn't to let the sarpint see his face when he was in 'em for fear of scaring it; an' when the mate wanted to leave him out o' the watch, he ses, 'No, he might as well have fits while at work as well as anywhere else.'

"We were about twenty-four hours from port, an' the sarpint was still following us; and at six o'clock in the evening the officers puffected all their arrangements for ketching the creetur at eight o'clock next morning. To make quite sure of it an extra watch was kept on deck all night to chuck it food every half-hour; an' when I turned in at ten o'clock that night it was so close, I could have reached it with a clothes-prop.

"I think I'd been abed about 'arf-an-hour when I was awoke by the most infernal row I ever heard. The foghorn was going incessantly, an' there was a lot o' shouting and running about on deck. It struck us all as 'ow the sarpint was gitting tired o' bread, and was misbehaving himself, consequently we just shoved our 'eds out o' the fore-scuttle and listened. All the hullaballoo seemed to be on the bridge, an' as we didn't see the sarpint there we plucked up courage and went on deck.

"Then we saw what had happened. Joe had 'ad another fit while at the wheel, and, *not knowing what he was doing*, had clutched the line of the foghorn, and was holding on to it like grim death, and kicking right and left. The skipper was in his bedclothes, raving worse than Joe; and just as we got there, Joe came round a bit, and, letting go o' the line, asked in a faint voice what the foghorn was blowing for. I thought the skipper 'ud have killed him; but the second mate held him back, an', of course, when things quieted down a bit, an' we went to the side, we found the sea-sarpint had vanished.

"We stayed there all that night, but it warn't no use. When day broke there wasn't the slightest trace of it, an' I think the men was as sorry to lose it as the officers. All 'cept Joe, that is, which shows how people should never be rude, even to the humblest; for I'm sartin that if the skipper hadn't hurt his feelings the way he did we should now know as much about the sea-sarpint as we do about our own brothers."

The Toll-House

It's all nonsense," said Jack Barnes. "Of course, people have died in the house; people die in every house. As for the noises—wind in the chimney and rats in the wainscot are very convincing to a nervous man. Give me another cup of tea, Meagle."

"Lester and White are first," said Meagle, who was presiding at the tea-table of the Three Feathers Inn. "You've had two."

Lester and White finished their cups with irritating slowness, pausing between sips to sniff the aroma, and to discover the sex and dates of arrival of the "strangers" which floated in some numbers in the beverage. Mr. Meagle served them to the brim, and then, turning to the grimly expectant Mr. Barnes, blandly requested him to ring for hot water.

"We'll try and keep your nerves in their present healthy condition," he remarked. "For my part I have a sort of half-and-half belief in the supernatural."

"All sensible people have," said Lester. "An aunt of mine saw a ghost once."

White nodded.

"I had an uncle that saw one," he said.

"It always is somebody else that sees them," said Barnes.

"Well, there is the house," said Meagle, "a large house at an absurdly low rent, and nobody will take it. It has taken toll of at least one life of every family that has lived there—however short the time—and since it has stood empty caretaker after caretaker has died there. The last caretaker died fifteen years ago."

"Exactly," said Barnes. "Long enough ago for legends to accumulate."

"I'll bet you a sovereign you won't spend the night there alone, for all your talk," said White suddenly.

"And I," said Lester.

"No," said Barnes slowly. "I don't believe in ghosts nor in any supernatural things whatever; all the same, I admit that I should not care to pass a night there alone."

"But why not?" inquired White.

"Wind in the chimney," said Meagle, with a grin.

"Rats in the wainscot," chimed in Lester.

"As you like," said Barnes, colouring.

"Suppose we all go?" said Meagle. "Start after supper, and get there about eleven? We have been walking for ten days now without an adventure—except Barnes's discovery that ditch-water smells longest. It will be a novelty, at any rate, and, if we break the spell by all surviving, the grateful owner ought to come down handsome."

"Let's see what the landlord has to say about it first," said Lester. "There is no fun in passing a night in an ordinary empty house. Let us make sure that it is haunted."

He rang the bell, and, sending for the landlord, appealed to him in the name of our common humanity not to let them waste a night watching in a house in which spectres and hobgoblins had no part. The reply was more than reassuring, and the landlord, after describing with considerable art the exact appearance of a head which had been seen hanging out of a window in the moonlight, wound up with a polite but urgent request that they would settle his bill before they went.

"It's all very well for you young gentlemen to have your fun," he said indulgently; "but, supposing as how you are all found dead in the morning, what about me? It ain't called the Toll-House for nothing, you know."

"Who died there last?" inquired Barnes, with an air of polite derision.

"A tramp," was the reply. "He went there for the sake of half-a-crown, and they found him next morning hanging from the balusters, dead."

"Suicide," said Barnes. "Unsound mind."

The landlord nodded. "That's what the jury brought it in," he said slowly; "but his mind was sound enough when he went in there. I'd known him, off and on, for years. I'm a poor man, but I wouldn't spend the night in that house for a hundred pounds."

He repeated this remark as they started on their expedition a few hours later. They left as the inn was closing for the night; bolts shot noisily behind them, and, as the regular customers trudged slowly homewards, they set off at a brisk pace in the direction of the house. Most of the cottages were already in darkness, and lights in others went out as they passed.

"It seems rather hard that we have got to lose a night's rest in order to convince Barnes of the existence of ghosts," said White.

"It's in a good cause," said Meagle. "A most worthy object; and something seems to tell me that we shall succeed. You didn't forget the candles, Lester?"

"I have brought two," was the reply; "all the old man could spare."

There was but little moon, and the night was cloudy. The road between high hedges was dark, and in one place, where it ran through a wood, so black that they twice stumbled in the uneven ground at the side of it.

"Fancy leaving our comfortable beds for this!" said White again. "Let me see; this desirable residential sepulchre lies to the right, doesn't it?"

"Farther on," said Meagle.

They walked on for some time in silence, broken only by White's tribute to the softness, the cleanliness, and the comfort of the bed which was receding farther and farther into the distance. Under Meagle's guidance they turned off at last to the right, and, after a walk of a quarter of a mile, saw the gates of the house before them.

The lodge was almost hidden by over-grown shrubs and the drive was choked with rank growths. Meagle leading, they pushed through it until the dark pile of the house loomed above them.

"There is a window at the back where we can get in, so the landlord says," said Lester, as they stood before the hall door.

"Window?" said Meagle. "Nonsense. Let's do the thing properly. Where's the knocker?"

He felt for it in the darkness and gave a thundering rat-tat-tat at the door.

"Don't play the fool," said Barnes crossly.

"Ghostly servants are all asleep," said Meagle gravely, "but I'll wake them up before I've done with them. It's scandalous keeping us out here in the dark."

He plied the knocker again, and the noise volleyed in the emptiness beyond. Then with a sudden exclamation he put out his hands and stumbled forward.

"Why, it was open all the time," he said, with an odd catch in his voice. "Come on."

"I don't believe it was open," said Lester, hanging back. "Somebody is playing us a trick."

"Nonsense," said Meagle sharply. "Give me a candle. Thanks. Who's got a match?"

Barnes produced a box and struck one, and Meagle, shielding the candle with his hand, led the way forward to the foot of the stairs. "Shut the door, somebody," he said; "there's too much draught."

"It is shut," said White, glancing behind him.

Meagle fingered his chin. "Who shut it?" he inquired, looking from one to the other. "Who came in last?"

"I did," said Lester, "but I don't remember shutting it—perhaps I did, though."

Meagle, about to speak, thought better of it, and, still carefully guarding the flame, began to explore the house, with the others close behind. Shadows danced on the walls and lurked in the corners as they proceeded. At the end of the passage they found a second staircase, and ascending it slowly gained the first floor.

"Careful!" said Meagle, as they gained the landing.

He held the candle forward and showed where the balusters had broken away. Then he peered curiously into the void beneath.

"This is where the tramp hanged himself, I suppose," he said thoughtfully.

"You've got an unwholesome mind," said White, as they walked on. "This place is quite creepy enough without you remembering that. Now let's find a comfortable room and have a little nip of whisky apiece and a pipe. How will this do?"

He opened a door at the end of the passage and revealed a small square room. Meagle led the way with the candle, and, first melting a drop or two of tallow, stuck it on the mantelpiece. The others seated themselves on the floor and watched pleasantly as White drew from his pocket a small bottle of whisky and a tin cup.

"H'm! I've forgotten the water," he exclaimed.

"I'll soon get some," said Meagle.

He tugged violently at the bell-handle, and the rusty jangling of a bell sounded from a distant kitchen. He rang again.

"Don't play the fool," said Barnes roughly.

Meagle laughed. "I only wanted to convince you," he said kindly. "There ought to be, at any rate, one ghost in the servants' hall."

Barnes held up his hand for silence.

"Yes?" said Meagle, with a grin at the other two. "Is anybody coming?"

"Suppose we drop this game and go back," said Barnes suddenly. "I don't believe in spirits, but nerves are outside anybody's command. You may laugh as you like, but it really seemed to me that I heard a door open below and steps on the stairs."

His voice was drowned in a roar of laughter.

"He is coming round," said Meagle, with a smirk. "By the time I have done with him he will be a confirmed believer. Well, who will go and get some water? Will, you, Barnes?"

"No," was the reply.

"If there is any it might not be safe to drink after all these years," said Lester. "We must do without it."

Meagle nodded, and taking a seat on the floor held out his hand for the cup. Pipes were lit, and the clean, wholesome smell of tobacco filled the room. White produced a pack of cards; talk and laughter rang through the room and died away reluctantly in distant corridors.

"Empty rooms always delude me into the belief that I possess a deep voice," said Meagle. "Tomorrow I——"

He started up with a smothered exclamation as the light went out suddenly and something struck him on the head. The others sprang to their feet. Then Meagle laughed.

"It's the candle," he exclaimed. "I didn't stick it enough."

Barnes struck a match, and re-lighting the candle, stuck it on the mantelpiece, and sitting down took up his cards again.

"What was I going to say?" said Meagle. "Oh, I know; tomorrow I——"

"Listen!" said White, laying his hand on the other's sleeve. "Upon my word I really thought I heard a laugh."

"Look here!" said Barnes. "What do you say to going back? I've had enough of this. I keep fancying that I hear things too; sounds of something moving about in the passage outside. I know it's only fancy, but it's uncomfortable."

"You go if you want to," said Meagle, "and we will play dummy. Or you might ask the tramp to take your hand for you, as you go downstairs."

Barnes shivered and exclaimed angrily. He got up, and, walking to the half-closed door, listened.

"Go outside," said Meagle, winking at the other two. "I'll dare you to go down to the hall door and back by yourself."

Barnes came back, and, bending forward, lit his pipe at the candle.

"I am nervous, but rational," he said, blowing out a thin cloud of smoke. "My nerves tell me that there is something prowling up and down the long passage outside; my reason tells me that that is all nonsense. Where are my cards?"

He sat down again, and, taking up his hand, looked through it carefully and led.

"Your play, White," he said, after a pause.

White made no sign.

"Why, he is asleep," said Meagle. "Wake up, old man. Wake up and play."

Lester, who was sitting next to him, took the sleeping man by the arm and shook him, gently at first and then with some roughness but White, with his back against the wall and his head bowed, made no sign. Meagle bawled in his ear, and then turned a puzzled face to the others.

"He sleeps like the dead," he said, grimacing. "Well, there are still three of us to keep each other company."

"Yes," said Lester, nodding. "Unless—Good Lord! suppose——"

He broke off, and eyed them, trembling.

"Suppose what?" inquired Meagle.

"Nothing," stammered Lester. "Let's wake him. Try him again. White! *White!*"

"It's no good," said Meagle seriously; "there's something wrong about that sleep."

"That's what I meant," said Lester; "and if he goes to sleep like that, why shouldn't——"

Meagle sprang to his feet. "Nonsense," he said roughly. "He's tired out; that's all. Still, let's take him up and clear out. You take his legs and Barnes will lead the way with the candle. Yes? Who's that?"

He looked up quickly towards the door. "Thought I heard somebody tap," he said, with a shamefaced laugh. "Now, Lester, up with him. One, two—Lester! Lester!"

He sprang forward too late; Lester, with his face buried in his arms, had rolled over on the floor fast asleep, and his utmost efforts failed to awake him.

"He—is—asleep," he stammered. "Asleep!"

Barnes, who had taken the candle from the mantelpiece, stood peering at the sleepers in silence and dropping tallow over the floor.

"We must get out of this," said Meagle. "Quick!"

Barnes hesitated. "We can't leave them here——" he began.

"We must," said Meagle, in strident tones. "If you go to sleep, I shall go—Quick! Come!"

He seized the other by the arm and strove to drag him to the door. Barnes shook him off, and, putting the candle back on the mantel-piece, tried again to arouse the sleepers.

"It's no good," he said at last, and, turning from them, watched Meagle. "Don't you go to sleep," he said anxiously.

Meagle shook his head, and they stood for some time in uneasy silence. "May as well shut the door," said Barnes at last.

He crossed over and closed it gently. Then at a scuffling noise behind him he turned and saw Meagle in a heap on the hearthstone.

With a sharp catch in his breath he stood motionless. Inside the room the candle, fluttering in the draught, showed dimly the grotesque attitudes of the sleepers. Beyond the door there seemed to his overwrought imagination a strange and stealthy unrest. He tried to whistle, but his lips were parched, and in a mechanical fashion he stooped, and began to pick up the cards which littered the floor.

He stopped once or twice and stood with bent head listening. The unrest outside seemed to increase; a loud creaking sounded from the stairs.

"Who is there?" he cried loudly.

The creaking ceased. He crossed to the door, and, flinging it open, strode out into the corridor. As he walked his fears left him suddenly.

"Come on!" he cried, with a low laugh. "All of you! All of you! Show your faces—your infernal ugly faces! Don't skulk!"

He laughed again and walked on; and the heap in the fireplace put out its head tortoise fashion and listened in horror to the retreating footsteps. Not until they had become inaudible in the distance did the listener's features relax.

"Good Lord, Lester, we've driven him mad," he said, in a frightened whisper. "We must go after him."

There was no reply. Meagle sprang to his feet.

"Do you hear?" he cried. "Stop your fooling now; this is serious. White! Lester! Do you hear?"

He bent and surveyed them in angry bewilderment. "All right," he said, in a trembling voice. "You won't frighten me, you know."

He turned away and walked with exaggerated carelessness in the direction of the door. He even went outside and peeped through the crack, but the sleepers did not stir. He glanced into the blackness behind, and then came hastily into the room again.

He stood for a few seconds regarding them. The stillness in the house was horrible; he could not even hear them breathe. With a sudden resolution he snatched the candle from the mantelpiece and held the flame to White's finger. Then as he reeled back stupefied, the footsteps again became audible.

He stood with the candle in his shaking hand, listening. He heard them ascending the farther staircase, but they stopped suddenly as he went to the door. He walked a little way along the passage, and they went scurrying down the stairs and then at a jog-trot along the corridor below. He went back to the main staircase, and they ceased again.

For a time, he hung over the balusters, listening and trying to pierce the blackness below; then slowly, step by step, he made his way downstairs, and, holding the candle above his head, peered about him.

"Barnes!" he called. "Where are you?"

Shaking with fright, he made his way along the passage, and summoning up all his courage, pushed open doors and gazed fearfully into empty rooms. Then, quite suddenly, he heard the footsteps in front of him.

He followed slowly for fear of extinguishing the candle, until they led him at last into a vast bare kitchen, with damp walls and a broken floor. In front of him a door leading into an inside room had just closed. He ran towards it and flung it open, and a cold air blew out the candle. He stood aghast.

"Barnes!" he cried again. "Don't be afraid! It is I—Meagle!"

There was no answer. He stood gazing into the darkness, and all the time the idea of something close at hand watching was upon him. Then suddenly the steps broke out overhead again.

He drew back hastily, and passing through the kitchen groped his way along the narrow passages. He could now see better in the darkness, and finding himself at last at the foot of the staircase, began to ascend it noiselessly. He reached the landing just in time to see a figure disappear round the angle of a wall. Still careful to make no noise, he followed the sound of the steps until they led him to the top floor, and he cornered the chase at the end of a short passage.

"Barnes!" he whispered. "Barnes!"

Something stirred in the darkness. A small circular window at the end of the passage just softened the blackness and revealed the dim outlines of a motionless figure. Meagle, in place of advancing, stood almost as still as a sudden horrible doubt took possession of him. With his eyes fixed on the shape in front he fell back slowly, and, as it advanced upon him, burst into a terrible cry.

"Barnes! For God's sake! Is it you?"

The echoes of his voice left the air quivering, but the figure before him paid no heed. For a moment he tried to brace his courage up to endure its approach, then with a smothered cry he turned and fled.

The passages wound like a maze, and he threaded them blindly in a vain search for the stairs. If he could get down and open the hall door——

He caught his breath in a sob; the steps had begun again. At a lumbering trot they clattered up and down the bare passages, in and out, up and down, as though in search of him. He stood appalled, and then as they drew near entered a small room and stood behind the door as they rushed by. He came out and ran swiftly and noiselessly in the other direction, and in a moment the steps were after him. He found the long corridor and raced along it at top speed. The stairs he knew were at the end, and with the steps close behind he descended them in blind haste. The steps gained on him, and he shrank to the side to let them pass, still continuing his headlong flight. Then suddenly he seemed to slip off the earth into space.

Lester awoke in the morning to find the sunshine streaming into the room, and White sitting up and regarding with some perplexity a badly-blistered finger.

"Where are the others?" inquired Lester.

"Gone, I suppose," said White. "We must have been asleep."

Lester arose, and, stretching his stiffened limbs, dusted his clothes with his hands and went out into the corridor. White followed. At the noise of their approach a figure which had been lying asleep at the other end sat up and revealed the face of Barnes. "Why, I've been asleep," he said, in surprise. "I don't remember coming here. How did I get here?"

"Nice place to come for a nap," said Lester severely, as he pointed to the gap in the balusters. "Look there! Another yard and where would you have been?"

He walked carelessly to the edge and looked over. In response to his startled cry the others drew near, and all three stood staring at the dead man below.

Keeping up Appearances

"Everybody is superstitious," said the night-watchman, as he gave utterance to a series of chirruping endearments to a black cat with one eye that had just been using a leg of his trousers as a serviette; "if that cat 'ad stole some men's suppers they'd have acted foolish, and suffered for it all the rest of their lives."

He scratched the cat behind the ear, and despite himself his face darkened. "Slung it over the side, they would," he said, longingly, "and chucked bits o' coke at it till it sank. As I said afore, everybody is superstitious, and those that ain't ought to be night-watchmen for a time—that 'ud cure 'em. I knew one man that killed a black cat, and arter that for the rest of his life he could never get three sheets in the wind without seeing its ghost. Spoilt his life for 'im, it did."

He scratched the cat's other ear. "I only left it a moment, while I went round to the Bull's Head," he said, slowly filling his pipe, "and I thought I'd put it out o' reach. Some men——"

His fingers twined round the animal's neck; then, with a sigh, he rose and took a turn or two on the jetty.

Superstitiousness is right and proper, to a certain extent, he said, resuming his seat; but, o' course, like everything else, some people carry it too far—they'd believe anything. Weak-minded they are, and if you're in no hurry I can tell you a tale of a pal o' mine, Bill Burtenshaw by name, that'll prove my words.

His mother was superstitious afore 'im, and always knew when 'er friends died by hearing three loud taps on the wall. The on'y mistake she ever made was one night when, arter losing no less than seven friends, she found out it was the man next door hanging pictures at three o'clock in the morning. She found it out by 'im hitting 'is thumb-nail.

For the first few years arter he grew up Bill went to sea, and that on'y made 'im more superstitious than ever. Him and a pal named Silas Winch went several v'y'ges together, and their talk used to be that creepy that some o' the chaps was a'most afraid to be left on deck alone of a night. Silas was a long-faced, miserable sort o' chap, always looking on the black side o' things, and shaking his 'ead over it. He thought nothing o' seeing ghosts, and pore old Ben Huggins slept on the floor for a week by reason of a ghost with its throat cut that Silas saw in his bunk. He gave Silas arf a dollar and a neck-tie to change bunks with 'im.

When Bill Burtenshaw left the sea and got married, he lost sight of Silas altogether, and the on'y thing he 'ad to remind him of 'im was a piece o' paper which they 'ad both signed with their blood, promising that the fust one that died would appear to the other. Bill agreed to it one evenin' when he didn't know wot he was doing, and for years arterwards 'e used to get the cold creeps down 'is back when he thought of Silas dying fust. And the idea of dying fust 'imself gave 'im cold creeps all over.

Bill was a very good husband when he was sober, but 'is money was two pounds a week, and when a man has all that and on'y a wife to keep out of it, it's natural for 'im to drink. Mrs. Burtenshaw tried all sorts o' ways and means of curing 'im, but it was no use. Bill used to think o' ways, too, knowing the 'arm the drink was doing 'im, and his fav'rite plan was for 'is missis to empty a bucket o' cold water over 'im every time he came 'ome the worse for licker. She did it once, but as she 'ad to spend the rest o' the night in the backyard it wasn't tried again.

Bill got worse as he got older, and even made away with the furniture to get drink with. And then he used to tell 'is missis that he was drove to the pub because his 'ome was so uncomfortable.

Just at that time things was at their worst Silas Winch, who 'appened to be ashore and 'ad got Bill's address from a pal, called to see 'im. It was a Saturday arternoon when he called, and, o' course, Bill was out, but 'is missis showed him in, and, arter fetching another chair from the kitchen, asked 'im to sit down.

Silas was very perlite at fust, but arter looking round the room and seeing 'ow bare it was, he gave a little cough, and he ses, "I thought Bill was doing well?" he ses.

"So, he is," ses Mrs. Burtenshaw.

Silas Winch coughed again.

"I suppose he likes room to stretch 'imself about in?" he ses, looking round.

Mrs. Burtenshaw wiped 'er eyes and then, knowing 'ow Silas had been an old friend o' Bill's, she drew 'er chair a bit closer and told him 'ow it was. "A better 'usband, when he's sober, you couldn't wish to see," she ses, wiping her eyes agin. "He'd give me anything—if he 'ad it."

Silas's face got longer than ever. "As a matter o' fact," he ses, "I'm a bit down on my luck, and I called round with the 'ope that Bill could lend me a bit, just till I can pull round."

Mrs. Burtenshaw shook her 'ead.

"Well, I s'pose I can stay and see 'im?" ses Silas. "Me and 'im used to be great pals at one time, and many's the good turn I've done him. Wot time'll he be 'ome?"

"Any time after twelve," ses Mrs. Burtenshaw; "but you'd better not be here then. You see, 'im being in that condition, he might think you was your own ghost come according to promise and be frightened out of 'is life. He's often talked about it."

Silas Winch scratched his head and looked at 'er thoughtful-like.

"Why shouldn't he mistake me for a ghost?" he ses at last; "the shock might do 'im good. And, if you come to that, why shouldn't I pretend to be my own ghost and warn 'im off the drink?"

Mrs. Burtenshaw got so excited at the idea she couldn't 'ardly speak, but at last, arter saying over and over agin she wouldn't do such a thing for worlds, she and Silas arranged that he should come in at about three o'clock in the morning and give Bill a solemn warning. She gave 'im her key, and Silas said he'd come in with his 'air and cap all wet and pretend he'd been drowned.

"It's very kind of you to take all this trouble for nothing," ses Mrs. Burtenshaw as Silas got up to go.

"Don't mention it," ses Silas. "It ain't the fust time, and I don't suppose it'll be the last, that I've put myself out to help my feller-creeturs. We all ought to do wot we can for each other."

"Mind, if he finds it out," ses Mrs. Burtenshaw, all of a tremble, "I don't know nothing about it. P'r'aps to make it more life-like I'd better pretend not to see you."

"P'r'aps it would be better," ses Silas, stopping at the street door. "All I ask is that you'll 'ide the poker and anything else that might be laying about handy. And you 'ad better oil the lock so as the key won't make a noise."

Mrs. Burtenshaw shut the door arter 'im, and then she went in and 'ad a quiet sit-down all by 'erself to think it over. The only thing that comforted 'er was that Bill would be in licker, and also that 'e would believe anything in the ghost line.

It was past twelve when a couple o' pals brought him 'ome, and, arter offering to fight all six of 'em, one after the other, Bill hit the wall for getting in 'is way, and tumbled upstairs to bed. In less than ten minutes 'e was fast asleep, and pore Mrs. Burtenshaw, arter trying her best to keep awake, fell asleep too.

She was woke up suddenly by a noise that froze the marrer in 'er bones—the most 'art-rending groan she 'ad ever heard in 'er life; and, raising her 'ead, she saw Silas Winch standing at the foot of the bed. He 'ad done his face and hands over with wot is called loominous paint, his cap was pushed at the back of his 'ead, and wet wisps of 'air was hanging over his eyes. For a moment Mrs. Burtenshaw's 'art stood still and then Silas let off another groan that put her on edge all over. It was a groan that seemed to come from nothing a'most until it spread into a roar that made the room tremble and rattled the jug in the wash-stand basin. It shook everything in the room but Bill, and he went on sleeping like an infant. Silas did two more groans, and then 'e leaned over the foot o' the bed, and stared at Bill, as though 'e couldn't believe his eyesight.

"Try a squeaky one," ses Mrs. Burtenshaw.

Silas tried five squeaky ones, and then he 'ad a fit o' coughing that would ha' woke the dead, as they say, but it didn't wake Bill.

"Now some more deep ones," ses Mrs. Burtenshaw, in a w'isper.

Silas licked his lips—forgetting the paint—and tried the deep ones agin.

"Now mix 'em a bit," ses Mrs. Burtenshaw.

Silas stared at her. "Look 'ere," he ses, very short, "do you think I'm a fog-horn, or wot?"

He stood there sulky for a moment, and then 'e invented a noise that nothing living could miss hearing; even Bill couldn't. He moved in 'is sleep, and arter Silas 'ad done it twice more he turned and spoke to 'is missis about it. "D'ye hear?" he ses; "stop it. Stop it at once."

Mrs. Burtenshaw pretended to be asleep, and Bill was just going to turn over agin when Silas let off another groan. It was on'y a little one this time, but Bill sat up as though he 'ad been shot, and he no sooner caught sight of Silas standing there than 'e gave a dreadful 'owl and, rolling over, wropped 'imself up in all the bedclothes 'e could lay his 'ands on. Then Mrs. Burtenshaw gave a 'owl and tried to get some

212

of 'em back; but Bill, thinking it was the ghost, only held on tighter than ever.

"Bill!" ses Silas Winch, in an awful voice.

Bill gave a kick, and tried to bore a hole through the bed.

"Bill," ses Silas agin, "why don't you answer me? I've come all the way from the bottom of the Pacific Ocean to see you, and this is all I get for it. Haven't you got anything to say to me?"

"Goodbye," ses Bill, in a voice all smothered with the bedclothes.

Silas Winch groaned agin, and Bill, as the shock 'ad made a'most sober, trembled all over.

"The moment I died," ses Silas, "I thought of my promise towards you. 'Bill's expecting me,' I ses, and, instead of staying in comfort at the bottom of the sea, I kicked off the body of the cabin-boy wot was clinging round my leg, and 'ere I am."

"It was very—t-t-thoughtful—of you—Silas," ses Bill; "but you always—w-w-was—thoughtful. Goodbye—"

Afore Silas could answer, Mrs. Burtenshaw, who felt more comfortable, 'aving got a bit o' the clothes back, thought it was time to put 'er spoke in.

"Lor' bless me, Bill," she ses. "Wotever are you a-talking to yourself like this for? 'Ave you been dreaming?"

"Dreaming!" ses pore Bill, catching hold of her 'and and gripping it till she nearly screamed. "I wish I was. Can't you see it?"

"See it?" ses his wife. "See wot?"

"The ghost," ses Bill, in a 'orrible whisper; "the ghost of my dear, kind old pal, Silas Winch. The best and noblest pal a man ever 'ad. The kindest-'arted——"

"Rubbish," ses Mrs. Burtenshaw. "You've been dreaming. And as for the kindest-'arted pal, why I've often heard you say—"

"*Hsh!*" ses Bill. "I didn't. I'll swear I didn't. I never thought of such a thing."

"You turn over and go to sleep," ses his wife, "hiding your 'ead under the clothes like a child that's afraid o' the dark! There's nothing there, I tell you. Wot next will you see, I wonder? Last time it was a pink rat."

"This is fifty million times worse than pink rats," ses Bill. "I on'y wish it was a pink rat."

"I tell you there is nothing there," ses his wife. "Look!"

Bill put his 'ead up and looked, and then 'e gave a dreadful scream and dived under the bedclothes again.

"Oh, well, 'ave it your own way, then," ses his wife. "If it pleases you to think there is a ghost there, and to go on talking to it, do so, and welcome."

She turned over and pretended to go to sleep agin, and arter a minute or two Silas spoke agin in the same hollow voice.

"Bill!" he ses.

"Yes," ses Bill, with a groan of his own.

"She can't see me," ses Silas, "and she can't 'ear me; but I'm 'ere all right. Look!"

"I 'ave looked," ses Bill, with his 'ead still under the clothes.

"We was always pals, Bill, you and me," ses Silas; "many a v'y'ge 'ave we had together, mate, and now I'm a-laying at the bottom of the Pacific Ocean, and you are snug and 'appy in your own warm bed. I 'ad to come to see you, according to promise, and over and above that, since I was drowned my eyes 'ave been opened. Bill, you're drinking yourself to death!"

"I—I—didn't know it," ses Bill, shaking all over. "I'll knock it—off a bit, and—thank you—for—w-w-warning me. G-G-Goodbye."

"You'll knock it off altogether," ses Silas Winch, in a awful voice. "You're not to touch another drop of beer, wine, or spirits as long as you live. D'ye hear me?"

"Not—not as medicine?" ses Bill, holding the clothes up a bit so as to be more distinct.

"Not as anything," ses Silas; "not even over Christmas pudding. Raise your right arm above your 'ead and swear by the ghost of pore Silas Winch, as is laying at the bottom of the Pacific Ocean, that you won't touch another drop."

Bill Burtenshaw put 'is arm up and swore it.

Then 'e took 'is arm in agin and lay there wondering wot was going to 'appen next.

"If you ever break your oath by on'y so much as a teaspoonful," ses Silas, "you'll see me agin, and the second time you see me you'll die as if struck by lightning. No man can see me twice and live."

Bill broke out in a cold perspiration all over. "You'll be careful, won't you, Silas?" he ses. "You'll remember you 'ave seen me once, I mean?"

"And there's another thing afore I go," ses Silas. "I've left a widder, and if she don't get 'elp from someone she'll starve."

"Pore thing," ses Bill. "Pore thing."

"If you 'ad died afore me," ses Silas, "I should 'ave looked arter your

214

good wife—wot I've now put in a sound sleep—as long as I lived."

Bill didn't say anything.

"I should 'ave given 'er fifteen shillings a week," ses Silas.

"'*Ow much?*" ses Bill, nearly putting his 'ead up over the clothes, while 'is wife almost woke up with surprise and anger.

"Fifteen shillings," ses Silas, in 'is most awful voice. "You'll save that over the drink."

"I—I'll go round and see her," ses Bill. "She might be one o' these 'ere independent—"

"I forbid you to go near the place," ses Silas. "Send it by post every week; 15 Shap Street will find her. Put your arm up and swear it; same as you did afore."

Bill did as 'e was told, and then 'e lay and trembled, as Silas gave three more awful groans.

"Farewell, Bill," he ses. "Farewell. I am going back to my bed at the bottom o' the sea. So long as you keep both your oaths I shall stay there. If you break one of 'em or go to see my pore wife I shall appear agin. Farewell! Farewell! Farewell!"

Bill said "Goodbye," and arter a long silence he ventured to put an eye over the edge of the clothes and discovered that the ghost 'ad gone. He lay awake for a couple o' hours, wondering and saying over the address to himself so that he shouldn't forget it, and just afore it was time to get up he fell into a peaceful slumber. His wife didn't get a wink, and she lay there trembling with passion to think 'ow she'd been done, and wondering 'ow she was to alter it.

Bill told 'er all about it in the morning; and then with tears in his eyes 'e went downstairs and emptied a little barrel o' beer down the sink. For the fust two or three days 'e went about with a thirst that he'd ha' given pounds for if 'e'd been allowed to satisfy it, but arter a time it went off, and then, like all teetotallers, 'e began to run down drink and call it pison.

The fust thing 'e did when 'e got his money on Friday was to send off a post-office order to Shap Street, and Mrs. Burtenshaw cried with rage and 'ad to put it down to the headache. She 'ad the headache every Friday for a month, and Bill, wot was feeling stronger and better than he ''ad done for years, felt quite sorry for her.

By the time Bill 'ad sent off six orders she was worn to skin and bone a'most a-worrying over the way Silas Winch was spending her money. She dursn't undeceive Bill for two reasons: fust of all, because she didn't want 'im to take to drink again; and secondly, for fear of wot he might do to 'er if 'e found out 'ow she'd been deceiving 'im.

She was laying awake thinking it over one night while Bill was sleeping peaceful by her side, when all of a sudden she 'ad an idea. The more she thought of it the better it seemed; but she laid awake for ever so long afore she dared to do more than think. Three or four times she turned and looked at Bill and listened to 'im breathing, and then, trembling all over with fear and excitement, she began 'er little game.

"*He did send it,*" she ses, with a piercing scream. "*He did send it.*"

"W-w-wot's the matter?" ses Bill, beginning to wake up.

Mrs. Burtenshaw didn't take any notice of 'im.

"He did send it," she ses, screaming agin. "Every Friday night reg'lar. Oh, *don't let 'im see you agin.*"

Bill, wot was just going to ask 'er whether she ''ad gone mad, gave a awful 'owl and disappeared right down in the middle o' the bed.

"There's some mistake," ses Mrs. Burtenshaw, in a voice that could ha' been 'eard through arf-a-dozen beds easy. "It must ha' been lost in the post. It must ha' been."

She was silent for a few seconds, then she ses, "All right," she ses, "I'll bring it myself, then, by hand every week. No, Bill sha'n't come; I'll promise that for 'im. Do go away; he might put his 'ead up at any moment."

She began to gasp and sob, and Bill began to think wot a good wife he 'ad got, when he felt 'er put a couple of pillers over where she judged his 'ead to be, and hold 'em down with her arm.

"Thank you, Mr. Winch," she ses, very loud. "Thank you. Good-bye, Goodbye."

She began to quieten down a bit, although little sobs, like wimmen use when they pretend that they want to leave off crying but can't, kept breaking out of 'er. Then, by and by, she quieted down altogether and a husky voice from near the foot of the bed ses: "Has it gorn?"

"Oh, Bill," she ses, with another sob, "I've seen the ghost!"

"Has it gorn?" ses Bill, agin.

"Yes, it's gorn," ses his wife, shivering. "Oh, Bill, it stood at the foot of the bed looking at me, with its face and 'ands all shiny white, and damp curls on its forehead. Oh!"

Bill came up very slow and careful, but with ''is eyes still shut.

"His wife didn't get the money this week," ses Mrs. Burtenshaw; "but as he thought there might be a mistake somewhere, he appeared to me instead of to you. I've got to take the money by hand."

"Yes, I heard," ses Bill; "and mind, if you should lose it or be robbed of it, let me know at once. D'ye hear? *At once!*"

"Yes, Bill," ses 'is wife.

They lay quiet for some time, although Mrs. Burtenshaw still kept trembling and shaking; and then Bill ses. "Next time a man tells you he 'as seen a ghost, p'r'aps you'll believe in 'im."

Mrs. Burtenshaw took out the end of the sheet wot she 'ad stuffed in 'er mouth when 'e began to speak.

"Yes, Bill," she ses.

Bill Burtenshaw gave 'er the fifteen shillings next morning and every Friday night arterwards; and that's 'ow it is that, while other wimmen 'as to be satisfied looking at new hats and clothes in the shop-winders, Mrs. Burtenshaw is able to wear 'em.

The Well

Two men stood in the billiard-room of an old country house, talking. Play, which had been of a half-hearted nature, was over, and they sat at the open window, looking out over the park stretching away beneath them, conversing idly.

"Your time's nearly up, Jem," said one at length, "this time six weeks you'll be yawning out the honeymoon and cursing the man—woman I mean— who invented them."

Jem Benson stretched his long limbs in the chair and grunted in dissent.

"I've never understood it," continued Wilfred Carr, yawning. "It's not in my line at all; I never had enough money for my own wants, let alone for two. Perhaps if I were as rich as you or Croesus, I might regard it differently."

There was just sufficient meaning in the latter part of the remark for his cousin to forbear to reply to it. He continued to gaze out of the window and to smoke slowly.

"Not being as rich as Croesus—or you," resumed Carr, regarding him from beneath lowered lids, "I paddle my own canoe down the stream of Time, and, tying it to my friends' door-posts, go in to eat their dinners."

"Quite Venetian," said Jem Benson, still looking out of the window. "It's not a bad thing for you, Wilfred, that you have the doorposts and dinners—and friends."

Carr grunted in his turn. "Seriously though, Jem," he said, slowly, "you're a lucky fellow, a very lucky fellow. If there is a better girl above ground than Olive, I should like to see her."

"Yes," said the other, quietly.

"She's such an exceptional girl," continued Carr, staring out of the window. "She's so good and gentle. She thinks you are a bundle of all the virtues."

He laughed frankly and joyously, but the other man did not join him. "Strong sense—of right and wrong, though," continued Carr, musingly. "Do you know, I believe that if she found out that you were not——"

"Not what?" demanded Benson, turning upon him fiercely, "Not what?"

"Everything that you are," returned his cousin, with a grin that belied his words, "I believe she'd drop you."

"Talk about something else," said Benson, slowly; "your pleasantries are not always in the best taste."

Wilfred Carr rose and taking a cue from the rack, bent over the board and practiced one or two favourite shots. "The only other subject I can talk about just at present is my own financial affairs," he said slowly, as he walked round the table.

"Talk about something else," said Benson again, bluntly.

"And the two things are connected," said Carr, and dropping his cue he half sat on the table and eyed his cousin.

There was a long silence. Benson pitched the end of his cigar out of the window, and leaning back closed his eyes.

"Do you follow me?" inquired Carr at length.

Benson opened his eyes and nodded at the window.

"Do you want to follow my cigar?" he demanded.

"I should prefer to depart by the usual way for your sake," returned the other, unabashed. "If I left by the window all sorts of questions would be asked, and you know what a talkative chap I am."

"So long as you don't talk about my affairs," returned the other, restraining himself by an obvious effort, "you can talk yourself hoarse."

"I'm in a mess," said Carr, slowly, "a devil of a mess. If I don't raise fifteen hundred by this day fortnight, I may be getting my board and lodging free."

"Would that be any change?" questioned Benson.

"The quality would," retorted the other. "The address also would not be good. Seriously, Jem, will you let me have the fifteen hundred?"

"No," said the other, simply.

Carr went white. "It's to save me from ruin," he said, thickly.

"I've helped you till I'm tired," said Benson, turning and regarding him, "and it is all to no good. If you've got into a mess, get out of it. You should not be so fond of giving autographs away."

"It's foolish, I admit," said Carr, deliberately. "I won't do so any more. By the way, I've got some to sell. You needn't sneer. They're not my own."

"Whose are they?" inquired the other.

"Yours."

Benson got up from his chair and crossed over to him. "What is this?" he asked, quietly. "Blackmail?"

"Call it what you like," said Carr. "I've got some letters for sale, price fifteen hundred. And I know a man who would buy them at that price for the mere chance of getting Olive from you. I'll give you first offer."

"If you have got any letters bearing my signature, you will be good enough to give them to me," said Benson, very slowly.

"They're mine," said Carr, lightly; "given to me by the lady you wrote them to. I must say that they are not all in the best possible taste."

His cousin reached forward suddenly, and catching him by the collar of his coat pinned him down on the table.

"Give me those letters," he breathed, sticking his face close to Carr's.

"They're not here," said Carr, struggling. "I'm not a fool. Let me go, or I'll raise the price."

The other man raised him from the table in his powerful hands, apparently with the intention of dashing his head against it. Then suddenly his hold relaxed as an astonished-looking maid-servant entered the room with letters. Carr sat up hastily.

"That's how it was done," said Benson, for the girl's benefit as he took the letters.

"I don't wonder at the other man making him pay for it, then," said Carr, blandly.

"You will give me those letters?" said Benson, suggestively, as the girl left the room.

"At the price I mentioned, yes," said Carr; "but so sure as I am a living man, if you lay your clumsy hands on me again, I'll double it. Now, I'll leave you for a time while you think it over."

He took a cigar from the box and lighting it carefully quitted the room. His cousin waited until the door had closed behind him, and then turning to the window sat there in a fit of fury as silent as it was terrible.

The air was fresh and sweet from the park, heavy with the scent of new-mown grass. The fragrance of a cigar was now added to it, and glancing out he saw his cousin pacing slowly by. He rose and went to the door, and then, apparently altering his mind, he returned to the window and watched the figure of his cousin as it moved slowly away into the moonlight. Then he rose again, and, for a long time, the room was empty.

★★★★★★

It was empty when Mrs. Benson came in some time later to say goodnight to her son on her way to bed. She walked slowly round the table, and pausing at the window gazed from it in idle thought, until she saw the figure of her son advancing with rapid strides toward the house. He looked up at the window.

"Goodnight," said she.

"Goodnight," said Benson, in a deep voice.

"Where is Wilfred?"

"Oh, he has gone," said Benson.

"Gone?"

"We had a few words; he was wanting money again, and I gave him a piece of my mind. I don't think we shall see him again."

"Poor Wilfred!" sighed Mrs. Benson. "He is always in trouble of some sort. I hope that you were not too hard upon him."

"No more than he deserved," said her son, sternly. "Goodnight."

2

The well, which had long ago fallen into disuse, was almost hidden by the thick tangle of undergrowth which ran riot at that corner of the old park. It was partly covered by the shrunken half of a lid, above which a rusty windlass creaked in company with the music of the pines when the wind blew strongly. The full light of the sun never reached it, and the ground surrounding it was moist and green when other parts of the park were gaping with the heat.

Two people walking slowly round the park in the fragrant stillness of a summer evening strayed in the direction of the well.

"No use going through this wilderness, Olive," said Benson, pausing on the outskirts of the pines and eyeing with some disfavour the gloom beyond.

"Best part of the park," said the girl briskly; "you know it's my favourite spot."

"I know you're very fond of sitting on the coping," said the man slowly, "and I wish you wouldn't. One day you will lean back too far

222

and fall in."

"And make the acquaintance of Truth," said Olive lightly. "Come along."

She ran from him and was lost in the shadow of the pines, the bracken crackling beneath her feet as she ran. Her companion followed slowly, and emerging from the gloom saw her poised daintily on the edge of the well with her feet hidden in the rank grass and nettles which surrounded it. She motioned her companion to take a seat by her side, and smiled softly as she felt a strong arm passed about her waist.

"I like this place," said she, breaking a long silence, "it is so dismal —so uncanny. Do you know I wouldn't dare to sit here alone, Jem? I should imagine that all sorts of dreadful things were hidden behind the bushes and trees, waiting to spring out on me. Ugh!"

"You'd better let me take you in," said her companion tenderly; "the well isn't always wholesome, especially in the hot weather.

"Let's make a move."

The girl gave an obstinate little shake, and settled herself more securely on her seat.

"Smoke your cigar in peace," she said quietly. "I am settled here for a quiet talk. Has anything been heard of Wilfred yet?"

"Nothing."

"Quite a dramatic disappearance, isn't it?" she continued. "Another scrape, I suppose, and another letter for you in the same old strain; 'Dear Jem, help me out.'"

Jem Benson blew a cloud of fragrant smoke into the air, and holding his cigar between his teeth brushed away the ash from his coat sleeves.

"I wonder what he would have done without you," said the girl, pressing his arm affectionately. "Gone under long ago, I suppose. When we are married, Jem, I shall presume upon the relationship to lecture him. He is very wild, but he has his good points, poor fellow."

"I never saw them," said Benson, with startling bitterness. "God knows I never saw them."

"He is nobody's enemy but his own," said the girl, startled by this outburst.

"You don't know much about him," said the other, sharply. "He was not above blackmail; not above ruining the life of a friend to do himself a benefit. A loafer, a cur, and a liar!"

The girl looked up at him soberly but timidly and took his arm without a word, and they both sat silent while evening deepened into night and the beams of the moon, filtering through the branches, surrounded them with a silver network. Her head sank upon his shoulder, 'till suddenly with a sharp cry she sprang to her feet.

"What was that?" she cried breathlessly.

"What was what?" demanded Benson, springing up and clutching her fast by the arm.

She caught her breath and tried to laugh.

"You're hurting me, Jem."

His hold relaxed.

"What is the matter?" he asked gently.

"What was it startled you?"

"I was startled," she said, slowly, putting her hands on his shoulder. "I suppose the words I used just now are ringing in my ears, but I fancied that somebody behind us whispered '*Jem, help me out.*'"

"Fancy," repeated Benson, and his voice shook; "but these fancies are not good for you. You—are frightened—at the dark and the gloom of these trees. Let me take you back to the house."

"No, I'm not frightened," said the girl, reseating herself. "I should never be really frightened of anything when you were with me, Jem. I'm surprised at myself for being so silly."

The man made no reply but stood, a strong, dark figure, a yard or two from the well, as though waiting for her to join him.

"Come and sit down, sir," cried Olive, patting the brickwork with her small, white hand, "one would think that you did not like your company."

He obeyed slowly and took a seat by her side, drawing so hard at his cigar that the light of it shone upon his fare at every breath. He passed his arm, firm and rigid as steel, behind her, with his hand resting on the brickwork beyond.

"Are you warm enough?" he asked tenderly, as she made a little movement. "Pretty fair," she shivered; "one oughtn't to be cold at this time of the year, but there's a cold, damp air comes up from the well."

As she spoke a faint splash sounded from the depths below, and for the second time that evening, she sprang from the well with a little cry of dismay.

"What is it now?" he asked in a fearful voice. He stood by her side and gazed at the well, as though half expecting to see the cause of her alarm emerge from it.

"Oh, my bracelet," she cried in distress, "my poor mother's bracelet. I've dropped it down the well."

"Your bracelet!" repeated Benson, dully. "Your bracelet? The diamond one?"

"The one that was my mother's," said Olive. "Oh, we can get it back surely. We must have the water drained off."

"Your bracelet!" repeated Benson, stupidly.

"Jem," said the girl in terrified tones, "dear Jem, what is the matter?"

For the man she loved was standing regarding her with horror. The moon which touched it was not responsible for all the whiteness of the distorted face, and she shrank back in fear to the edge of the well. He saw her fear and by a mighty effort regained his composure and took her hand.

"Poor little girl," he murmured, "you frightened me. I was not looking when you cried, and I thought that you were slipping from my arms, down—down—"

His voice broke, and the girl throwing herself into his arms clung to him convulsively.

"There, there," said Benson, fondly, "don't cry, don't cry."

"Tomorrow," said Olive, half-laughing, half-crying, "we will all come round the well with hook and line and fish for it. It will be quite a new sport."

"No, we must try some other way," said Benson. "You shall have it back."

"How?" asked the girl.

"You shall see," said Benson. "Tomorrow morning at latest you shall have it back. Till then promise me that you will not mention your loss to anyone. Promise."

"I promise," said Olive, wonderingly. "But why not?"

"It is of great value, for one thing, and—But there—there are many reasons. For one thing it is my duty to get it for you."

"Wouldn't you like to jump down for it?" she asked mischievously. "Listen."

She stooped for a stone and dropped it down.

"Fancy being where that is now," she said, peering into the blackness; "fancy going round and round like a mouse in a pail, clutching at the slimy sides, with the water filling your mouth, and looking up to the little patch of sky above."

"You had better come in," said Benson, very quietly. "You are developing a taste for the morbid and horrible."

The girl turned, and taking his arm walked slowly in the direction of the house; Mrs. Benson, who was sitting in the porch, rose to receive them.

"You shouldn't have kept her out so long," she said chidingly. "Where have you been?"

"Sitting on the well," said Olive, smiling, "discussing our future."

"I don't believe that place is healthy," said Mrs. Benson, emphatically. "I really think it might be filled in, Jem."

"All right," said her son, slowly. "Pity it wasn't filled in long ago."

He took the chair vacated by his mother as she entered the house with Olive, and with his hands hanging limply over the sides sat in deep thought. After a time, he rose, and going upstairs to a room which was set apart for sporting requisites selected a sea fishing line and some hooks and stole softly downstairs again. He walked swiftly across the park in the direction of the well, turning before he entered the shadow of the trees to look back at the lighted windows of the house. Then having arranged his line he sat on the edge of the well and cautiously lowered it.

He sat with his lips compressed, occasionally looking about him in a startled fashion, as though he half expected to see something peering at him from the belt of trees. Time after time he lowered his line until at length in pulling it up, he heard a little metallic tinkle against the side of the well.

He held his breath then, and forgetting his fears drew the line in inch by inch, so as not to lose its precious burden. His pulse beat rapidly, and his eyes were bright. As the line came slowly in, he saw the catch hanging to the hook, and with a steady hand drew the last few feet in. Then he saw that instead of the bracelet he had hooked a bunch of keys.

With a faint cry he shook them from the hook into the water below, and stood breathing heavily. Not a sound broke the stillness of the night. He walked up and down a bit and stretched his great muscles; then he came back to the well and resumed his task.

For an hour or more the line was lowered without result. In his eagerness he forgot his fears, and with eyes bent down the well fished slowly and carefully. Twice the hook became entangled in something, and was with difficulty released. It caught a third time, and all his efforts failed to free it. Then he dropped the line down the well, and with head bent walked toward the house.

He went first to the stables at the rear, and then retiring to his room for some time paced restlessly up and down. Then without removing his clothes he flung himself upon the bed and fell into a troubled sleep.

3

Long before anybody else was astir he arose and stole softly downstairs. The sunlight was stealing in at every crevice, and flashing in long streaks across the darkened rooms. The dining-room into which he looked struck chill and cheerless in the dark yellow light which came through the lowered blinds. He remembered that it had the same appearance when his father lay dead in the house; now, as then, everything seemed ghastly and unreal; the very chairs standing as their occupants had left them the night before seemed to be indulging in some dark communication of ideas.

Slowly and noiselessly he opened the hall door and passed into the fragrant air beyond. The sun was shining on the drenched grass and trees, and a slowly vanishing white mist rolled like smoke about the grounds. For a moment he stood, breathing deeply the sweet air of the morning, and then walked slowly in the direction of the stables.

The rusty creaking of a pump-handle and a spatter of water upon the red-tiled courtyard showed that somebody else was astir, and a few steps farther he beheld a brawny, sandy-haired man gasping wildly under severe self-infliction at the pump.

"Everything ready, George?" he asked quietly.

"Yes, sir," said the man, straightening up suddenly and touching his forehead. "Bob's just finishing the arrangements inside. It's a lovely morning for a dip. The water in that well must be just icy."

"Be as quick as you can," said Benson, impatiently.

"Very good, sir," said George, burnishing his face harshly with a very small towel which had been hanging over the top of the pump. "Hurry up, Bob."

In answer to his summons a man appeared at the door of the stable with a coil of stout rope over his arm and a large metal candlestick in his hand.

"Just to try the air, sir," said George, following his master's glance, "a well gets rather foul sometimes, but if a candle can live down it, a man can."

His master nodded, and the man, hastily pulling up the neck of his shirt and thrusting his arms into his coat, followed him as he led the way slowly to the well.

"Beg pardon, sir," said George, drawing up to his side, "but you

227

are not looking over and above well this morning. If you'll let me go down, I'd enjoy the bath."

"No, no," said Benson, peremptorily.

"You ain't fit to go down, sir," persisted his follower. "I've never seen you look so before. Now if—"

"Mind your business," said his master curtly.

George became silent and the three walked with swinging strides through the long, wet grass to the well. Bob flung the rope on the ground and at a sign from his master handed him the candlestick.

"Here's the line for it, sir," said Bob, fumbling in his pockets.

Benson took it from him and slowly tied it to the candlestick. Then he placed it on the edge of the well, and striking a match, lit the candle and began slowly to lower it.

"Hold hard, sir," said George, quickly, laying his hand on his arm, "you must tilt it or the string'll burn through."

Even as he spoke the string parted and the candlestick fell into the water below.

Benson swore quietly.

"I'll soon get another," said George, starting up.

"Never mind, the well's all right," said Benson.

"It won't take a moment, sir," said the other over his shoulder.

"Are you master here, or am I?" said Benson hoarsely.

George came back slowly, a glance at his master's face stopping the protest upon his tongue, and he stood by watching him sulkily as he sat on the well and removed his outer garments. Both men watched him curiously, as having completed his preparations he stood grim and silent with his hands by his sides.

"I wish you'd let me go, sir," said George, plucking up courage to address him. "You ain't fit to go, you've got a chill or something. I shouldn't wonder it's the typhoid. They've got it in the village bad."

For a moment Benson looked at him angrily, then his gaze softened. "Not this time, George," he said, quietly. He took the looped end of the rope and placed it under his arms, and sitting down threw one leg over the side of the well.

"How are you going about it, sir?" queried George, laying hold of the rope and signing to Bob to do the same.

"I'll call out when I reach the water," said Benson; "then pay out three yards more quickly so that I can get to the bottom."

"Very good, sir," answered both.

Their master threw the other leg over the coping and sat motionless. His back was turned toward the men as he sat with head bent, looking down the shaft. He sat for so long that George became uneasy.

"All right, sir?" he inquired.

"Yes," said Benson, slowly. "If I tug at the rope, George, pull up at once. Lower away."

The rope passed steadily through their hands until a hollow cry from the darkness below and a faint splashing warned them that he had reached the water. They gave him three yards more and stood with relaxed grasp and strained ears, waiting.

"He's gone under," said Bob in a low voice.

The other nodded, and moistening his huge palms took a firmer grip of the rope.

Fully a minute passed, and the men began to exchange uneasy glances. Then a sudden tremendous jerk followed by a series of feebler ones nearly tore the rope from their grasp.

"Pull!" shouted George, placing one foot on the side and hauling desperately. "Pull! pull! He's stuck fast; he's not coming; *P-u-ll!*"

In response to their terrific exertions the rope came slowly in, inch by inch, until at length a violent splashing was heard, and at the same moment a scream of unutterable horror came echoing up the shaft.

"What a weight he is!" panted Bob. "He's stuck fast or something. Keep still, sir; for heaven's sake, keep still."

For the taut rope was being jerked violently by the struggles of the weight at the end of it. Both men with grunts and sighs hauled it in foot by foot.

"All right, sir," cried George, cheerfully.

He had one foot against the well, and was pulling manfully; the burden was nearing the top. A long pull and a strong pull, and the face of a dead man with mud in the eyes and nostrils came peering over the edge. Behind it was the ghastly face of his master; but this he saw too late, for with a great cry he let go his hold of the rope and stepped back. The suddenness overthrew his assistant, and the rope tore through his hands. There was a frightful splash.

"You fool!" stammered Bob, and ran to the well helplessly.

"Run!" cried George. "Run for another line."

He bent over the coping and called eagerly down as his assistant sped back to the stables shouting wildly. His voice re-echoed down the shaft, but all else was silence.

LEONAUR

ALSO FROM LEONAUR
AVAILABLE IN SOFTCOVER OR HARDCOVER WITH DUST JACKET

MR MUKERJI'S GHOSTS by S. Mukerji—Supernatural tales from the British Raj period by India's Ghost story collector.

KIPLINGS GHOSTS by Rudyard Kipling—Twelve stories of Ghosts, Hauntings, Curses, Werewolves & Magic.

THE COLLECTED SUPERNATURAL AND WEIRD FICTION OF WASHINGTON IRVING: VOLUME 1 by Washington Irving—Including one novel 'A History of New York', and nine short stories of the Strange and Unusual.

THE COLLECTED SUPERNATURAL AND WEIRD FICTION OF WASHINGTON IRVING: VOLUME 2 by Washington Irving—Including three novelettes 'The Legend of the Sleepy Hollow', 'Dolph Heyliger', 'The Adventure of the Black Fisherman' and thirty-two short stories of the Strange and Unusual.

THE COLLECTED SUPERNATURAL AND WEIRD FICTION OF JOHN KENDRICK BANGS: VOLUME 1 by John Kendrick Bangs—Including one novel 'Toppleton's Client or A Spirit in Exile', and ten short stories of the Strange and Unusual.

THE COLLECTED SUPERNATURAL AND WEIRD FICTION OF JOHN KENDRICK BANGS: VOLUME 2 by John Kendrick Bangs—Including four novellas 'A House-Boat on the Styx', 'The Pursuit of the House-Boat', 'The Enchanted Typewriter' and 'Mr. Munchausen' of the Strange and Unusual.

THE COLLECTED SUPERNATURAL AND WEIRD FICTION OF JOHN KENDRICK BANGS: VOLUME 3 by John Kendrick Bangs—Including twor novellas 'Olympian Nights', 'Roger Camerden: A Strange Story', and ten short stories of the Strange and Unusual.

THE COLLECTED SUPERNATURAL AND WEIRD FICTION OF MARY SHELLEY: VOLUME 1 by Mary Shelley—Including one novel 'Frankenstein or the Modern Prometheus', and fourteen short stories of the Strange and Unusual.

THE COLLECTED SUPERNATURAL AND WEIRD FICTION OF MARY SHELLEY: VOLUME 2 by Mary Shelley—Including one novel 'The Last Man', and three short stories of the Strange and Unusual.

THE COLLECTED SUPERNATURAL AND WEIRD FICTION OF AMELIA B. EDWARDS by Amelia B. Edwards—Contains two novelettes 'Monsieur Maurice', and 'The Discovery of the Treasure Isles', one ballad 'A Legend of Boisguilbert'and seventeen short stories to cill the blood.